SYDNEY SCOTT

EVERNIGHT PUBLISHING ®

www.evernightpublishing.com

Copyright© 2025

Sydney Scott

ISBN: 978-0-3695-1152-2

Cover Artist: Jay Aheer

Editor: Stephanie Marrie

SYDNEY SCOTT

DEDICATION

For my friends, one of the greatest sources of love in my life.

SYDNEY SCOTT

LOVING THE LIBRARIAN

Willow Creek, 3

Sydney Scott

Copyright © 2025

Chapter One

~Millie~

A light melody of musical notes drifted through the air and pierced Millie's subconscious, alerting her to the start of another day. Reaching over to her phone, she slapped at the screen until the classical ringtone stopped.

Blinking, she watched as dust mites drifted through the air. She wished she were still asleep. "It's too early," she grumbled to herself.

It was certainly far too early to be so maudlin, but Millie couldn't help it. Rolling over to the other side of her bed, she brushed the cold sheets, sighing wistfully as her fingers smoothed over the cotton fabric. Sometimes, in the hazy state of consciousness that existed between when her alarm went off and when she was truly awake, Millie would pretend that her special someone was there with her in bed, making her breakfast in her small kitchen, or showering to prepare for his day. Eventually, those flights of fancy would vanish as reality set in. She couldn't even have a dog or cat because she was allergic. Neither fish nor reptiles interested her, so alone she stayed. *Perpetually.*

With a sigh, Millie pushed the tangled mess that was her toffee brown hair out of her face and sat up, scanning the small bedroom of her apartment. The light yellow walls created a sunny atmosphere, something that became increasingly necessary to brighten her mood every morning. Her eyes moved from the walls devoid of family pictures to the sparse amount of furniture. Other than her bed, a dresser, and a cozy reading chair, Millie's room consisted of nothing but shelves of books. Her own story was a bit of a sad tale, so she surrounded herself with ones that had happier endings. Escaping into a good book was and always had been her favorite coping mechanism.

Millicent Legare was born in a small town near Georgia's southern border, but she was raised in Willow Creek. Her parents, or rather, the people who raised her, lived in the small town and brought Millie up after her birth mother decided she didn't actually want to have a child and left. Her birth mother had given baby Millie over to the care of her older brother, Bo Legare, and his wife, Beatrice.

Millie's aunt and uncle hadn't wanted a child of their own either, but they fulfilled "their Christian duty" by raising her until she graduated from high school. Apparently, that duty didn't include doing more than providing a roof over her head and the occasional meal. *It was more than some other people had*, she reminded herself. While she had been grateful for not being out on the streets, she hadn't considered living with her aunt and uncle in the Willow Creek mobile home community much better.

Most people who lived in the trailer park were nomadic or kept to themselves. She was one of only a handful of children among the seventy homes, so her upbringing was a lonely one. Her aunt and uncle changed jobs a lot, and up until she was old enough to look after herself, they left Millie in the care of a neighbor or the daycare. Yet even that didn't provide many social opportunities for her. School had been Millie's saving grace for multiple reasons, but the biggest one was meeting Gigi Davenport and Jo Farrow.

Gigi and Millie met way back in kindergarten and had been the best of friends ever since. On the very first day, the teacher had asked each student to stand up, recite their name, and tell everyone what their favorite color was. Millie had been so nervous that her stomach churned as she waited for her turn. When another little girl before her announced that her favorite color was "rainbow," Millie immediately relaxed. She was pleased that someone else loved all of the same colors that she did.

When the pretty, auburn-haired little girl came up and introduced herself, Millie grew nervous again. Gigi wore the prettiest pink dress that Millie had ever seen. The girl's hair was done in two perfect pigtails with matching pink ribbons. Millie's hair was always matted and tangled, her clothes always too big or too small for her body and full of holes, which made her feel undeserving of the little girl's friendship. Millie compared herself to others, always feeling less than, but Gigi wouldn't let her shrink into herself and insisted that they sit together at lunch. When she discovered that Millie's birthday was the same as hers, Gigi declared them best friends for life.

Jo joined their little group two years later. While the tough tomboy scared Millie at first, Gigi insisted that they get to know her. When they did, they found out that not only did Jo share their January birthday, but the gruff girl was actually very friendly and cool. Jo shared all sorts of knowledge that Gigi and Millie didn't have access to. They couldn't get enough of it, and the three instantly became best friends, staying that way ever since.

School also saved Millie because it introduced her to reading. Her parents had no love for books, always preferring to watch TV or go out to the bar while she stayed home alone. Millie was the exact opposite, reading as soon as she was able to decipher words on a page. She loved to get lost in a story, any story. It didn't matter what genre it was as long as it had a happy ending and was different from her real life. She started bringing home books from school as often as her teachers would let her, and when they had a field trip to the library in third grade and were able to sign up for their own checkout card, Millie's fate was sealed. From that moment on, she knew she wanted to do something with books, but in order to do that, she would need to get a good education first.

It had always been obvious that there was no way her "parents" would have the money to send her to college, so Millie worked hard at school to get scholarships and got a part-time job down at the grocery store as soon as she was fifteen. Once she was accepted by the same college as Gigi, Millie got a couple of jobs on campus to help pay for her room and board. Gigi's parents were well-off and paid for their daughter's off campus apartment as well as her education, something Millie had always envied. Gigi had offered to let Millie live with her for free, but that hadn't sat right with her, so Millie worked as hard as she could to chip in for rent while also saving a little bit of money for the future.

With all the working she had to do, it took her five years to graduate, but she was proud of herself for having done it all on her own. After graduation, she took her degree in library science back to Willow Creek to snag an open position as the assistant librarian there. Millie loved her job and couldn't imagine working anywhere else. She just wished her personal life was as fulfilling as her professional one.

A beep from her phone pulled Millie from the thoughts of her past. She glanced over at her small nightstand, past the small hill of beloved paperbacks, wondering who the message was from and hope blooming in her chest at the possibilities. That same hope wilted when she saw the dating app notification. Back in January, she, Gigi, and Jo made a pact to step outside their comfort zones and challenge themselves both personally and professionally. After eight months of earnest work, Millie hadn't made much progress in either area.

The head librarian, Mrs. Hammersmith, was friendly, but also intimidating. The older woman's encyclopedic knowledge and years of experience always outweighed Millie's contributions. Though Millie was passionate about starting an outreach program to get books to members of the community who were housebound or had limited access to the library, she had been too nervous to present her idea to her boss and the board of trustees. Millie's dating life wasn't faring much better. She had been on several dates since signing up for the apps, but none had worked out.

"Maybe this time will be different," she mused as she swiped on her phone. One of the four apps her friends had helped her set up Millie opened a message from a guy that lived one town over in Drysdale, but she immediately regretted it. "Ugh, seriously?" she grumbled at the picture of the man's flaccid penis. "At least get it hard first."

Slamming her finger on the phone as quickly as possible, she closed the message and blocked the user. Millie had never seen so many male appendages as she had in the last seven months. Tossing her phone to the side with a sigh, she threw her bedsheets back and padded over to her bathroom to start getting ready for the day.

After brushing her teeth and combing the knots from her hair, she made her way over to the closet. As her fingers trailed over the various thrift store finds, Millie glanced around at the empty racks near the back, wondering if there would ever come a time when there were more than just her own clothes in there. She couldn't help her mind from picturing a certain set of men's suits next to her dresses and sweaters, but she shook her head to get rid of the image.

It was like her brain was an Etch a Sketch, constantly drawing something that would remind her of Ford, Gigi's brother, only for her to have to erase it before her heart had time to latch onto the picture of the man she'd always felt was perfect for her. Truth be told, her heart had been firmly latched onto Ford Davenport since she was old enough to realize that boys didn't have cooties, or not to care about those cooties anyway.

The number of times Millie was allowed to visit Gigi's home had been few, so she didn't get to see Ford as often as she would have liked. Her friend didn't admit it, but Millie knew the reason she wasn't able to visit Gigi much was because she lived in the trailer park. The Davenports lived in one of the nicest parts of town in a house that could have fit at least six of Millie's, and they didn't like the idea of their daughter hanging out with someone of a lower class.

The Davenports were very influential and important people in the Willow Creek community. Millie was the opposite. Luckily, the Davenport children never treated her as such. Whenever she had been around the house, Ford was always polite to Millie, offering her snacks before he would join his friends at the park to play baseball, her eyes always following along after him as she longed to do.

As Millie grew, so did her crush on Ford. By the time she was a freshmen in high school and Ford was a senior, Millie was full-on in love with him, creating stories in her head about how he would take her to prom or blow her a kiss from the gym floor during assemblies when the baseball team was up on risers to get everyone pumped for their upcoming season. Neither of those things ever happened, of course, nor did any of the other hundreds of her fantasies in the years that followed. They never would. Gigi had been right to tell Millie not to waste her time with Ford when it came up at their twenty-eight birthday celebration earlier that year. Ford was a successful lawyer from a highly influential family, and she was a librarian whose "parents" moved away from her as soon as they were able.

It was the idea of what her parents could have been that Millie missed more than anything, not the people themselves. Growing up with no money and little food would have been a lot more bearable to her if there was someone who loved her, but that hadn't been the case. A week before she went off to college, her "parents" announced that they were moving north to Indiana. Millie didn't blame them for wanting to go somewhere they would have an easier time finding jobs, but it still stung that they hadn't thought to tell her until they had already made their decision.

Once they were gone, they would drop a line occasionally to tell her where they had landed, and she would send them Christmas and birthday cards. Yet more often than not, the cards would come back unopened and "return to sender," the address no longer correct. Millie had never felt loved by either Bo or Beatrice. The only people who ever made Millie feel loved were her two best friends, but they were both coupled up now with partners of their own. Though they still hung out together, it just wasn't the same.

Millie shook off the loneliness that plagued her daily and got back to choosing her outfit for the day. After another moment of browsing, she fingered the ruffled white blouse and beige, tweed skirt she often wore to work, pulling both from their hangers and getting dressed. Slipping her feet into her brown heels, Millie returned to the bathroom to do her hair and makeup. Her routine consisted of nothing more than a few swipes of mascara, a little face powder, and some lip gloss.

As she stared at her reflection, Millie thought to try something different, perhaps a more mature look to attract a man. She quickly wrinkled her nose at the idea. "Nah," she told the Millie in the mirror. She hated wearing makeup and would rather be alone that be with someone who preferred her face painted. Whipping her long hair into a high ponytail, she grabbed her phone off the bed and walked out of the small bedroom into the even smaller kitchen.

The apartment was tiny, and while she could afford a bigger place, Millie didn't need the space, nor did she have the desire to spend more on rent than she needed to. *When you grow up with nothing, you come to expect nothing, and while you can take the girl out of financial insecurity, but you can't erase the years of struggling and money anxiety from the girl.* Millie had a small nest egg going, but she never allowed herself to touch it unless it was for something absolutely necessary like getting her bike fixed up, fancy ingredients for a new recipe she wanted to try, or for trips with the girls.

Vacations with Gigi and Jo were probably the most extravagant thing she paid for, and even those were still always reasonable. Weekends at the coast didn't cost that much. Millie knew at least part of the reason why they did those easy trips was because her friends knew how money conscious she was. They were the greatest friends a girl could ask for. Even though Millie was happy that both had found someone to love and share their lives with, she envied them and pitied herself at the same time. Even before her friends had found their matches, she'd mostly on her own. Gigi had her busy social life, Jo had her hook-ups, and Millie had her books. She hoped these dating apps worked out sooner rather than later because she was tired of being alone.

After having a quick breakfast scramble and glass of orange juice, Millie said goodbye the ghosts of the fictional characters that were her only roommates and was out the door. A short path down the stairs of her small block apartment building led her out to the courtyard, where she locked up her bike. The sunlight glinted off the metal of her turquoise beach cruiser. The small baskets covered in flowers that rested in the front and back that she used for carrying her bags when she went grocery shopping sat empty until she tossed her purse in the front.

Millie lived close to the library. The weather in Willow Creek was always fairly moderate, which made biking to work a no-brainer. It saved her money, got her exercise, and, above all, cheered her up. She had always wanted a bike when she was growing up, but she didn't have the money for one. As soon as she got to college, Millie bought a used bike to get around campus and had been in love with that mode of transportation ever since. Her current bike had been more than she liked to spend, but it was a purchase she would happily make again and again because of how much joy the simple act of riding a bike brought into her somewhat lonely life.

Millie undid the bike and hopped on the cruiser she nicknamed "Eleanor," meaning "bright, shiny one," and started off toward work. She passed along the maple-lined streets, looking forward to the time when the leaves would change from dark green to vibrant reds and yellows, and inhaled the fresh air as it whirled past her face. Always wanting to be friendly, she waved to people she knew and some she didn't. After all, she never knew who needed a little brightness in their day.

As she passed by a small park, Millie saw a couple enjoying a picnic breakfast as they snuggled up against one another. *Maybe someday that will be you?* Millie hoped that someday happened soon because, though she was always happy to provide a little brightness into everyone else's day, she could also use a little for herself.

Chapter Two

~Ford~

The sun blazed through the glass windows of Ford's office, pushing his already painful headache closer to migraine territory. Despite the glare, he walked over to the large wall of glass that offered a beautiful view of the river that ran through most of town. Why they named the town Willow Creek and not Willow River was anybody's guess, but it wasn't his job to figure that out. Currently, Ford's job was to find a way to justify one of his corporate clients denying sick time to their employees. *Fucking deplorable.*

For Ford, corporate law was a soul-sucking endeavor, and after the last seven years of doing it at his father's law firm, he was beyond over it. His days passed in a haze of finding tax loopholes, justifying lower pay and substandard benefits for employees, or trying to dodge unsafe work environment claims for his clients. Ford wasn't sure how his father had lasted so long in this business without losing his mind. Then again, the two of them were very different people.

Clifford Alan Davenport III was very unlike the man he had gotten his name from. Ford's father was happy to help his clients do what was necessary to increase their profit margins and their own salaries, even if it came at the expense of the everyday person because it lined his own pockets as well. While Ford had grown up as a beneficiary of his father's work, he's never admired it. Unfortunately for him, it had always been a forgone conclusion that Ford would follow in his father's footsteps and go into corporate law. While Ford had been happy to go along with that plan in the past, he was less on board with that decision with each passing year.

Ford had enjoyed learning the law at Duke University, his father's alma matter, and had a great time leading some of the other students in study groups or mock trials that dealt with fighting for a righteous cause. Once it came time to practice law, however, he found that the good times had ended, and he was simply performing a job to live up to his parent's exceedingly high expectations. That was how it went from the very day he started at Davenport and Atwater. Ford arrived at the office, did his job, played the part he was born and raised to play, and then he went home to his big, empty house where he sat and wondered just how he had become so utterly pathetic.

Late at night, while he lay in his oversized bed, Ford would sometimes dream of what his life could look like if he cared less about his parent's expectations and was free to do what he wanted. He would dream of living in a house that wasn't so cold and impersonal, but one that felt cozy and lived-in, with knickknacks and personal items scattered about instead of blank walls, empty shelves, and furniture that some decorator had deemed "in style."

In his dream life, Ford would wake up in the morning looking forward to his day and climb down to a small kitchen nook, inhaling the smell of freshly baked bread and warm apples wafting from the oven as his wife made him his favorite breakfast: apple cinnamon coffee cake. He would walk up to her and rub his face into the side of her neck before pouring them each a cup of coffee, then they would enjoy breakfast with one another and head off to work.

Ford would be working for clients who needed help at his own law firm, and his wife would go to her job doing something to help the community, just like him. He was never clear on exactly what that was because he was never clear on the type of woman he would end up marrying. If it were up to his parents, he'd still be with his ex or someone like her. That was never going to happen. After years of dating the same type of girl and not caring for them, Ford had given up on love and dedicated himself to his job. He had been in a relationship once, but fortunately he ended it before the two of them progressed any further.

Presley hadn't been someone he was in love with, but she was just the type of girl he'd been expected to marry. She was pretty, polished, and connected to high society. They got along well enough and had known each other a while, so when she had floated the idea that the two of them should date, Ford sort of shrugged and went along with it. Clifford and Theodora Davenport had been over the moon that their twenty-five-year-old son was finally going out with one of their friend's daughters, but he didn't share their excitement. In fact, he had practically tightened the noose that was already around his neck, but because he had always been the dutiful son, Ford went along with it.

Ford was certain that he would probably be married and already divorced by now if he hadn't come to his senses. Thank goodness he did. It hadn't been an easy breakup, with pretty much everyone except for his sister trying to convince him to keep dating Presley because they were "perfect for one another," but the woman was vain and self-centered. He didn't want to be the perfect match for someone like that.

The fallout had taken a while to settle, but it was worth it to not be with a woman his heart had never belonged to. Ford was fairly certain she had never given him her heart either, but they hadn't talked much in the years since. That was fine with him. The firm he wanted to start was where all his focus went these days, but even that seemed doomed to fail, just like his past relationship. Ford sighed as he pulled the blinds shut, his heart heavy with the knowledge that his dream wasn't possible in the light of day. At least, not anymore.

Ford grabbed his things and walked out of the office to meet his sister. She called and mentioned it was important. Unlike their overbearing jerk parents, Ginny was nothing but sunshine. Thinking of his awesome sister still wasn't enough to lighten his mood as he drove toward The Happy Kettle, his sister's tearoom, to pick her up. Even after she'd slide into his car and started chatting with him about something that was going on with her friend, Jo, and the entire time they climbed the steps up to Jo's apartment, Ford couldn't help drifting back to the moment he realized his dream might not come to fruition.

Two months earlier, Ford had met with the executor of his grandfather's estate, an old colleague of Clifford Davenport I. The man only kept up his law practice to be in charge of his deceased friends' business dealings after they were gone. Ford remembered walking into the elderly man's office, taking in the dust and old law books that lined the bookshelves on the walls before he sat down to discuss the trust Ford's grandfather had set up for both him and his sister, Ginny.

Unlike Ginny's trust that she got the minute she turned twenty-four and had used to help pay for renovations to her tearoom, Ford's had more stipulations to fulfill in order to access the money. Leave it to Grandpa to act like an asshole from beyond the grave. That didn't matter anymore because, in a few months, Ford would turn thirty-two. He had already worked at the law firm for more than the required five years, and he was an equity partner. The three things required of him would be checked off. Ford could take the money, open his own firm, and finally escape from under the thumb of his demanding father.

"Good morning, Ford," Jonah Burgess called, peering over the top of his bifocal lenses.

Ford took the seat across from the bald gentleman and shook his hand. "Good to see you again, Mr. Burgess," he replied, all polite smiles. "You mentioned something about my trust. Are we allowed to release the money early? My birthday is soon enough." Ford didn't like the desperation he heard in his voice, but he was excited about starting his own firm. With all his extra cash tied up in his current firm's equity, he needed that money.

Burgess raised his head up higher, resembling a turtle peeking out of its shell. "Well, that's the thing," he replied with a click of his tongue. "I'm afraid we've hit a bit of a snafu."

"What kind of snafu?" Ford asked, instantly switching into asshole lawyer mode so they could plow through whatever problem was holding up his trust.

"The marriage kind," the man answered ominously, spinning the trust contract over to him and pointing to a section he hadn't seen before.

Ford read the additional stipulation that he be married by his thirty-second birthday and scoffed. "That's not legal," he insisted, even as his mind whirred and searched through his mental law library to see if he was actually right about that.

"I can assure you it is," tutted Burgess, pointing a wrinkled finger to all the necessary signatures, notarization, and legal filing number. "Your grandfather wanted to ensure that not only were you helping to maintain the law firm, but that you were also dedicated to continuing the family lineage."

"This is bullshit," Ford barked, but held up his

hands when he caught the man's offended expression. "Apologies, sir. I know you don't care for foul language"

"I certainly do not," chided Burgess, straightening himself in his worn leather seat. He shuffled the papers together before passing them over to Ford. "You're free to look over the papers and challenge anything you like, but I can assure you, the only way you are seeing the money your granddaddy left you is if you put a ring on some girl's finger." He gave Ford an appraising once-over. "Or guy. No judgement from me."

"Appreciate it," Ford muttered, collecting the papers with a sigh and slipping them into his briefcase. "I will definitely be challenging this." With that, he stormed out the door with every intention of making sure that last stipulation was erased from the contract. Two months and a few failed court challenges later, Ford was still at square one. Only this time, his birthday was only a few weeks away, and he was nowhere near getting married.

As he came back to the present, he smiled. At least the case Ford was thinking of taking on was interesting enough to keep his mind off the fact that he'd be stuck at his father's firm for the rest of his life. The prospect of helping his sister's friend get compensation for having to deal with sexual harassment made him feel a little lighter. Helping members of the community rather than countless money-making entities felt right. If only he got to do it for the rest of his life.

Tabling that dream for another time, Ford concentrated on the discussion going on around him. At the moment, he and a few others had found their way into Jo's apartment and were talking through her case. Ford was certain she could win, especially if they could get other victims to come forward.

"I don't think I could afford to pay you your hourly rate though," Jo told him, her blue eyes betraying defeat. Before Ford could address her concerns, Jo's boyfriend Archer jumped in.

"I'll pay it." The man's gesture was admirable, but ultimately unnecessary.

"No need," Ford explained, causing Jo's head to whip back in his direction. "I'll do it pro bono." He was required by his firm to do a certain number of hours of pro bono work anyway, so this would be killing two birds with one stone.

"What?" Jo and Archer blurted out at the same time.

Ford nodded and smiled reassuringly, shrugging like it was no big deal. This was the kind of work he loved to do, that he was meant to do. "Trust me, this is the type of law I enjoy practicing. Helping people instead of protecting corporations," he muttered, the dream of his own firm slipping further and further away from him.

"Thank you," Jo gushed. The gratitude coming off of her was just the dopamine hit he needed to keep trying to make his dream a reality. It might take a few more years of working for his father to make it happen, but no matter the cost, he needed to get his own firm so he could help people like her who needed quality representation at an affordable price.

"Knock-knock," someone sang from the doorway. Ford glanced over to see Millie peeking her head in from behind the doorway, and his smile automatically widened at the sight of the sweet woman. Her brown eyes widened behind her thick-framed glasses as she scanned the cramped apartment. "Whoa. Full house."

Jo smiled at the woman and ushered her inside. "Might as well come in and join us."

Millie pushed the door open to reveal two huge brown bags in her arms that she struggled to carry. Ford quickly hustled over and lifted both bags. "Let me get those for you," he told her before carrying them over to the counter in Jo's small kitchen.

"Thanks," Millie replied shyly, her doe eyes shining behind her glasses. Millicent Legare was a sweet little thing and had been friends with his sister Ginny for just about forever. Ford had always liked Millie. There wasn't a mean bone in the woman's body. If she had been Catholic, she would be up for sainthood.

"Something smells amazing," Ginny remarked, joining him in the kitchen to help unload the bags. Something did smell amazing, much better than any of the preordered meals he had waiting in his fridge at home.

"Oh, it's nothing special," Millie mumbled as she came into the apartment and shut the door. Ford peeked over his shoulder at her and smiled. She was wearing a very Millie-like outfit: a burgundy, corduroy overall dress with a white t-shirt underneath, her white canvas sneakers appearing a little worse for wear. Her long toffee hair was in a braid, and she twisted the ends of it with one hand while she held out a small tin for Ford to take and shrugged. "I thought Jo might get hungry later, and I wanted her to have a home-cooked meal."

"More like a few home-cooked meals." Ginny smiled at her friend as she unloaded multiple food containers onto the counter. It looked like Millie had spent an entire day cooking up a storm for Jo. *Yup, definitely a saint.*

"I like taking care of people." Millie's cheeks blushed from all the attention, and Ford couldn't help but smile at the sight of it. His sister's friend was actually pretty adorable when he thought about it, which apparently he hadn't ever done before but was definitely doing now. "Besides, I figured you had at least one other person here, so I made enough food for two."

Jo smiled at her friend and walked over to give her a hug. "Thanks, Mills. You're the best." Jo reached over and grabbed one of the containers from Ford's hand, smiling when she opened the lid to see some kind of cookies. "You have to try one of these," she told her boyfriend before handing him a cookie.

Ginny grabbed one for herself as well and offered one to Ford. He was never going to turn down a cookie, especially one of Millie's creations. They were guaranteed to be amazing. She was always cooking or baking for his sister, and he occasionally got to reap the rewards as well. The cookie was soft, yet crispy. After inhaling the chocolate scent, he chomped into it and groaned at just how delicious it was. *Why was this woman a librarian and not a baker?*

"I'm jealous of your future husband, Mills," he heard Jo say. "With food like this always coming out of your kitchen, he'd be one lucky guy."

"You think so?" Millie asked Jo, her eyes meeting his for a moment before sliding back to her friend.

"Oh yeah," Ford chimed in, nodding and making a grab for another cookie. "I don't know any guy who wouldn't love to be married to a girl like you. I'm surprised someone hasn't snapped you up already." He popped the cookie into his mouth and chewed it. After the second or third bite, he finally felt the impact of his words. Who wouldn't love to be married to a girl like Millie? *Married. To Millie.*

"Thanks," Millie replied.

Ford stared at Millie for a moment while she talked with Jo. It was sometimes hard to tell behind the lenses of her glasses, but her big, round eyes were the color of coffee and cream. Her lips and cheeks were rosy as she played with her braided hair. She was the girl-next-door type, as sweet as her cookies. Millie was loyal, reliable, and loved to help others, so maybe she would want to help him.

Ford reached for his third cookie. He should probably stop if he didn't want to deal with a sugar crash later, but they were just so delicious and he needed a distraction from the crazy idea that was turning over in his head. Millie spoke some more before walking out the door, but she remained in his thoughts regardless. All Ford could think about was whether or not she would go along with the crazy scheme his brain has concocted.

Jo turned to him with an annoyed expression, but that must be from having to deal with so many people in such a confined space. "Okay, so what are the next steps with all this?" She gestured to notebooks full of her observations of sexism and harassment at her workplace.

Ford shook the thoughts of marrying Millie out of his head and walked over to the pile, picking them all up. "If it's all right with you, I'll take these and make copies, look through them, and get a timeline set up for you." After opening his leather briefcase, he stuffed them inside and pulled out a business card for Jo. "Here's my number. Feel free to call if you think of anything else you have. I'll call you with an update early next week."

"Thanks, Ford." Jo gave him a grateful, but tired smile.

"You're welcome." Ford made his way toward the door. "I need to get back to the office."

Ginny nodded at him and grabbed her stuff. "Drop me on the way," she commanded. Since he loved his sister, he nodded and started down the stairs. He chuckled at the idea that had been rolling around in his brain. "What's so funny?"

"Oh, nothing," he lied, leading her over to his electric SUV. "Probably just having a mental breakdown." After the years trying to be someone he wasn't, he was long overdue for one.

"At least wait until after your birthday." Ginny smirked. "I already got you a present and I'm not sure you can take it with you to the looney bin."

"Har-har." He opened her door and let her inside.

Hours later, as he lay in bed at night dreaming of that life he always wanted but couldn't have, the crazy idea from earlier wiggled its way to the forefront of his mind and set up camp. When he dreamed of his wife making breakfast, he realized she was no longer faceless. This time, she resembled Millie. Ford barely slept that night, but it wasn't the fear of losing his dream that kept him awake. It was the wild notion that maybe he could convince Millie to marry him, and then his dream could become reality.

Chapter Three

~Millie~

Millie's two best friends stared back at her from across the table at The Happy Kettle, Gigi's tearoom and the spot they were currently meeting at for lunch. Millie had just finished practicing the presentation she planned on giving to her boss and the board about her outreach program that evening. She hoped that the bright smiles on her friend's faces meant that she had done a good job.

"So, do you think they'll go for it?" Millie continued to twist her fingers together in her lap, a nervous habit from her youth that she had never quite managed to shake.

"Are you kidding? They're going to love it. Your program is well-thought-out and fills a gap in the community, as far as public library services is concerned." Gigi reached over and squeezed her twisting fingers to get them to stop. Gigi was always doing things to help her, even something as small as keeping her from fidgeting.

"Agreed," Jo added, pulling her blonde curls up into a bun. "If they don't go for it, they're a bunch of dumbasses."

Millie chuckled at her friend. Of the three of them, Jo definitely had the most colorful language and would regularly make Millie blush. "I think I'll leave that comment out of my presentation, but thank you." She took a sip of the black tea and milk that sat next to her empty lunch plate. "I'm still pretty nervous."

The board of trustees meeting was that night and while Millie had rehearsed the presentation in front of her mirror a few times and just now in front of her friends, it was going to be much harder to do it in front of her bosses, the board members, and anyone from the community who decided to show up.

"Don't be," Gigi insisted. "You're going to do so great, and we'll be there in the audience for moral support."

Millie gulped, not sure if her friends being there would make her more or less apprehensive about the whole thing. "Who's we?"

Jo started ticking off fingers as she went down the line of people. "Well, the two of us, obviously. Gigi is bringing Cooper and his gran. I'm bringing Archer and Pops." That was a lot of people, but at least Millie knew them and there were all very friendly. Maybe she wouldn't be so nervous after all.

"Ford's coming too," Gigi mentioned offhandedly. As if her brother coming was no big deal.

"Ford's coming?" Millie squeaked. Her earlier nervousness was back in full force at the thought of her almost lifelong crush possibly witnessing her make a fool of herself.

"Strange, I know," Gigi remarked. "I mentioned it to him when we were at dinner the other night and he said he'd be there."

"I bet lawyers get off on going to all kinds of public meetings." Jo smirked. "City councils, home owner's association gatherings, town budget approvals. Oh baby, civic duty talk is so hot," she said huskily, fanning herself.

Millie tossed a small lump of bread at her. "You're so dumb," she told her friend while giggling.

Millie was thankful to Jo for lightening the mood. Nerves aside, the idea of Ford's presence also provided a whole other reason for butterflies to flutter in her stomach. Millie wasn't allowing herself to indulge in her crush anymore, but that was difficult to manage when she's seen his big smile, sandy brown hair, and jade eyes so often lately. He seemed to be everywhere she was and pushing feelings aside when they were literally staring her in the face was impossible. The combination of his good looks and kind and caring personality, always did a number on her heart and her libido.

"You love it." Jo gave her another big smile. Someone was paid to bus the table, but The Happy Kettle was more like a second home at this point, so they gathered their plates and teacups together on the table. Millie had always felt silly letting someone clean up after her, especially in such a familiar place.

"Speaking of love," Gigi began with a sly smile as she turned to Millie. "How's life on the apps, Mills? Do you have any more dates lined up?"

Millie sighed and plopped her cloth napkin on the table. "Well, let's see. I do have one date lined up, but I'm not sure it will pan out. I have also gotten two new dick pics since Monday." She frowned. "So there's that."

"Ew," Gigi cried.

Jo asked, "How were they?"

Millie gasped. "Gross, Jo."

"What do you mean gross? C'mon, you don't have to date the person attached to it. You could just use him for a night of fun while you search for Mr. Right." Jo's tone was too easygoing. For Millie, sex was a *very* big deal. Her friends just didn't know exactly how big, and she couldn't blame them for that because she was the one who kept the whole thing secret for their entire friendship.

"I'm not normally one for hookups." Gigi scrunched up her nose for a moment before she continued. "But maybe Jo is right. I mean, why not have a little fun while you're looking for love? At the very least, it might relax you."

"I don't know," Millie mumbled, thankful that the tearoom was mostly empty.

"It's not like it would be the first one you've ever had, right?" Jo asked with a chuckle, but her laughter died when she noticed that Millie wasn't laughing. "You have had a one-night stand before, right Mills?"

"Um, well..." Millie faltered, apprehension swirling in her stomach along with her lunch.

"It's not a big deal." Gigi flashed her a small, sympathetic smile. She was always coming to Millie's defense when she needed it.

Jo slapped Millie on the shoulder. "Totally. No big deal, and no time like the present to pop that one night stand cherry."

Gigi pulled a face at their friend's description, but she nodded. "Exactly. No time like the present to try something new."

Millie's fingers twitched. She tried to quell the fear that was bubbling up with the realization that she should probably stop lying to her friends. "About that," she muttered, staring up at the ceiling for a moment to gather courage before admitting the truth. Millie leaned closer to her friends and lowered her voice to just above a whisper. "I haven't popped my other cherry either."

Her friends were shocked, their jaws almost to the floor and their eyebrows at their hairlines. The two stared at each other before turning back to her. "Why didn't you ever tell us?" Gigi asked, slightly affronted.

"Yeah, what the hell?" Jo added. "I thought we were friends."

"We are friends," Millie insisted, grabbing both of their hands and squeezing them. Fortunately, neither of them pulled away, but their twin looks of betrayal pierced Millie's heart like a dagger. It was understandable. She had kept the truth to herself for a long time, and she couldn't say she wouldn't feel the same way if one of them had kept a similarly large secret. "We're best friends. It's just kind of hard to admit to it after a certain age."

Gigi huffed. "You could have told us a long time ago."

She was right. Millie could have told them from the beginning, but they had made assumptions and she had been too embarrassed to correct them. Sex was a normal part of relationships, so the fact that she hadn't participated in that part of it yet made her feel even weirder about her social life than she already did. How could she explain that to a woman who, up until a few months ago was hooking up with a different guy every week, and another who had been the most eligible bachelorette in the city until she got with her current boyfriend?

"I know, I know. I'm sorry, you guys," she professed, her voice as contrite as she could make it. "It's just that when you both assumed I did it with Brian Miller when we kind of dated in college, I didn't want to correct you. It was silly that I dated someone for six months and we never progressed past the occasional groping session." It was less silly now that she was older and knew better, but at a time when everyone had already lost their virginity, it felt like a much bigger deal.

Jo let out a low whistle. "Wow." Millie winced and braced herself for her friend's judgement. "That's pretty cool, Mills."

Millie gulped. "Really?" Never in a million years did she expect her friend to say that.

"Totally. We should plant some velvet ropes around your hoo-ha and charge admission," Jo quipped, a bright smile on her face. "The world's last know virgin. Only $5.95 for a peek behind the meat curtains."

Gigi barked, but covered her mouth immediately.

"Ha, ha," Millie replied, knowing very well Jo was just messing with her. Still, the joke hit a little harder than Jo probably intended. Millie knew she wasn't the last known virgin at her age, but it sure felt like it sometimes.

"Seriously though, Mills. Why the wait?" Jo asked. "Sex is definitely not as big a deal as most people make it out to be. It's just two consenting adults enjoying each other's bodies."

"I don't know."

Even as she said it, Millie knew why she had waited, but it might sound silly to her friends who had parents and now partners who loved them very much. Even Gigi's parents, who had always been a little too hard on their daughter, still loved her. How could she explain to her friends that she wanted to feel something for the person she was with, wanted to mean something to them in a way she never had to anyone else? Millie wanted the first person she had sex with to love her, or at least, have the potential to love her. Unfortunately, she had never even gotten close to that. Now it had been built up in her head so much that it was this big deal. She didn't know what to do about it. It was like she had carried around a fifty-pound weight on her back and had no idea of how to get rid of it.

"I guess I just want to feel something, not love necessarily, but something close to it for the person I have sex with. I've only ever felt that way with..." She stopped and stared at her friends. Millie didn't have to finish that sentence for them to know she was talking about Ford. "Anyway, with the way my dating is going, that probably won't happen, so maybe I should just hire an escort or something. Get it over with."

"Um, no," Jo insisted. Then she pulled out her

phone and started scrolling. "At the very least, I'll reactivate my Tinder account and hook you up with a guaranteed good lay."

Millie placed her hand over Jo's. "Appreciate the thought, but I don't think I could have sex with someone you already did. No offense." Even though Millie knew there wouldn't have been feelings involved on Jo's end, she was grossed out by the idea of being with a guy her friend had already screwed.

Jo rolled her eyes at Millie, but smiled anyway. "Fine, but don't ever say I didn't try to help."

Millie glanced over at Gigi, who was tapping her chin lightly. "Some of the guys across the street seem nice. I could ask Cooper to vet his coworkers and see who might be a good fit," she offered with a smile.

Millie's head hit the table with a loud *thunk*. "Please don't ask your fiancé to pimp me out to his coworkers," she mumbled against the linen fabric. She lifted her head and sighed. "Can we just forget I ever said anything?"

"Nope," Gigi answered automatically.

"No chance of that happening," Jo proclaimed, but after seeing how tired the whole conversation was making Millie, she nodded. "We can agree to table any more discussion about your V-card until after your presentation though."

"A small reprieve, but I'll take it." Millie gathered her things and stood up from the table. "I'll see you guys tonight then?" She shouldered her handbag. Millie was one of those women who carried a mom purse even though she had no children. If anyone wanted a hand wipe, tissue, spot cleaner, snack, mint, or just about anything else, then Millie was their girl.

"Absolutely," Gigi chirped. She stepped over to Millie to give her a hug, her familiar peaches and cream scent wafting over and helping to relax her after such an awkward conversation.

"Archer and I will be there and do our best to stay awake," Jo snarked before pulling Millie into a big bear hug. "Thanks for telling us, Mills. I know it wasn't easy for you."

"Of course," Millie replied. "Catch you guys later." Millie walked outside and hopped onto Eleanor to make her way back to the library. She was pushing her lunch hour to the limit, which probably wasn't the wisest thing to do the day of her presentation, but if the wind was with her, she'd make it back just in time.

****

As it turned out, Millie had arrived back to the library just in the nick of time and spent the rest of her work day alternating between excitement and nausea at having to give a presentation in front of a bunch of people. After her shift ended, Millie had just enough time to run to the bathroom to freshen up before she had to head upstairs to the conference room. She tried her best to tame her hair, but after all her biking, it was a mess. Millie grabbed a tie from her purse and pulled the strands into a messy braid before grabbing her powder and trying to take the shine off of her cheeks and forehead. After a few swipes of lipstick and a re-up of her almond scented deodorant, she was ready to go.

Millie grabbed her laptop and headed upstairs to get ready. When she walked into the room that was lined with wood paneled walls and blue Berber carpet, her eyes widened. All seven board members and Mrs. Hammersmith, the head librarian, were seated at the front of the room. There were a few average citizens sprinkled here and there in the audience, but it was the large group of people crowded in the front that had captured her attention. Sitting in the first row of chairs were Gigi, her fiancé Cooper, and his grandmother Mags. Next to them was Jo, her partner Archer, and her father Bob, along with a few guys who Millie was pretty certain were mechanics from his auto shop.

Finally, in the second row seated all by himself was Ford. His thumbs were flying across the screen of his phone, but he stopped suddenly and turned around. Time seemed to stand still when his beautiful, light green eyes met hers. Millie's breath caught in her throat, and she melted at the sight of him. Ford always looked good, and tonight was no different. He looked impeccable in his navy suit and brown tie with his sandy brown hair neatly styled. Millie yearned to run her fingers through it, both to feel how silky it was and to mess it up just a little.

When Ford shot her a bright smile, his white teeth shining in the fluorescent light, time started again, her heartbeat ticking the seconds away at an alarming rate. Millie had to remind herself for the billionth time in her life that he wasn't for her. She returned the smile though, and made her way to the front of the room, sitting on the empty seat in front of Ford and twisting her fingers while she waited for the meeting to start.

"You're going to do great, Millie." Ford's face was so close to hers that she could see the shadow of stubble on his strong jaw and smell his citrusy cologne. The fragrance of sun-kissed oranges reminded her of warm summer days when the world was happy and relaxed. She wanted to lean into him to get a bigger hit in hopes of gathering up a little of that blissful sensation for herself.

"Thank you," she replied quietly. Instead of sniffing his neck like the weirdo she was, she smiled and ducked bashfully.

The board chairman called the meeting to order. After going over old business, he asked for any new business to come forward. Millie was the only one on the agenda, so she stood and made her way to the front. After hooking up her laptop, she took a deep breath and proceeded to tell the board all about her idea for a book outreach program. She had done a lot of research and even called a few libraries in other towns and states that had similar programs to get logistics. Millie spoke about her own love of reading and how hard it had been to get to and from the library while growing up in the mobile home park. She laid out her plans for a sort of mobile library service where members of the community could reserve books and then volunteers or library staff could check them out and deliver the books for them.

"Books can be such a lifeline for people who don't otherwise have a way to interact much with the outside world. Imagine being able to bring the latest bestseller to someone who is housebound due to an injury or disability, or provide vital information to people in the more rural areas of the community who might otherwise not be able to get it. With the Library Outreach Program, we can contact people and make sure that no matter what situation someone may find themselves in, they still have access to information and entertainment. When it comes to reading, everyone should have access. Thank you."

Millie concluded her presentation and blushed when her friends and their family members stood up and cheered. Ford stood as well and whistled loudly before clapping and smiling at her. She beamed at him, wondering where his sudden enthusiasm for books came from, and gathered her material before heading back to her seat. Millie's heart was beating quickly once again from the adrenaline rush of her presentation. When Ford squeezed her shoulder, her pace accelerated even more.

"That was amazing. I knew you could do it, Millie," he gushed. After all that direct attention, she couldn't stop blushing.

"Thanks, Ford." Millie placed her hand over his, giving it a light squeeze and enjoying the skin to skin contact with him more than was probably wise for someone who could never have him. The touch had been brief, but the feel of his warm hand under hers had sparks shooting up and down her arm as her heart continued to kick against her ribs. "I'm glad you came," she whispered, wishing more than anything that the circumstances of their upbringings had been different so that she might actually have a chance with him.

"I wouldn't have missed it for anything," Ford told her happily. When his phone rang, his smile faded away as he pulled the device out, frowning at it before glancing back at her. "Sorry. I need to get back to the office."

"This late?" Millie wondered. It was almost seven o'clock. He worked so hard, and she wondered when he ever had time to do anything else.

"No rest for the wicked," Ford joked with a sad smile before gathering his briefcase. He squeezed her shoulder one last time. "Good luck with the results."

Millie's eyes never left his retreating form until the door shut behind him, cutting off her view. She turned back to the rest of the meeting and tried to listen, but was having a hard time of it, her body still buzzing from her presentation. *Or was it from being so close to Ford?* When the meeting was over, the board and her boss adjourned for the night. Her friends came over to congratulate her on a job well done.

"When do you find out if they approve the program or not?" Gigi asked as she leaned against Cooper, whose arms were wrapped around her middle.

Millie squashed her envy and smiled at her friend. "They discuss it for a bit, and after the next budget meeting, I'll get an answer." It wasn't a long wait, but Millie knew she was going to go a little crazy until she had her answer.

"What?" Jo asked incredulously. "I thought they were deciding tonight. Please tell me I don't have to come to another meeting. I loved listening to you, Mills, but the rest of this thing was a total snoozefest."

Archer laughed at his girlfriend and stuck out a hand to Millie. "Don't listen to Jo. We'll come back and support you anytime," he promised, shaking Millie's hand before gathering Jo in his arms and kissing her cheek.

Millie smiled politely and moved on to thank everyone else for coming before saying her goodbyes and heading out to her bike. On her ride home, she replayed her presentation in her mind, pretty pleased with how the whole thing went. She got across every point she had wanted to make and she hadn't stuttered or mumbled once. Surprisingly, having Ford there actually helped rather than hindered her ability to speak publicly. There was no better motivation than not wanting to mess up in front of the man you loved. *Used to love,* Millie reminded herself. She shouldn't love someone who was so out of her league, but as she pedaled her legs and drifted along the streets toward home, she couldn't help but think about Ford, and when she did, love was the only word that came to mind.

Chapter Four

~*Ford*~

The firm was already buzzing with activity, everyone flitting around their offices and cubicles like the good worker bees they were, as Ford stepped away from the heavy walnut doors that led into the law offices of Davenport and Atwater with a sigh. He trudged toward his own large office, pulling his shoulders back to try and psych himself up for the work day. Ford pasted on his "everything is A-Okay" smile and greeted the various administrators, interns, and paralegals as he moved through the corridors of the mid-size firm.

It was unusual for a firm that size to be in a smaller city, but his father and his law partner had made quite a name for themselves in their early days in corporate law, boosting the already strong reputation his grandfather had created. Now people traveled to them instead of the other way around. Ford's presence didn't elicit the same level of awe and admiration from other lawyers and clients, but he didn't care. It probably had something to with the fact that his heart just wasn't in it anymore, if it ever had been.

Law school had been wonderful, and it had painted a pretty picture to him and his fellow graduates. They would be going out into the world and making a real difference for the little guy, protecting people from getting taken advantage of, fighting the good fight and all those other platitudes that meant nothing when the reality didn't quite match. Occasionally with his pro bono work, Ford did get to make a difference in someone's life, but those times were rare. More often than not, he was either trying to get lawsuits tossed out of court or convincing a rightfully indignant employee of a corporation or business to settle for pennies on the dollar.

Ford did his job and always followed the law, but at the end of the day, he didn't have that feeling of making the world a better place like he had hoped he would. Having his own firm had been a pipe dream and not something he might have even considered in the past, but after witnessing his sister defy their parents by getting engaged to a mechanic instead of a doctor or lawyer, well, it had been on his mind more and more as of late. Now, he had the desire, but he still needed to money to make it happen.

"Good morning, Mr. D," his assistant Kevin sang. He handed Ford a sleek mug with the law firm logo printed on it that was brimming with rich, black coffee.

"Good morning to you, Kevin." Ford raised the mug to his lips, taking a sip of the aromatic liquid and enjoying the slight burn as it slid down his throat. Hopefully the caffeine would kick in soon and put him in a better mood. "You are allowed to call me Ford," he reminded the slight, younger man for the hundredth time since he had started a little over a year ago.

"I know," Kevin replied with a sly smile. "But I like Mr. D. It sounds powerful." The man's smile showed off his bright teeth, but the sight was gone in a flash as his assistant spun around, grabbing a tablet from his desk. "I've already sent your schedule for the day to your phone. It's pretty light for a Thursday and with the settlement from the Bollinger case going through, your court appearance has been cancelled, so you're free until lunch."

"Wonderful." Ford tried to sound convincing, but wasn't so sure he pulled it off. Ford hadn't stepped into a courtroom in almost two years. Most of his clients preferred to settle out of court. Though Ford didn't love all the work that went along with preparing for a trial, he did miss litigating in front of actual people instead of in a conference room. Now he had all morning to spend checking in on existing corporate clients or actively searching for new ones, neither of which sounded very compelling.

"There's one other thing." Kevin leaned in closer to Ford. "Your father is in your office." A *yikes* expression flitted across his face. Ford stifled his chuckle. Just about everyone in the office was afraid of his father, himself included, but it was still entertaining to observe how everyone reacted to the man's foreboding presence.

"Thanks for letting me know." Ford patted Kevin's shoulder and walked toward his office door. "Buzz me in ten if he's still in there."

"Will do, Mr. D," Kevin chirped before taking a seat at his desk.

Ford took a deep breath to fortify himself before pushing open the dark wooden door to his office. He strode in to see his father sitting at the couch against the wall, his thumbs flying over the screen of his phone.

"You're late, Clifford," he stated without glancing up from the device.

Ford hated being called that, but he brushed that aside to deal with the sinking feeling in his stomach. His parents only used his full name when he was in trouble or they expected something from him, usually something he didn't want to do. He glanced at his watch and saw that the time read just past 8:30 AM. Most lawyers at his firm didn't show up until nine o'clock unless they had court, but apparently he was expected to do better. He tried to play off his father's comment with a shrug as he walked over to his desk and dropped his briefcase on top of the polished wood surface.

"Sorry about that." Ford removed the coat of his

brown suit and hung it over his chair. "Traffic was a mess," he joked. Traffic in Willow Creek was basically nonexistent except for the times when a town festival shut down some of the roads, but those occurred only sporadically.

His father finally glared up at him, narrowing his light brown eyes.

"Amusing," he replied flatly before standing up and walking toward the desk, his patent leather shoes shining. There wasn't a wrinkle to be found on his black suit.

Ford could understand why people found him intimidating. The man always appeared completely put together. He was on the taller side, just over six feet, and he always wore a fine suit. Not one strand of his salt and pepper hair was ever out of place. His expression was always serious, causing anyone who glanced at him to immediately be put on the defensive. Overall, his father's appearance screamed power and money while his expression screamed, "I can and will bury you alive." Ford pushed down the lump of fear that always developed in his gut when his father was in his office. *The man never comes to you, you always come to him.* The fact that he was in the room before Ford had even arrived was telling.

Ford sat down at his desk and tried to look calm in the face of such an imposing figure. "What can I do for you, Dad?"

His father didn't bother sitting in the chair across from him, but instead placed his hands on the edge of Ford's desk and leaned in slightly. "I'm here to talk about your pro bono hours."

Ford sighed with relief. The founding partners insisted that every lawyer in the office perform several hours of pro bono work for the community so that they could tout themselves as an altruistic firm. Ford always got his hours in and then some, especially now with all the work he was putting in on Jo's case. His father must just have missed Ford's record of it.

"I've already done all my hours for the month," Ford stated firmly, turning on his laptop and clicking over to his email. "I can resend the email to your assistant—"

His father held up a hand. "Don't bother. I already have it."

Ford raised his brow in confusion. "Then what's the problem?" No matter what he did or how much he lived his life according to his parent's wishes, Ford still couldn't do anything right.

His father sighed and gave him a stern look. "The problem is that you are performing too many hours of pro bono work," he reprimanded. "You are spending far too much time on cases that don't bring in any money and not enough time helping the paying clients. I've seen your billable hours. It's not a good look for the firm."

Ford almost scoffed, but then remembered who was in front of him. "I suppose I don't understand how it isn't a good look for the firm for one of its partners to be doing good works. I still serve my other clients, and I help people who need it at the same time." Ford's pro bono work was what kept him sane, so cutting back wasn't an option for him.

His father speared him with a glare. "While some may find your more charitable nature compelling, I do not. Neither do the other partners. Do your minimum pro bono and be done with it," he commanded, raising back up to his full height and buttoning the jacket of his suit. "And since you have overperformed for August, you can take September off. Focus on the clients who actually pay for you to be here."

Ford wanted to dispute him, but any argument

died on his tongue when he saw the unblinking stare on the man's face. "Yes, sir," he acquiesced, hating himself for being such a coward.

Ford had never been able to stand up to the man, but he wanted to so very badly. It was pitiful that an almost thirty-two-year-old man was afraid of his father, but here he was, hiding himself away again. Ford would still work on Jo's case, he just wouldn't send the logged hours to his father. He gave Jo his word and he intended to keep it.

"Good boy," his father said. "Oh, and your mother will be calling with a list of potential dates for you to bring to her charity group's masquerade function next month." Ford opened his mouth to protest but swallowed it when he spotted his father's raised hand. "Just does us all a favor and agree to someone of her choosing." The elder Davenport turned toward the door, but stopped and peeked over his shoulder to stare him in the eye. "I expect great things from you, Ford. Don't disappoint me again." With those parting words that felt like a knife in the gut, his father strode from the office.

Ford exhaled with relief at no longer being under his father's intense scrutiny, but his chest felt tight with the knowledge that unless he lived the life as specifically as his father laid out for him, he would always be a disappointment to the man. He was already a disappointment to his mother due to his lack of enthusiasm when it came to dating one of her society matches, but at least she only bothered him when he needed to show up somewhere with a woman on his arm. His father, on the other hand, never let up. Ford was already exhausted from the day and he'd only been there ten minutes. He rested his head in his hands for a moment before a knocking at the door drew his attention.

It was Kevin with a fresh cup of coffee and a

donut. "I thought you might want these after, you know," he began, wincing at what he would have known was a tense interaction.

Ford had a sweet tooth and his assistant always seemed to know when he needed a pick-me-up. "Thanks, Kev." Ford took the offered mug and glazed donut. He appreciated the small ways that showed him that some people cared about him, even if they were kind of paid to do so. He took a sip of the fresh brew and glanced over at the donut. Ford was in the mood for something sweet, but the donut wouldn't lighten his mood. He needed to get out of this place, and not just for the moment. He needed out permanently, and he only had one way to do that. "You said my morning was free until lunch, right?"

"Yes," Kevin replied with a small smile. "Going to play hooky?"

Ford chuckled, but he stood up from his desk and grabbed his keys and briefcase. "I don't know what you're referring to, Kevin, but on the off chance anyone asks to see me, let them know I'm meeting with a very important client downtown."

"Of course, boss." Kevin gave him a jaunty salute and shut the door behind them. "Enjoy your client meeting."

"Thank you," Ford chirped before striding through the halls, making sure to avoid the corner offices of his father and the other partners.

Once he was outside, he smiled and enjoyed the feel of the warm summer sun on his face. He quickly walked to his SUV and opened the driver door, sliding against the buttery, soft leather of the seat and starting the car. The drive to the Willow Creek Library only took fifteen minutes. With any luck, he would be able to get in a little visit with Millie and be back in the office before anyone noticed he was gone. Ford wasn't too worried about his father finding out. Now that the man had already said his piece, he probably wouldn't be coming to see Ford again anytime soon.

Ford parked the car and stepped out, making his way toward the automatic doors of the old brick library. Birdsong rang as he passed by the dogwood and ash trees that surrounded the front of the building, and a smile pulled across his face as he imagined the chorus heralded in a new era, one where he was free of the burdens laid down on him by his parents. Ford walked into the large building, nodding to an older woman who was perusing through the newspapers the library always had available. His feet took him up to the circulation desk, where he spotted Millie. Her dark-rimmed glasses slid down her nose as she peered at the computer screen in front of her.

Ford gave her the once-over while she was still oblivious to his presence. Millie wore a gray tweed dress with a ribbon tied in a bow at the collar. Some might say she dressed a little old-fashioned, but it worked for him. Her clothes hugged her curvy frame. Ford shook his head. *Why are you thinking about her curves?* A marriage between them would be a business arrangement, nothing more. He gazed upon her brown hair which was pulled back, giving him an unobstructed view of the heart-shaped face that contained beautiful brown eyes, rosy cheeks, and plump lips. *What would they taste like?* He thought before shaking his head again. *Focus,* he scolded. *Business Arrangement.*

Millie huffed at the screen and pushed her glasses up closer to her eyes. She shook her head at the device in frustration, and he couldn't help chuckling at her. She was actually kind of adorable when she was distressed. Millie's surprised gaze shot up to his. "Ford," she cheered, the melodic tone of her voice soothing his frayed nerves after the meeting with his father. "What are you doing here?"

Ford pushed out his lips in a mock pout. "Not happy to see me?"

Millie slapped at his arm lightly from across the circulation desk. "Of course I am," she insisted before coming out from behind the desk and giving him a quick hug.

Ford had hugged Millie many times. They were friends, well, if not friends they were at least friendly, so a hug wasn't unusual, but this one felt different. Maybe it was because she was familiar and he needed a bit of comfort, but he found himself sinking into the embrace, weirdly enjoying the feeling of her body against his and the two of them fitting perfectly together. Ford gave himself a little mental smack in the face to keep things on track. He couldn't get distracted by just how nice it felt to have her so close.

Millie finally stepped out of the hug and glanced up at him, her eyes wide and a peaceful smile across her face. "Did you come in just to say hi, or did you need help finding a book?" she asked. For a split second, he considered telling her the truth, which was that he had come here because wanted to see if she was up for a marriage of convenience, but he kept all of that to himself. Seeing her look so happy made him question his idea. Everyone knew Millie was all about romance. There's no way she would ever want to marry a man she didn't love.

Trying to think of an actual reason for him to be there, he held up his briefcase for her. "I need to do a little research for a case," he lied.

"Oh, okay." Her brow furrowed slightly. "Well, do you know where the books are? I mean, we have the maps on the walls, but it's easy for most people to get lost in this place." She shrugged and laughed.

Ford smiled impishly at her. "Do you think you could show me? I do get turned around anytime I'm in here," he told her. The truth was he didn't often come to the library, but he didn't want to admit that. He also didn't want to roam around the place like a fool, and it wasn't like he could just turn around and leave after only being here a few minutes.

"You'd think a lawyer would be smart enough not to get lost anywhere," Millie teased as she led him back to the research section. "I'm surprised your law firm doesn't have its own law library. I know most stuff is on the internet now, but you'd think your father would have a lot of his old books at the office for everyone to use."

He shrugged. "That would be a smart idea," he said, knowing full well that there was an extensive law library already located at the firm. "I'll mention it to him."

"Just don't say it was my idea," she requested in a low voice. "I don't think your father likes me very much."

Ford played dumb. "I'm not sure that's true."

He didn't want to confirm her fear, even though it was a known fact. It wasn't necessarily that his father didn't like her, it was that he didn't even rate her at all because she wasn't someone important enough to him. Hell, his father couldn't even be bothered to remember her actual name most of the time.

Millie snorted and crossed her arms once they were at the stacks of books he needed. "Half the time he calls me Mildred, and the other half he calls me Millet. *Millet*, Ford. That's not a name, it's a grain," she argued, more amused than upset.

Ford smiled at her sadly. "Don't take it personally, Millie. My father is just kind of a dickhead," he admitted. The man was way worse than that, but there was no need to get caught talking crap about his own father. Everyone in town knew who Ford was and what family he came from, so there was no way that it wouldn't get back to his parents.

Millie giggled but tried to cover it with a cough. "You shouldn't say things like that," she scolded lightly, scanning the empty library to make sure no one heard him swearing. She was too pure for this world and definitely too pure for an arranged marriage. "Anyway," she continued with a smile. "I should get back to work and let you get to your research."

"Thanks for all your help," he replied and watched as she gave him a small wave and walked back to the front of the library.

Ford pulled a few useful books that he could take some notes from for some of his current cases, but most of the time the words just blurred together on the page. Even though he'd already ruled her out as a potential wife, he couldn't stop thinking about Millie. It was probably because she was the exact opposite of every woman that his parents had ever thrown at him. Millie was down-to-earth, humble, and genuine. She deserved a lot better than what he had to offer. Ford was back to square one after all.

Chapter Five

~Millie~

The crowd at the used book fair that was taking place on the lawn in front of the library was sparser than Millie would like, not only because it meant less money for the library, but because it meant fewer people coming to her bake sale table and buying the cookies, cupcakes, and brownies that she had spent every night this week baking. Last Thursday, her boss and the board of trustees had gotten back to her about her outreach program with an email telling Millie that they loved her idea, but the budget was about ten thousand dollars short of being able to afford the additional supplies and labor to get the project off the ground.

They welcomed her to try and raise the additional funds herself, but that meant either dipping into her savings, something she was loathe to do since that was her financial safety net, or asking the community for donations, something that was just as difficult. Businesses already donated to the library, and those funds were allocated for other things, so Millie had to get creative and try and come up with the money another way. The problem was she only had just over a month to do it or she would have to start the whole approval process over again. Sometimes working in civil service was a drag. There were so many rules and regulations, so much bureaucratic red tape when it came to funding that it slowed projects down or held them up altogether.

A library patron passed by her table and eyed the peanut butter chocolate chip cookies she had made the night before, so Millie put on her best smile and approached the woman. "Good afternoon," she greeted politely. "Would you be interested in buying a cookie or other treat? All proceeds go toward helping fund a new library outreach program."

The woman smiled at her. "How much for a cookie?"

Millie grabbed the donation box and held it out to the older woman. "It's donation-based, so whatever you would like to give is accepted and appreciated." She hoped this woman would dig deep and give a decent amount or she would never make that donation deadline.

The woman reached into her small clutch purse and pulled out a one-dollar bill, slipping it into the donation box with a smile before grabbing a cookie. "Good luck with your bake sale, dear," she told Millie as she walked away down the sidewalk.

"Thank you," Millie called as she popped open the lid of the box and inspected her total haul. She had been out in the heat for the last three hours and she only had about twenty-five dollars to show for all her effort. "Only nine thousand nine hundred and seventy-five more to go," she mumbled to herself. At this rate, she would spend all her free time baking and still not reach her goal for another few years.

"Well, look who we have here." Millie smiled automatically as she turned toward the sound of her friend's voice. Gigi approached, every bit the southern belle in her floral dress and heels, a large brimmed hat shading her from the afternoon sun. Her arm was looped through Cooper's. Millie sighed wistfully at what a handsome couple they made.

"Hey guys." Millie waved while trying to tamp down the sadness she felt at not having someone of her own yet. *Someday soon*, she hoped. "What brings you two to the library?

Gigi smirked. "Well, my best friend told me that people who come to the used book sale early in the day get all the good finds."

Millie smiled at Gigi, remembering the advice she had given her friend the day before. As a librarian, Millie also had the advantage of being able to browse the donated books before the sale even started, and she already had five new romance novels she had purchased sitting in her bag that she would start reading later.

"That they do. Speaking of good finds," Millie mentioned, splaying her arms widely to showcase the mountain of baked goods she spent most of her week making. "I have plenty of goodies here, if you all are interested. Care for something sweet?"

"I already have my something sweet," Cooper smirked, slinging his arms around Gigi's shoulder and pulling her closer to him so he could kiss her cheek.

Gigi shoved him away, but Millie didn't miss the smile and blush that spread across her face. "Anyway," her friend babbled, her cheeks getting pinker by the second. Gigi could pretend all she liked, but Millie knew how much she loved Cooper and all the attention he gave her. Millie could hardly blame her friend. Cooper was a good man and treated her well. As far as Millie was concerned, he might as well be a unicorn and Gigi should hold onto him with both hands. Gigi continued to gawk at all the treats on the table, her eyes widening as she did. "My god, Mills. When did you find the time to bake all of these?"

Millie shrugged and twisted the end of her ponytail. "I just did it after work, and a little in the morning. It's not a big deal." Millie glanced to the side, not enjoying the attention that was being drawn to her or her lack of a social life.

"It's a huge deal," Gigi insisted, drawing Millie's eyes back up to her friend's. "You're working so hard for your goal. That's amazing." Gigi studied the wide variety of treats, but a frown pulled her lips down at the corner.

"Did you take any downtime for yourself at all though?"

Gigi peeked up at her and gave her the same look she always gave Millie when she thought her friend wasn't taking enough care of herself. It was probably the same look she would use on her future children to get them to spill all their secrets. Those hypothetical children were screwed because the stern look was very effective and had Millie shuffling nervously.

"I enjoy baking," she replied, suddenly self-conscious. "It's not like I have a whole lot else going on anyway." *Sadly.*

Millie didn't love being on dating apps. She did have one date scheduled, but the guy had messaged so infrequently that she wasn't sure he was actually interested in her all that much. With no other relationship prospects on the horizon, Millie didn't have much choice but to at least give the guy a shot.

"I thought you had a date lined up?" Gigi asked, her expression optimistic.

"I do, but I'm not so sure he's all that keen. I think he's just in it for a hookup," Millie admitted, her face reddening when she remembered Cooper was right there. She was definitely not comfortable talking about that sort of thing in front of him. "Can we talk about this another time?" She begged her friend, flicking her gaze to the woman's fiancé.

Gigi seemed to finally catch on and gave her a small smile. "Totally, but right now can we please talk about how badly I need to buy one of your caramel walnut brownies in the next five seconds?" she asked, picking up a napkin and brownie before slipping five dollars into the donation box. Gigi took a bite and groaned. "Oh my god. I have dreams about these brownies after every time you bring them to our girl's nights."

"I'm glad you like them," Millie replied, eager to jump on the subject change. Anything to keep from having to talk about her pathetic social life. "I roasted the walnuts before I added them to the batter. It adds some depth to the flavor." Gigi nodded happily at Millie's baking babble and fed Cooper a bit of the brownie.

Cooper's eyes widened as he chewed. "Damn, Millie. These are amazing," he groaned, flicking his gaze to Gigi with a smirk. "Think you can teach my fiancée how to bake?"

"I know how to bake," Gigi argued, slapping him on the arm playfully. "I can make you brownies if you want, though it may take time away from other activities." Gigi shot Cooper a sultry glance and his eyes widened.

The man pulled out his wallet and dropped a twenty on the table before grabbing another four brownies and cradling them in his large hand. "Don't you worry about baking me a thing, Peach," he reassured Gigi before popping an entire brownie into his mouth.

Another library patron walked up to the table, saving Millie from the envious feeling that rose in her chest every time she witnessed her friends with their beaus. *Will I ever have that?* Maybe not, but at least she still had her friends. That knowledge wasn't as comforting as it once might have been. Surely their close relationships would change with marriage and babies, but Millie tried hard not to think about the inevitable increase in her loneliness.

With a smile at Gigi and Cooper, Millie turned toward the other patron, an older man she had helped many times and knew well. "I'll be right with you, Mr. Knight," she told him before glancing back at her friends. "Thanks for coming, guys."

"Of course." Gigi waved the gesture away like it

was nothing, but it was not nothing to Millie. She could count on few people in her life, so she greatly appreciated the people she did have and anything they could do to show they cared. "Text a picture of you in your dress before you go on your date later, okay."

"Sounds good." Millie still wasn't loving the idea of her date. She hoped she could scrounge up some enthusiasm for it by the time it rolled around. Millie waved goodbye to her friends before turning to Mr. Knight. "What can I get you for you, Harry?"

The gentleman rubbed his balding head. "I'll take two vanilla cupcakes," he answered, fishing a few dollars from his pocket. "My wife will be so excited that I not only got three new mysteries for her at the book sale but a couple of cupcakes as well."

Millie put the cupcakes on a small paper plate and handed them over to the man. "Well, I thank you for your donation and I hope Mrs. Knight enjoys her books and the treat. Have a wonderful day," she replied with a friendly smile.

"You too, Miss Millie." Mr. Knight used the name most library patrons knew her as, and it brought a small smile to her face. The library did bring people into her life, even if they were only there for a book and a nice snack. The man shoved his money into the donation box and walked away, books under his arm and the cupcakes in his hand.

Another three hours later and most of the food was gone, but there were a few of her peanut butter blossom cookies left. Maybe she would be drowning her sorrows in the treat later that night if her date didn't go well. Millie shook her head. *It won't go well if you don't have the right attitude*, she reminded herself. It was hard to have a brighter outlook when none of her other dates had gone well though. Comparing all of them to Ford probably didn't help either, but even without that, there had never been a spark of interest with any of the guys. Millie hadn't had much in common with them. Not a lot of local men her age were searching for marriage and babies right away, but she was. Millie was tired of being single, but single was what she was doomed to be.

With a defeated sigh, Millie finished packing up the leftover treats. Once that was finished, she picked up the donation box and opened it up to start sifting through the cash. She pulled out mostly one-dollar bills, smiling at the occasional five and perking up when she came across a twenty-dollar bill, but it wasn't anywhere near where she needed to be to get the program up and running.

Millie walked the donation box into the library and brought it to her boss, Marsha, feeling proud of all her hard work. "I made just over four hundred dollars," she bragged, handing over the locked box with a small smile. "Just twenty-five more bake sales that are as successful as this one, and I'll make my goal." There was no way she was going to be able to pull that off in four weeks, but she was still going to try. Maybe she could come up with another idea, but she had limited fundraising experience.

"That's a great start," the older woman mentioned as she smoothed down her short, blonde bob. "I'm sure you'll get there eventually, dear."

Millie nodded, not quite as confident as her boss. "Maybe I can sell some of my own books online," she suggested.

The thought of parting with any of her books, saying a permanent goodbye to what felt like old friends, made her chest feel tight. Every book she owned was precious to Millie because it had brought her joy, even if only momentarily. She enjoyed revisiting those stories and those worlds again and again, but at the end of the day, if it made the outreach program a possibility, it would be worth parting with them.

"That's definitely an idea." Her boss walked the donation boxes from the book and bake sales into the office, putting them into the safe. She turned to Millie with a bright smile. "I'm sure you'll put that big brain of yours to work and come up with a way to make the money."

"Thanks." Millie wasn't quite sure she was going to reach her goal, but she appreciated her boss cheering her on.

As she packed up her things and headed out to her bike, she wondered if maybe Gigi or Jo would have fundraising ideas. It was definitely something worth exploring with her friends, though she was a little afraid of what Jo might come up with. Probably selling a kidney on the black market or something equally as dark. Millie was willing to do a lot to make the outreach program happen, but she wasn't ready to part with any of her organs. At least, not yet, but she might change her mind if she hadn't met her goal by the end of the four weeks.

There were a lot of people in Willow Creek who needed the same lifeline that had saved her when she was young, and she didn't want to leave any of them behind. She knew how awful that felt, and if she could prevent even one person from feeling abandoned, she had to do it. Millie tried to clear all that from her thoughts as she rode home. She would think about all that tomorrow. Right now, she had a date to get psyched up for.

****

The Italian restaurant was absolutely lovely and the perfect setting for a romantic meetup. Dim lighting from wall sconces and candles on the white linen-topped tables created a warm atmosphere. Millie smiled as the hostess escorted her to a table. After her little pep talk to herself earlier, she was actually kind of looking forward to meeting her date, hoping that maybe they would hit it off and she would soon have what her friends did, a partner who loved her. With her excitement renewed, Millie had been sure to order a driver to drop her off so that she wouldn't be late. Now she was about five minutes early, just enough time to grab a seat and settle her nerves. The ride had been pretty pleasant considering she rarely spent time in cars, but there was no way she was riding her bike to a date, let alone one in a fancy restaurant.

The hostess smiled and let her know that the server would be with her shortly before leaving. Millie scanned the open and inviting dining area, which was filled with people wearing nice suits and beautiful dresses. She didn't feel comfortable at such a nice place, but she felt less like a sore thumb as she smoothed down the silky material of her halter dress. Her new haircut and contact lenses helped her blend in too.

That afternoon, Millie had stopped at the salon and asked that her lengthy locks be transformed into a wavy, long bob that reached just to the tops of her shoulders. It was a nice change and definitely helped keep her cool during this late summer heat. It was a last-minute decision to try and shake things up for her date. Maybe a new cut would bring a new bit of luck her way. Millie loved her new hairdo, but her contacts were much less enjoyable. She had always had them, but never bothered to try them out since she liked her glasses so much. While she enjoyed not having the frames sitting on her face, the contacts itched. She had to blink a few times every now and then to adjust them.

A server came by and asked for her drink order. Not wanting to be rude, Millie simply ordered some water and waited patiently for her date before asking for anything else. After a few minutes had passed, she slipped her phone out of her purse and checked the time. The man she had been chatting with, Greg, was only five minutes late, so she pushed her phone aside and hummed along to the Italian orchestral music that was playing in the restaurant.

The server came back a while later with her water and a drink menu. "Are you sure I can't get you a glass of wine?" he asked, slipping her the list.

Millie bit her lip and checked the time. Her date was now fifteen minutes late, which was still forgivable, but she was getting more and more nervous with each passing minute. Normally she didn't drink much, mostly due to the cost, but she thought a little liquid courage could be in order to quell the increasingly anxious feeling in her chest.

"Um, what do you recommend? Normally my friends bring the wine," she admitted to the younger man.

He smiled politely. "Well, that depends on your tastes, the flavor notes you want to experience, whether you like dry or sweet..." he trailed off.

"Can you bring me a glass of something sweet and not too expensive?" she asked, her fingers twisting in her lap.

"Of course," he answered. "I'll be right back with a glass of one of our lower-end port wines. It's not cheap, but it's the most affordable wine we have."

Another few minutes passed. The server came back with her drink before leaving her to herself again. Millie lifted the glass of burgundy liquid to her nose and inhaled. It smelled like wood and nuts, not something she found particularly enticing, but she downed the glass all at once, coughing and scrunching up her nose in distaste afterward.

"Blergh." She shook her body as the wine rolled over her tongue, wishing she had some dark chocolate to chase away the flavor. Millie might not like the way it tasted, but after a minute or so, her body felt warm and a little tingly as well as slightly more relaxed. "I guess that did the trick," she joked to herself and glanced at her phone.

Greg was almost half an hour late at this point, so Millie picked up her phone and opened the Hooked on You app. She tried to open their message thread, but it wasn't there anymore. Puzzled at the sight, she navigated over to her list of matches and saw that his name and small profile picture had disappeared as well. Millie stared at her phone in confusion for a minute or two, wondering if the app was malfunctioning or if she had accidentally erased something before she finally figured out what had happened. She'd been ghosted. Ghosted on the app and stood up for the date. Was this a prank, or was flaky Greg just acting like he had the whole time they were messaging? Moisture pooled in her eyes but she blinked it away, almost pushing out one of her contacts.

Millie sniffed and glanced down at her outfit, suddenly feeling ridiculous with her halter dress, new hair, and contacts. Every time she psyched herself up for the possibility of meeting someone, she was let down. Love was always out of reach, and her heart sank with the knowledge that it probably always would be. She ducked and took a deep breath to try and keep the despair that was creeping in at bay, but it was tough when she seemed to only experience one disappointment after another.

Her server came over once again and regarded her with sympathy in his eyes. How pathetic she must appear, sitting there playing dress up only for no one to join her. "Did you want another glass now, or did you want to wait for the rest of your party to arrive?"

With a punch of her finger, Millie closed the dating app on her phone and glanced up at the server. "I'll take another glass now," she told him decisively. "The rest of my party isn't coming, so I guess I'll have to party all on my own."

"I'll be right back with that and a menu," the server replied.

Millie shook her head. "Just the wine please."

She picked up a hard breadstick and snapped the end off with her teeth. The server nodded and walked away as she munched on the complimentary snack. Millie wasn't going to waste any of her money on fancy food, but she liked the way the wine was making her feel. It helped blur the edges of the pain and humiliation that were filling her body. Maybe if she drank enough, she could erase the feeling that she would always be alone, never being loved, and never feeling wanted.

Chapter Six

~Ford~

The dim lighting in Primo Bracio was more conducive to a romantic rendezvous than it was a meeting with a potential client, but when the owner of Pet Palace, the state's largest pet food retailer asked to meet with you and named the place, you went were you were told. That was the reason Ford was currently at the expensive Italian restaurant on a Saturday night, sitting across from one of the most disagreeable men he had ever met.

Most of his colleagues actually had lives and they weren't the boss's son, so they were able to enjoy their weekend while he was out schmoozing, the part of his job he probably hated most. Mercifully, the dinner was almost over and he would be able to pack it in for the evening. If he got home early enough, maybe he could squeeze in a run before bed and feel like he had actually accomplished something that day. Their server dropped off the receipt for dinner, one Ford would be sure to submit for a tax write off like his father taught him, and smiled at the gentleman across from him.

"Well, Mr. Thornton, I want to thank you for your time this evening." Ford hoped he didn't sound as phony as he felt. In his opinion, there was nothing pleasant about discussing the best ways to minimize employee benefits in order to streamline profits for the boss and a board of investors.

The slick-haired man smiled, showing off expensive veneers. "Thank you for dinner," he said, standing and buttoning his suit jacket. It was easily a ten-thousand dollar suit, but after growing up with a man who wore a similar uniform nearly every day, Ford wasn't as impressed as others might be. Thornton stuck his hand out to shake his, and Ford took it, briefly clasping the man's hand to signal an end to the evening. *Thank God.* "I'm looking forward to working with you and your team."

"As am I," Ford lied smoothly. Thornton hadn't been happy with his business' current legal team for various reasons and wanted to jump ship to his father's firm. Ford was tasked with landing the client. Like the good little soldier he was, he spent the last two hours wining and dining the man to make a case for him to do just that. Ford gestured for his new client to exit the more private back parlor that was reserved for important guests of the restaurant, and they made their way toward the front. "I'll send the contracts over to your assistant Monday morning."

"Wonderful," the man replied.

Ford smiled politely as they made their way through the restaurant, but he stopped short when he saw a familiar face sitting at a table all alone. Well, the face was mostly familiar, but Millie looked different tonight. Ford noticed her shorter haircut immediately, but it took him another moment to realize that she wasn't wearing her glasses either. Her hair fell in waves, stopping just above her mostly bare shoulders, and she was wearing a knockout red dress that showed off a substantial amount of cleavage that had his blood pumping a little harder than it had been.

"Ford?"

The voice startled him, and Ford peeled his attention away from a surprisingly sexy Millie to look at his new client. "Sorry, sir. It's someone I know," he stuck out his hand one last time and the two men shook hands. "I'll talk to you again soon."

Thornton leered at Millie for a moment before

turning back to him. "Ah, well then. Enjoy your evening," he said with a wink. Ford was tempted to poke the man's eyes out of his head just for ogling Millie and implying something untoward. *Whoa,* he thought, rearing back at the sudden possessiveness he felt toward his sister's friend. *Where had that come from?*

"Uh, you too," Ford replied distractedly, relaxing the hands he hadn't realized had been balled into fists at his side. He made sure Thornton was gone before he turned and strolled over toward Millie. She was sitting at a table for two, nibbling on the end of a breadstick with three empty wine glasses and one almost completely full glass of water in front of her. *Was she on a date?* He stopped when he was next to her, and she tilted her head back to look at him with glassy eyes. "Mind if I join you?" he asked politely. Ford wasn't sure what had possessed him to come over to speak with her, but he couldn't leave without at least saying hello to the woman who had occupied his thoughts more often than not lately.

Millie's eyes widened and smiled sweetly. "Ford. You're here," she bubbled, pointing to the other chair with her breadstick. "I would love for you to join me. You can sit there. No one else is sitting there." A small hiccup escaped her mouth.

He frowned as he sat across from her. Despite the light tone of her voice as she babbled to him, the sadness in her eyes told another story. "You're eating alone?"

Millie shook her head and squeezed her eyes shut when she stopped. "I'm always eating alone." She scanned the room for a moment before reaching out to the near-empty bread basket and grabbing a hard garlic stick, chomping a bite off the end of it, and chewing it slowly. "S-s'okay though. I made a new friend," she slurred. Seconds later her eyes widened with glee at the sight of a server who had come up to the table. "There he is. Ford this is my new friend Anthony. Anthony, this is Ford."

"Good evening, sir," the younger man said politely before glancing over at Millie with an exasperated expression. "Are you all done, ma'am? Or would you finally like to order some food?"

Millie held up one of her empty wine glasses. "Can I get another one of these?" she asked, swaying a little in her seat. "It's forgetful juice," she whispered to Ford.

"Interesting," he told her with a smile before turning to the waiter. "Could you just bring us the check, please?" Millie had obviously had a good amount of wine and not nearly enough food. There was no way Ford would let her drink herself into a stupor.

The server sighed with relief and nodded. "My pleasure," he mumbled before taking off.

Ford glanced at the empty glasses and her hazy eyes and frowned. "How much wine have you had, Millie?" He was more than a little concerned. Millie wasn't known as much of a drinker, and here it looked like she had polished off at least three glasses of wine.

Millie held up three fingers, then added another. "I had this many glasses, but I need more because it's not working anymore."

Ford felt his brow furrow. "What's not working?"

"The forgetful juice, silly." Millie sighed heavily. "It's not working anymore because I can still remember being all alone." She sniffed and appeared so completely heartbroken that it caused his own heart to crack a little. "I got stood up," she admitted shakily.

The server dropped off the bill and Ford pulled out three hundred dollars in cash. That more than covered the four glasses of wine and however many breadsticks she had consumed as well as a decent tip for the server. After slipping the money into the billfold, he reached across the table and grabbed Millie's hand. It was warm, soft, and fit perfectly in his own. Ford tried not to think too hard about why he was noticing that sort of thing and soldiered on.

"I'm sorry you got stood up, sweet girl." The nickname fell off his lips automatically, probably because he pitied her. It would be impossible for anyone not to empathize with the look of devastation on her face. Millie was the sweetest woman he'd ever met, and she definitely deserved better than being stood up. "Can I give you a ride home?"

Millie nodded slowly. "Okay." She stood suddenly, grabbing the end of the table to steady herself.

Ford shot up out of his own chair and wrapped his arm around her waist to steady her. Millie blinked up at him with a grateful smile, but the sadness lingered in her eyes. "Thanks, Ford. You're a good guy," she declared as he steered the two of them to the exit.

The night had cooled off slightly, and when he saw goosebumps break out on Millie's skin as they left the restaurant, he paused their walk and took off his jacket to put it over her shoulders. She sniffled and hiccupped at the same time. He hated that she felt she had to drink so much to numb her feelings, but she was an adorable mess, and he couldn't help smiling down at her.

Millie tilted her head back to look at him and blinked a few times. "You're blurry," she mumbled and rubbed at her eyes, smearing her eye makeup a little.

Ford chuckled and led her over to his car, opening the passenger door and helping her slide down. "Let's get you home then and you can put your glasses back on and see me better," he said as he shut her door.

After rounding the hood, he slid into his own seat and glanced to the side to see Millie staring at him, a peaceful expression. "I don't need glasses to see you."

She smiled dreamily before closing her eyes. "I can see you even with my eyes shut."

Ford wasn't sure if it was the alcohol that was talking or if she meant something more by it, but for a moment he couldn't breathe. *Did she see him? Did anyone?* When most people looked at him, they saw the dutiful son and successful lawyer, but he liked to think he was more than that. It was probably just all the wine that had Millie speaking like she knew him. Reaching across her, Ford buckled her in.

"Let's get you home," he told her, steering the car to the small block of apartments she lived in. Ford had dropped her off once or twice in all the years he'd known her, but not many.

Twenty minutes later, he had parked along the street and was helping her along the uneven sidewalk, a little surprised that he still knew exactly how to get to her place. When the heel of Millie's shoe got stuck in a crack for a third time, Ford impatiently swept her up in his arms and strode over to the front of her building. He gazed down at her, liking the way her body felt against his, her head resting on his shoulder as her arms wrapped around his neck. A peaceful smile came over Millie's face and she sighed contentedly as he cradled her in his arms.

Ford was a little confused because he was feeling the same sense of calm, but he just attributed that to his own glass of wine at dinner and tiredness. He had to put Millie down so that she could fish her keys out of her purse and open the door to her the building. Once she had, he helped her up the stairs, and after watching her struggle to get her key in her lock, he gently took them from her and opened her apartment, pushing the door open for her. He then watched attentively as she stepped inside and kicked her heels off across her small living room.

Millie glanced over her shoulder at him. "You can come in if you want." She waved him in as she walked over her tiny kitchen.

Ford knew there was no real reason for him to do so, but he found himself stepping inside anyway, shutting the door behind him before scanning her apartment. It was much cozier and lived-in than his house, with walls of books and small keepsakes on display. In the middle of the room sat a comfy, dark green sofa with a cream-colored knitted throw blanket tossed along the top. The whole apartment was very Millie, charming and pleasant with little touches of brightness here and there. Her small feet padded across the hardwood floor as she approached him with a cookie tin. She popped off the lid and held it out to him.

"I don't have any shortbread," she said, her tone filled with regret. Shortbread was Ford's favorite, and her remembering that was both surprising and touching.

Ford smiled at her and took one of the peanut butter blossom cookies she offered. "I like other cookies just fine, Millie, but I appreciate your thoughtfulness."

Millie nodded and put the tin down on her counter, rubbing her eyes again. "I'm going to take out my eyeballs," she mumbled before walking into her room.

Ford assumed she meant her contacts. After she left, he walked over to one of her bookshelves, eating the salty sweet cookie as he did. Most of the shelves were covered in books, but there was one that was filled with picture frames. Ford looked at every single one, noticing that each held a photo of Millie with her friends. There were no pictures of her parents or any other friends, just Gigi and Jo. *Did she have no one else?* Ford knew she grew up with little money, but other than that, she didn't talk about herself much, preferring to let other people soak up all the attention instead.

A yelp from her bedroom had him jumping back and rushing over to the open door. Ford managed to keep himself from peeking inside, not wanting to invade her privacy. "You all right in there, Millie?" he called.

"Fine," she replied. "Stupid boob tape."

Ford had no idea what she was saying and he tried hard not to think about the magnificent pair of breasts that had been on display in her halter dress. Instead he tried diverting his thoughts to the contracts he needed to review on Monday to squash the desire he felt stirring low in his belly. Yup, that did the trick. Nothing like legalese to kill a man's libido, though why it was waking up after so long at thoughts of Millie was a mystery. It must just be his years of celibacy in effect.

After the long day he'd had, the couch in front of him practically called his name, so Ford sat down to give his tired feet a break and glanced over the books she had stacked on the coffee table. He chuckled at some of the titles of her romance novels. *The Dastardly Duke* or *The Mischievous Marquees* had him stifling a giggle. Apparently, Millie had a type when it came to books. He wondered if she had a type when it came to men. Ford had abandoned his idea about marrying her, but now that he was in Millie's space, surrounded by her books and furniture, it was back at the forefront of his mind. Maybe she would be okay with a sham marriage. Her dating life was clearly not going so well, so she could be willing to help him out for now.

Millie shuffled back into the room wearing slippers, pajama shorts, and a baggy t-shirt that was covered in books and read "I have no shelf control." Her makeup was gone and her glasses were back, her hair pulled into a little ponytail on top of her head. She flopped down next to him on the couch and rested her head against the back of it. Then, tired and dejected, she peeked over at him. Her glasses slipped down her nose, and he couldn't stop himself from reaching over to push them back up.

"There's Millie," he crooned so tenderly that he almost didn't recognize his own voice. Something about Millie brought out the softer side of him, and for someone who spent most of their day trying to be a hard ass, it was a nice switch.

"Here's me," she answered tiredly, covering her yawn. "Thanks for the ride home. Now I can use the ride share money I saved for my library program."

Ford studied her curiously. "I thought the library was paying for that," he remarked.

Millie shook her head quickly before she used both hands to hold it in place. "Ugh, no more shaking." She winced. Millie definitely had too much to drink if she was feeling dizzy. One of her brown eyes opened. "The library doesn't have enough money in the budget, so I have to raise it myself. Needing money sucks," she huffed.

"Yeah, it does," he commiserated. Ford needed money for his own firm. She needed money for her library program. The little devil on his shoulder whispered, *if she's married to you, she can have your money*. He waited for the angel to pop up telling him not to drag such a caring woman into his messy bullshit, but it never showed. Once again the idea took root in his mind. "How much do you need for your program?"

Millie's brow furrowed. "Um, I need about ten thousand dollars."

Ten thousand? Ford could see how someone who grew up without money might think that number was insurmountable, but it was doable if he knew the right people, which he did. Ford smiled at just having found the way to get her on board with this whole marriage scheme. He could introduce her to the right people, and she could legally bind herself to him for the next year. Not a fair trade off, but it was something. He turned in his chair to face her and broach the subject, only to find her dead asleep, her glasses crooked from the way her head rested on the couch. Yup, she was adorable, and she was just what he needed to finally get his life in order.

Ford stood and slipped his arm under her knees to lift her before carrying her into her bedroom and laying her down, pulling her quilt up to her chin to tuck her in. He gently removed her glasses and put them on her nightstand. "Sleep well, sweet Millie," he murmured, and smiled when she appeared to sigh happily in reply. He walked into the kitchen and poured her a glass of water and grabbed two ibuprofen from her medicine cabinet, leaving both on her nightstand for her to take in the morning. She was going to need them.

Ford made his way back out to the couch and kicked off his oxford shoes, grabbing the throw blanket and pulling it over himself as he tried to get comfortable enough to sleep. There was no way he was leaving, not when he'd finally figured out a way for all of this to work out in his favor. It would work out in her favor too, with her library program soon fully funded and able to get up and running in no time. As he tried to fall asleep, Ford started coming up with the beginnings of a plan to convince her to marry him, ignoring that small part of him that knew he wasn't doing it simply for the money from his trust, but for a chance to be with such a sweet woman as well.

Chapter Seven

~Millie~

A clinking sound awoke Millie. She rolled over in her bed, the bright streaks of sun beaming in from the window hitting her face, causing her to whine and pull her covers over her eyes to block out the intrusive daylight. Her head was pounding, like there were a bunch of tiny men with huge hammers swinging away at each part of her brain and making it throb. Millie wanted nothing more than to disappear back into unconsciousness, but now that she was awake, there was no way she would be able to go back to sleep. She gingerly explored her mouth with her tongue. Her teeth felt fuzzy and she tasted of dried wood chips, but more than that, she was extremely thirsty. *Why am I so darn thirsty?*

Tiny snippets of memory from the night before starting floating to the front of her mind, and she cringed at them. Millie had gotten stood up, then she drank too much, and she remembered Ford being there, but she was fairly certain she dreamt that last part. How did she even get home? She knew for sure that she was in her own bed because she recognized the scent of her lavender linen spray, and when she opened one eye and glanced down at herself, she saw that she was wearing her own pajamas. She had the *why* and the *where*, but not the *how*. How had she come to be in her apartment? The clinking sound happened again. Millie's eyes widened under her bedsheets for a moment before she shut them again. Still too bright, but was she not alone?

Millie eventually pulled the sheets down and climbed out of bed slowly to keep herself from passing out from the dizziness and pain that the movement caused. Then she shuffled over to the doorway of her bedroom. She peeked out and saw Ford standing in her kitchen. His clothes were wrinkled and his hair was disheveled, but other than that, he looked perfect, exactly as he had the night before. So she hadn't dreamt him after all.

Oh god, how embarrassing. She had inadvertently gotten drunk and he had to bring her home. Did she hit on him? Confess her feelings? Her cheeks warmed at the thought she'd humiliated herself in front of him, but there was nothing she could do about it now except pretend it didn't happen. Millie made to walk out into the kitchen, but the funky taste in her mouth had her spinning around to go the other way.

The nightstand had a cup of water and two pain pills on top, so she grabbed those along with her glasses before heading into her tiny bathroom. She downed the water and the medicine, then used the bathroom, and washed up. Millie took a good look at herself in the mirror while she brushed the night before off her teeth. Her hair was a mess and she resembled roadkill. She spat her toothpaste into the sink and swished some mouthwash around to get rid of the funky taste in her mouth. It was too bad she couldn't do the same thing with her memories from the night before. It would be nice to scrub away the pain and rejection she felt until everything was sparkling again, although to be fair, her life hadn't been sparkling for a while, maybe not ever.

After redoing her hair into a tiny ponytail, Millie walked out of the bathroom and through the bedroom doorway to confront her savior from the night before. As she passed by her couch, she saw that the cushions were a little lumpy and her throw blanket was bunched up at one end. Ford must have folded his six-foot frame onto her tiny sofa and slept there. She couldn't imagine why he stayed instead of going home to his amazing house, but she was grateful to not be waking up alone after such a horrible night.

"Good morning," she called, flinching at the sound of her gruff voice that was raspy from all the drinking. Millie hated not sounding like herself.

Ford turned at her call. He had been at the stove scrambling what looked to be eggs and cheese in one of her pans. His eyes seemed a little tired, but even with light purple bags underneath them, he was still the most handsome man she'd ever laid eyes on. A small smile came across his face as she continued to stare at him.

"How are you feeling?" he asked, keeping his voice low for her, something she greatly appreciated. The men with hammers had softened their blows, but they were still there.

Millie lightly shrugged and walked to the sink to fill her glass with more water. "I've been better," she admitted, turning on the faucet. She took a few big gulps of water and turned back to him. "I think this is my first official hangover. Do I get a prize or anything?"

Ford smiled and tilted the pan to show off his creation. "You get cheesy eggs and whatever bread I can find," he explained. "I didn't want to make too much noise banging around your kitchen, but I least wanted to get something started so you could get some food in your belly once you woke up."

Millie slid into one of the chairs of her small dining table. She had purchased the table and all four mismatched chairs at the thrift store downtown when she first moved into the apartment. She cleaned them and polished the wood, liking the fact that she was saving money and giving second life to something no one else wanted. If only someone would do the same thing for her.

Millie caught Ford staring at her intently. He had never been inside her apartment before, but he looked good there. He looked good everywhere, and while she had pictured him in her space before, albeit under much sexier circumstances, it was still nice to see him there now.

"Thank you for making breakfast." She tried pouring all of the sincerity she felt into her voice. "And for last night. I don't remember much, but I remember you being there and you obviously helped me get home in one piece. I'm grateful that you did."

"Of course," Ford replied, sounding almost offended that she was thanking him for going above and beyond the best friend's brother call of duty. "It was my pleasure."

Millie chuckled humorlessly. "I doubt I was much of a pleasure to deal with last night," she confessed. She probably said so many stupid things, but she was too afraid to ask him in case she actually had. "I hope I didn't throw up in your car or anything."

Ford shook his head. "Nothing like that. I was happy to help you, Millie." He turned back to the eggs to finish scrambling them. She remembered she had something in the refrigerator that would be the perfect "thank you" for his helping her.

Millie stood up, a little too quickly and winced at the pain in her head. Luckily, the medicine was starting to kick in, so it while moving around sucked, it wasn't going to make her pass out or want to throw up anymore. She padded over to the fridge and pulled out the leftover apple cinnamon coffee cake she had made a few days prior, lifting the foil covering and showing it to Ford.

"Do you want some coffee cake? It's not freshly made, obviously." She gestured to the state of her, which was undoubtedly a sight to be seen. "But it'll still taste good if I warm it up a little, maybe add some butter."

Ford beamed at her. "I would love some." He reached into her cabinet and grabbed two plates. "It's always been my favorite."

Millie took the plates from him and served up a slice on each, popping the first one in the microwave. Her brow furrowed in confusion. "You've had it before? Does the downtown bakery make it?" Millie wasn't aware of the local bakery making the same coffee cake she did, though she never had reason to visit the place much since she enjoyed her own baking much better.

Ford shook his head slowly, his cheeks turning a little pink. "Um, no." He started rubbing the back of his neck. "You made it a couple of times when you were living with Ginny in college and I had some when I was there for a visit. I think you were probably in class or something, but I always ate like two or three servings anytime they were available."

Millie giggled softly. "That was you? Oh my gosh, I feel so awful now because I thought Gigi was eating it all and I stopped making coffee cake after a while."

She grabbed the first plate from the microwave and passed it to Ford. He took it from her and served up some eggs and grabbed a fork, passing both back to her. She enjoyed working in tandem in the kitchen with him. He was a natural, and it was nice to have a partner, even in something as simple as making breakfast.

Ford nodded to the dining table. "You start eating. I'll join you in a sec," he told her, grabbing a glass of water for himself.

"Thanks." Millie slipped back into her chair and salted her eggs. When she lifted the fork to her mouth and the first bite hit her tongue, she was in heaven. The scramble was perfectly soft and pillowy, with just the right amount of cheddar cheese to add some zing. "This is delicious," she told him as he sat down with his own plate. "Thanks again."

Ford cut off a bite of cake and lifted it to him mouth, his expression nervous. "You don't have to thank me so much, Millie. I'm happy to do it," he promised before stuffing the cake in his mouth. He groaned and closed his eyes as he chewed while she tried very hard to remember that she wasn't supposed to be attracted to or in love with him anymore. "When I get to eat stuff like this, I feel like I should be thanking you. Besides, friends help each other out, right?"

The corners of her mouth twitched with a smile, but she suppressed it. His use of the word "friends" was a nice reminder that Millie needed to move on, but it still made her feel good that he recognized that, at the very least, they did have a friendship of sorts. It was a good thing that this kind of thing didn't happen that often though. Mornings like this were just putting ideas in her head. Ideas like marriage and babies with a man who would never see her as anything other than his sister's friend.

"I guess so," she mumbled, not sure what else to say.

"Since we're friends and we've just established that friends help one another, I wanted to talk to you about a mutually beneficial opportunity," he imparted, sounding more like the successful lawyer he was.

Millie nodded slowly to keep her head from hurting. The medicine and food were helping, but not as quickly as she would have liked. "What kind of opportunity?" she asked, taking a bite of coffee cake.

"Well," he began, rubbing his jaw. Millie willed herself to stay focused on his words and not the powerful hands that she wanted all over her body. "I know you need money for your library program…"

Millie held up her hand to stop him. "I don't want to accept money from a friend for this," she stated firmly. "I want to raise the funds myself if I can." She might feel differently when the deadline got closer, but there were a lot of avenues she hadn't explored yet, not very lucrative ones, but still. Millie hated handouts. They reminded her of where she came from and that some people still saw her as low-class and needy.

Ford smiled. "I thought you might say that, but that's not what I'm proposing."

"What are you proposing?" she asked before taking a sip of water. Millie couldn't imagine what his idea was. Maybe something involving his mother's charity group. Millie wanted to raise funds, but the idea of having to interact with his mother for more than a few minutes soured her stomach more than her hangover had.

"Marriage," he told her, his expression completely serious.

Millie choked on her water. Ford sprang up and out of his seat to rub her back. Her eyes watered and her breathing was ragged, but eventually she had coughed up all the water and was finally able to calm down enough to take a deep breath before she addressed him. "I'm sorry, I must still be drunk because I could have sworn you said you were proposing marriage."

Ford peered at her sheepishly. "I did."

Millie's brow furrowed and she tilted her head at him. As much as she might wish it were the case, there was no way she was lucky enough that he had suddenly realized he had harbored an all-consuming love for her and couldn't stand not being married to her a minute longer, so it must be something else.

"I think I'm going to need a little clarification." She rubbed her temples, trying to get rid of the throbbing that flared up again and make sense of what he was saying.

Ford took a deep breath and started to explain his own monetary quandary. He needed money to start a new firm, but his trust money was tied up until he got married. Yes, that was legal and yes, he had already exhausted all his court challenges. Now he needed to get married or in a month, his money would go to a charity and his dream of opening his own law firm would go with it. Millie frowned at the idea of him not getting everything he wanted. There was no doubt that Ford came from privilege, but he also worked incredibly hard to get where he was, and wanting to open a firm that would help people in need was noble and something she wanted to support.

"So, how exactly would the two of us getting married be mutually beneficial?" The idea of being married to Ford had her insides warming and turning to mush. Though just being married to him would be enough for her, he didn't know that. Millie wanted to hear what else he had to say.

"Well, I would have my money and could give it to you," he said, and barreled forward before she could protest. "But I know you don't want that. As my wife, you would benefit from my connections. I could introduce you to a lot of people with a lot of money that they would happily give to the library and write it off as a charitable donation."

Millie's head bobbed as she absorbed everything. "And we'd have to be married for a year?" A year married to a man who she loved desperately but who would never love her. That sounded equal parts heaven and hell. Millie wasn't quite sure where she landed on the whole concept yet.

"Yup. One year and then we could separate. Clean

and easy." He peeked at her cautiously. "What do you say?"

What did she say? Her body and heart said, sign me up. Marrying Ford had been a dream of hers since she was little and part of her wanted nothing more than to live that dream, but her mind was more cautious, telling her this whole scheme had the potential for disaster. "I don't know, Ford. That's a big commitment," she admitted. It was a big commitment. If it were anyone other than him she wouldn't even consider it, but this was Ford, and she loved him. Millie took a deep breath. "I'll think about it."

Ford nodded and stood. "Yes, do that," he replied quickly as he grabbed his jacket and backed toward her apartment door. "I won't bug you again, but you know, time is of the essence and all that."

Millie nodded as he walked out of her apartment and stared at the door long after he left. When Millie thought about the story of her life, she never would have guessed that the whole marriage of convenience trope would show up, but here it was and she had a decision to make. Those stories always ended happily, but that was fiction and this was real life. There was only one way this would end, and that was with her heartbroken. Even knowing that, why did she long to say yes?

****

"I'm getting married," Millie blurted out to Gigi and Jo three days after her morning with Ford. The three of them had moved their girl's night to Tuesday because Cooper was taking Gigi away for a trip this weekend. Millie wished romantic getaways like that were in her future, but she would have to settle for a fake marriage to a man she had real feelings for. *Close enough*, she guessed. Millie stood in front of where her friends sat on the couch and took in their blank stares. A sigh escaped her mouth and she waved toward her. "Come on, now. Out with the questions."

Two of Millie's best friends in the whole world glanced at one another for moment, where they had silently agreed to let Gigi perform the interrogation. Smart considering she was the gentler of the two. Millie knew she required a soft touch because of how sensitive she was, but it was even more necessary now when her emotions were all over the place. "Okay. Let's cover all the main ones like who are you marrying and why?"

"I'm marrying your brother so he can get his trust money," Millie stated as if it wasn't the single most ridiculous thing she had ever said to them. She winced at the women's raised brows. "More explanation required?"

Jo held her thumb and forefinger centimeters apart. "Yeah, just a smidge."

"Okay, here goes." Millie proceeded to give the two of them the same spiel Ford had given her, with all the details she could remember. When she was finished, Jo's eyes were wide with amusement, but Gigi had a far more concerned expression.

"Ford didn't tell me any of this," Gigi griped. "That's not important now though. I'll deal with Ford later, but Millie, honey, you can't do this." Her voice was steady and her tone firm. Though Millie understood it came from a place of love, it rankled her all the same.

"Why not?" Millie challenged, crossing her hands over her chest from where she stood in her apartment. This was her decision to make, not theirs. Millie wasn't exactly sure when she had decided to marry Ford Davenport, and while she still wasn't convinced it was the best idea, everything in her urged her to say yes. For once, she was going to let her heart guide her instead of always doing what was pragmatic.

Jo frowned. "You can't because it wouldn't be a

real marriage, Mills."

Millie scoffed. "Lots of people don't have real marriages," she alleged. "Ford needs to get married and he can help me raise money for the library. It's a total win-win." It was a great plan except for the part where her heart got crushed in the end when they inevitably divorced and she was alone again, but that was a problem for future Millie. Present-day Millie had Ford wanting to marry her, and she wasn't going to let that chance pass her by.

"No, it's a win-lose," Gigi argued. "Ford gets what he needs, but you don't. Millie, you are the most fanciful and romantic woman I have ever known. How can you settle for less than what you want? Less than you deserve?"

Millie tried not to let her friend's words get to her, but they did. Millie did want romance and the happily ever after, but this was as close as she was going to get and she needed to take the leap before he found someone else to marry. "You guys don't get it," she told them, her throat thick with emotion. "You've always had people in your lives who loved you. I haven't. I still don't."

"We love you," Jo shot back. "Do we not count?" Her friend sounded genuinely offended, and Millie wished she had chosen her words better. She loved her friends and was grateful for their love too, but it wasn't the same.

"Of course you guys count," Millie cried as she sat down on the coffee table, taking one of each of their hands in hers. "You're my best friends. I love you and without you, I would have nothing, but it's different and you know it. You both already found your person."

Gigi grimaced. "You can still find your person, Mills. I feel like you're giving up too soon." Part of Millie agreed with her friend, but the other part that had been lonely and on too many bad dates recently disagreed. That part was always the loudest.

"Maybe I am giving up too soon, but it doesn't feel like it," she huffed, tears welling in her eyes. "I've tried to meet people the natural way, and I've been using these stupid apps. I've been on terrible date after terrible date until, finally, I got stood up completely the other night. My mom didn't want to keep me, my aunt and uncle didn't stay with me. I can't even get a guy to show up for a date anymore. I have all this love inside of me, and nobody wants it. No one wants me." A few tears escaped and she swiped at them angrily. "And Ford may not want me, but he needs me to help make his dream happen. What's so wrong about helping the person you love make their dreams come true?"

Millie's friends looked at her with sympathy. "Nothing is wrong with that, sweetie," Gigi admitted, squeezing her hand. "But you shouldn't have to sacrifice your own happiness for it either."

Millie shrugged. "I'm not happy now, and at least this way I get to spend a little more time with him before…" she trailed off, not wanting to talk about the end of their marriage before it even began.

"I don't like this. Not one bit," Jo stated firmly, moving to sit next to Millie on the coffee table. "But if it's what you want, I'll support you because you are my friend and I love you."

"You will?" Millie and Gigi asked at the same time.

Jo nodded. "I will, and so will you," she told Gigi, who didn't look quite as convinced. "We'll support Millie because she has supported us even when we've made bad decisions, like the time you tried to dye your hair blonde and it looked bright orange." She smiled as she reminded Gigi of the disaster that was her clown-colored hair one summer.

"Or the time Jo tried to iron out her curls and burned off a chunk of her hair," Gigi added, a small smile finally coming across her face.

"Why are all your bad decisions hair-related?" Millie asked, feeling a little better now that she had her friends support.

"Because irons and hair dye are cheaper than therapy," Jo answered with a chuckle. The three of them laughed because it was true. When any of them had faced any kind of life crisis, something happened to their hair. Heck, even Millie's recent hair cut was because she felt like her social life needed a little pick up.

When their laughter died down, Millie squeezed their hands again. "Thanks you guys. Your support means a lot." The two women nodded and they spent the rest of the evening avoiding the topic of her impending nuptials, probably so as to not stir up any more emotions from her. She was grateful for the reprieve, but her friends not bringing it up didn't stop her from thinking about it all night long. Millie was getting married. Now she just had to go tell the groom.

Chapter Eight

~Ford~

Four days. It had been four days since Ford had clumsily proposed a fake marriage deal to Millie and he hadn't heard a peep from her. He was tempted to go down to the library and ask her where her head was at, but he also wanted to give her the space to think about it. Truthfully, he was also a little afraid of her refusal. The more time that passed since his proposal, the better he felt about this whole thing. Just two friends helping one another out for a little while before parting ways and going about life as usual again.

A year was no big deal. People always said life was short, and that was true in a sense, but it was also long and this would probably just end up being a fun anecdote they told other people at parties. *I was married once, but it was for money and only lasted a year.* That story was actually pretty common in the circles he ran with, so he would just end up another clichéd, divorced lawyer. At least he'd have his practice by then and wouldn't have to deal with the demands of his father anymore.

A buzz from his intercom caused Ford to jump in his seat and he quickly hit save on the document he was working on and closed it. If anyone saw the outline for his own firm on his screen or there was even one whiff of him leaving, he would be ousted and the other lawyers would start calling around to try and get him blackballed by clients. It would serve him right for working with such cutthroat maniacs to begin with, but he needed to keep the goodwill toward him going until he secured the capital, office space, and clients for his new firm. Ford was confident that a few of the smaller, more reputable businesses would want to come with him, and he already had a list of co-workers in mind that he wanted to poach, mostly paralegals and administrators, but he couldn't risk coming right out and asking anyone to jump ship until he was absolutely ready to go.

The intercom buzzed again and Ford shook himself from his thoughts and hit the button to speak to his assistant. "What is it, Kevin?" he asked hurriedly. He wanted to get back to his plans, but until Millie accepted his proposal, it was kind of a waste of time anyway.

"Is that any way to speak to your favorite assistant?" Kevin asked, clicking his tongue. "I swear he's not always this grumpy." When someone else tittered over the line, Kevin muttered, "Maybe *you* can cheer him up."

Ford sighed. "My apologies. What can I do for you, Kevin?"

"That's more like it," the young man replied more cheerfully. "I have a Miss Millie Legare here to see you. Should I send her in or can I keep her? She is just the cutest little thing. I want to scoop her up and put her in my pocket."

Ford could hear Millie giggle through the intercom, and a smile spread across his face. She came to say yes to his proposal, he just knew it. His chest filled with excitement, and he pumped his fist. Was he getting ahead of himself? Definitely. But confidence was key to being a lawyer, and Ford was in no shortage of it.

"You can send her in," he told Kevin before standing and buttoning his suit jacket. A quick glance in the reflection of his glass windows confirmed that Ford still looked as good as he had when he got ready that morning. Millie wouldn't be marrying him for his looks anyhow, but he still wanted to look presentable for his future fake bride.

When the door opened and Millie stepped inside, Ford smiled and gestured for her to come in. She was wearing one of her classic Millie outfits, a bright ruffled blouse with a dark navy skirt, bright leggings and a beret on her head. She was the most adorable librarian he had ever seen. If she had been working at his childhood library, he probably would have spent a lot more time reading.

Ford cleared that strange thought from his head and nodded at her. "It's nice to see you again, Millie."

"You too," she replied, smiling politely. Millie held a tin in her hand and he would bet his luxury vehicle it was filled with cookies. "I made you these."

Ford reached out and took the tin, smiling at her as he did. "Thanks, Millie." He opened the lid and saw the entire container filled with his favorite pecan shortbread cookies inside. The thoughtfulness of this woman seemed to know no bounds, especially when it came to showering her friends with baked goods.

When Ford looked up from the tin to her face, he noticed her anxious expression. She twined her fingers together. "I remembered you said they were your favorite, but that was a long time ago, so maybe that's changed."

Ford shook his head. "No. No, they're still my favorite." He reached in and took a bite of one of the cookies. It was soft, buttery, and had the roasted pecan flavor he loved. In short, it was the perfect cookie. He grinned as he swallowed it down before grabbing another. "These are amazing, Millie. Thanks again." He noticed her shuffling, so he escorted her over to the couch in his office to help put her at ease. "Why don't we sit down?"

Millie followed him and sat, but when he came to

sit next to her, she stood up quickly. "I think I need to walk while I say this," she told him, stretching her fingers out and back rapidly.

Oh, no. She was nervous, so she must be here to deliver bad news. The cookies she made were a consolation prize and just like that, the image of him in his own firm went up in a puff of smoke. Millie started pacing back and forth, glancing at him occasionally before finally coming to a stop in front of him. She stared at him and he stared back, slightly curious as to how he'd never noticed just how beautiful she was. *Not helpful*, he reminded himself. Then he readied himself for rejection.

Millie took a deep breath and exhaled slowly. "I'll marry you, but we have to agree on some rules first or it will get complicated for..." Her eyes darted to the side. "Reasons."

A slow smile spread across his face. "So you're saying yes, but you want rules. Should I draw up a contract?" With as much as he was worth, it would be smart to draw up a prenuptial agreement at least, but Millie would never take advantage of him and he didn't want to insult her by suggesting it.

Millie sighed and finally came to sit next to him. "No, I don't want anything that formal," she admitted, picking at a piece of lint on her skirt. "I get it if you do though. I know you're an important person and I'm...well, me."

Ford frowned, not liking the way she disparaged herself. "You're important too, Millie," he told her, realizing they weren't just empty words. Millie was like a ray of sunshine on an otherwise dreary day. She always thought of others and did everything she could to help them. The fact that she was in front of him accepting his offer proved that. "I don't need anything formal either. Now, why don't you tell me about these rules of yours?"

Millie's head bobbed, causing her silky waves to bounce as she reached into her giant purse and pulled out a folded piece of notebook paper. "I like lists," she told him as she unfolded it. Once it was all smoothed out, she raised it up to her face, adjusted her glasses, and began. "First, I want to do all the fundraising for the library program myself. You can introduce me to the right people, but I have to convince them to donate all on my own."

"Seems reasonable," he remarked.

Ford wanted to help her with her goal, but he could also understand her need to do it herself. Being his own person was important, and he wanted to get away from his father's influence, so he got where she was coming from. He gestured for her to continue, smiling when she cleared her throat. She was acting very professional, and while it should have been a signal for him to do the same, her cuteness had a more relaxing effect on him, and he leaned back into the couch, stretching his arm out behind her.

"Second, I already told Jo and Gigi about it. I assume they'll tell their partners, but other than that, I want the fakeness of it all to stay between us. I don't want the whole world to know about the marriage not being real," she explained.

Ford wasn't surprised she had told her friends. He agreed that he didn't want to world to know his marriage was a sham, at least not until it was over. The idea of it being over tightened his chest, and he rubbed his chest to try and ease the ache. *Probably just heartburn.*

"Okay. Anything else?" So far all her rules were very doable. Millie was doing him such a big favor that she could be asking for a whole lot more and Ford would give it to her, but she was never thinking about herself like that. He admired it, but he also wondered if maybe he was taking advantage of her kindness a bit.

A shaky exhale blew out from between Millie's lips, lips he suddenly couldn't stop staring at. They looked soft and plump. Ford would bet a large amount of money that she tasted as sweet as she acted. "I assume we'd get married in the courthouse as soon as possible so that you can get the paperwork taken care of and everything." He nodded, trying to clear his mind of his thoughts of Millie's taste. While he attempted to do that, she continued. "I'm fine with that, but I have one request for our wedding day."

"Name it," he requested. There wasn't anything she could say at this point that he wouldn't agree to.

The paper with her rules dropped to her lap. She started twisting her fingers together, something he had come to recognize as a nervous habit. "I want to wear a wedding dress."

He raised a brow at this. Ford hadn't expected the request, and while it wasn't out of line, he just sort of assumed they'd get married in the clothes they wore to work. A nice, small lunchtime wedding before heading back to the office.

Millie sighed. "It's just that," she started to explain, licking her lips. His eyes tracked the movement of her tongue and his mind got snagged on her lips again for a minute before he realized she was talking again. "This might be the only time I ever get married, and I would like to wear a wedding dress if that's okay."

The pain in his chest came back, but this time Ford knew it wasn't heartburn. Millie was a sweetheart, probably the most romantic person he'd ever met, and here she was giving up all her dreams of the perfect love and the perfect wedding to help him out. There was no way he could go through with this and keep a clear conscience. Having his own firm was important to him, but it wasn't so important that he would ask her to make a sacrifice she didn't want to make.

"I don't want you giving up your dreams of romance to help me with my dream of a law firm," he told her. "I can find another way." There was no other way, but that was his problem, not hers.

"I'm not giving up my dreams," she insisted, her hand darting out to cover his. Her voice was steady, but her eyes told another story. "Just delaying them for a year. Besides, my last date never showed, so it's not like I'm beating men away with a stick anyway."

Ford nodded, still hating the feeling that he was getting the better deal out of the two of them, but he understood that Millie was a grown woman. He wasn't going to tell her she couldn't make her own decisions. "If you're sure, then we'll do this, but I want you to know you can back out at any time before the wedding and there will be no hard feelings. I promise."

Millie nodded. "I won't back out. I have one question, though, about touching and stuff." She squinted, shifting awkwardly on the couch.

"Touching?" he asked, finding her discomfort both amusing and endearing. "I assume you mean acting like a married couple in public, yes?"

Millie blushed, making her already rosy cheeks even redder. "Um, yeah, that," she said, pulling her hand back to fidget with the other in her lap.

Ford reached over and placed one of his hands over hers to still them before taking her hand back and lacing their fingers together. His hand tingled, the sensation reverberating through his arm. Something in his body that had before been completely untethered became grounded. He must just be feeling settled now that he was getting his firm, that was all. It had nothing to do with the pretty woman who currently stared up at him like he hung the moon and stars.

Ford gulped. "I think we can manage things like this, don't you?" he asked, holding up their joined hands. Millie nodded and he continued. "So, we've got hand-holding, and we already know we can hug comfortably. I guess the only thing left to do is see if we're comfortable kissing."

"Kissing?" she squeaked.

He couldn't help but smile. "Well, yeah. I'm not a huge fan of public displays of affection, but I think a kiss here and there would show people how real this is." Ford hadn't planned on kissing Millie, but she brought up the touching and well, he had been thinking of her lips for almost her entire visit, so yeah, he kind of wanted to see what kissing her would be like.

Millie licked her full lips slowly, further escalating his desire to taste her. "I, um…" She paused, taking a deep breath. "I think I can handle a little kiss." With wide, cocoa eyes, she stared up at him. He wanted to dive into those brown depths, swim in the warmth and comfort inside until he drowned in it.

"Just a little kiss," he whispered, drifting closer to her.

Millie closed her eyes before he even got close, her serene, hopeful expression causing him to smile. She was such a sweet girl. After taking in her blissful expression one last time, Ford finally brushed his lips lightly against hers, enjoying the feel of the delicate skin there. The kiss was chaste and didn't last more than a few seconds, but it was enough to have him thinking about how good it would feel if he could take it further. Millie was right. They needed to keep some boundaries in place or things would get messy.

After finally pulling back, Millie blinked up at him with a tender smile. "Thank you," she whispered, gazing at him like he'd just given her the greatest gift she'd ever received.

Ford simply nodded, unsure what exactly it was she was thanking him for, but feeling a swell of gratitude himself. He had kissed a good amount of women, but never before had one looked up at him the way Millie had, let alone thanked him. "Was there anything else you wanted to talk about?"

With a shy smile, she shook her head slowly and gathered her bag. "I think that covered everything. You can just text me the day and time of our appointment at the courthouse and I'll be there." Millie stood and walked toward the door, but he called her before she left completely.

"Millie," Ford began as he remembered her romance books. "Aren't you supposed to tell me not to fall in love with you?"

Millie's eyes widened before she laughed somewhat hysterically. "Ha, I don't think there's any danger of that happening." She shook her head and walked out of his office. As Ford watched her retreating form, thoughts lingering on their kiss, he wasn't so sure that was true. The danger of falling in love with Millie was suddenly all too real.

****

Family dinners at Ford's parents' house had never been relaxed or easygoing. His folks were almost always formal, interrogating either his sister Ginny or himself about either their personal or professional lives. No matter what the siblings discussed, they were never good enough for either their mother or father. Case in point, both of his parents were currently frowning at their future son-in-law as he held Ginny's hand and smiled at her. Any other parents would be thrilled to see their daughter in such a loving relationship, but not Clifford and

Theodora Davenport. The fact that Cooper was a good man with a solid job and was deeply in love with Ginny didn't matter because his was an auto mechanic and his only family connection was his grandmother Mags. Cooper's gran was a stand-up lady, but she wasn't a society matron.

Dinner had been tense, but it was better than the after-dinner drinks they were currently enjoying on the porch in the fading evening light. At least food had been enough of a distraction from the lack of hospitality his parents afforded Ginny and Cooper, but now they had nothing but glasses filled with bourbon. There wasn't enough alcohol in the world to make this night any easier.

It was a warm day, and while the shade of from the large trees and roof overhang provided enough shelter from that, it hardly eased the discomfort Ford was currently feeling. He was sweating from nerves because tonight he was going to be telling his mother and father that he was getting married in two days in the courthouse to a woman they definitely would not approve of. There would be a lot of questions and protests of his decision, but it wouldn't change his mind. Getting his own firm was worth dealing with his parents' potential hysteria.

Ford didn't need to wait for a lull in conversation because frankly, there was none. The sound of crickets would have been comical if the whole experience wasn't so incredibly awkward. With a deep breath and the idea of being able to step out of his father's shadow, Ford cleared his throat to gather everyone's attention. When four pairs of eyes met his, he almost lost his nerve, but one glance at his sister gave him the courage to push forward. Ginny had defied their parent's wishes, and while her relationship with them was definitely very strained, she was happier than he had ever seen her. Clearly, it had been worth it for her and it would be worth it for him too.

"I have an announcement to make," he began, pushing down the smoked perch from dinner that was threatening to make a reappearance.

"We already know about you signing the Thornton account," his father explained, appearing slightly irritated that Ford might be trying to get extra kudos for doing his job.

"It's not that." Ford glanced at his sister to see her biting her lip. Ginny looked equal parts afraid for him and thrilled at their parents' potential freak-out. "I'm getting married."

"Congratulations!" Ginny exclaimed, coming over to give him a hug. When her arms were wrapped around him, she leaned up to whisper in his ear. "Hurt Millie, and I'll kill you." She leaned back with a polite smile on her face, but her eyes belied her true emotions. His sister was definitely not happy about his plan, but he had expected that. Ginny had always been fiercely protective of Millie, but didn't she realize he would never hurt her friend? Millie was his friend too.

"I guess matrimony is contagious," Cooper joked, offering his hand. He pulled Ford in for a bro hug and slapped his back. "Hurt Millie, and Gigi will kill you. And I'll help her bury the body." Ford leaned back and saw the same expression as his sister's. Wow, they were a good match.

Ford shuffled and ran his hand through his sandy brown hair. He dared to glance at his parents, not surprised by his mother's shock, but his father's shrewd expression gave him pause. It was as if he knew Ford was plotting something and he was already trying to put the pieces of the puzzle together. He knew his father well, which was why he made sure all his moves to start his own firm were protected against any intrusion by his old man.

His father's expression cleared and he smiled. "So, who is the lucky girl?"

"Yes, Ford. Who is this girl? As far as I know, you haven't even been seeing anyone." His mother appeared slightly hurt that he hadn't let her in on his secret love affair. Though it was regrettable, it was a necessary part of the plan.

"It's Millie," he boasted. "I knew you might not approve of the pairing, so we've been keeping our relationship very private to spare any hurt feelings in case things didn't work out, but they have. We're actually getting married at the courthouse this Friday."

"Millie? As in Millicent Legare?" his mother scoffed. "You can't be serious!"

Ford was enraged on behalf of his future bride. He may not be in love with Millie, but she was an amazing person who did not deserve any derision by his parents or anyone else. "I'm completely serious. You are welcome to come to the ceremony. It will be held at two o'clock." Ford gulped and willed his body to stop sweating, but it couldn't be helped. His father's narrowed gaze that was currently boring into him was unnerving. Ford had never been able to lie to the man and it was difficult to do it now, but he was willing to do whatever it took to start building the life he actually wanted.

"We certainly will not be there!" his mother shrieked. "We won't be there because it isn't happening." She turned to her husband. "Clifford, you have to stop this."

Ford's father gave him one last contemplative look before turning to his wife. "He's a grown man, Thea. He can make is own mistakes." He glanced back at Ford. "And there is no doubt that is what you are making, a mistake."

"Millie is not a mistake," he and Ginny shot back at the same time. He gave his sister a small smile, and she nodded appreciatively in reply.

"Maybe not, but marrying her certainly is," his father drawled before dragging his wife indoors. "Come Thea. We'll deal with this another way." The ominous words rang in Ford's ears until the slamming of the porch door brought him back into himself.

Ginny glanced at him sympathetically. "Fun stuff." She leaned against her fiancé who was always there, ready to support her when she needed it.

"Definitely went better than I expected, though Dad was already plotting something," he speculated as he scratched at the stubble along his jaw.

Cooper snorted. "As long as I live, I will never understand rich people." He wrapped his arms around Ginny and kissed the top of her head. "I'm just glad you didn't have any crazy rules that forced you to get married before you met me."

"Me too," she said, turning to kiss her fiancé on the lips. Ford looked away, not wanting to intrude on their private moment and also because he was a little envious. He had been so singularly focused on work for so long that he forgot what it was like to be in a relationship, not that he'd ever had one as loving as his sister's. "Ready to go?"

"I've been ready to go since we got here," the man declared. Ford couldn't help but chortle in reply.

"Same," he muttered as they dropped their glasses inside and made their way out to their vehicles.

After giving Cooper a goodbye nod, Ford hugged his sister. Then he turned to his vehicle, only for Ginny to stop him. "I was serious about what I said earlier, Ford. If you hurt Millie…"

"What could I possibly do to hurt Millie? I'm not

a monster, Gin," Ford cried. He knew it was more about protecting her friend than anything else, but still. Millie was stronger than most people gave her credit for and marrying him had been her decision. Ford wasn't forcing anything on her.

"I know." Ginny sighed, rubbing her hand on his arm. "But I also know how hard Millie's life had been. I don't want her to go through anything she doesn't have to."

"I'll look after her," Ford vowed. "I promise I won't hurt her." The conviction of his statement settled into his bones until he felt stronger than he had moments ago. *What is that all about?*

"I'm holding you to that," his sister warned him before walking over to hop on the back of Cooper's motorcycle. Ford watched as they tore out of their parent's driveway, the promise to his sister still on his mind. Millie was strong, but she was precious too. He never wanted to do anything to destroy that. What he'd thought would be an easy solution to his money problems might not be so easy after all.

Chapter Nine

~Millie~

When she pictured her wedding day, Millie had always dreamt of an open space filled with wildflowers and her groom standing under a big willow tree, waiting with baited breath for her to arrive next to him. Then they would exchange their vows of love and devotion while the sun came up. Afterwards, they would have a big wedding breakfast, celebrating their union with friends and family. Millie had definitely not pictured getting married in Willow Creek City Hall, and she had no family with her, but she did have her friends and her dress was perfect.

It hadn't taken Millie long to find a wedding gown because she had known the exact one she had wanted to wear for the last four years. It hung in the window of the bridal store downtown every spring, and every spring Millie would ride her bike past the shop to stare at it, dreaming of a day when she could go in and buy it. Yesterday had been that day. She was lucky that the white gown with embroidered flowers all over it and off-the-shoulder sleeves hadn't needed any alterations. Even though it took a fairly sizeable dent out of her savings, it was worth it to at least have one part of her dream wedding with her that day. Millie also had the dream groom, but it wasn't the same when Ford was there because he needed her to fulfill some ridiculous terms of his trust.

Millie put aside that last thought and tried to enjoy the moment with her friends. Gigi flitted around her like a hummingbird, making tiny adjustments to her hair every few seconds. The flurry of movement was making Millie nervous, so she finally swatted her friend away with a gentle wiggle of her hand.

"Stop fussing over me, Gi. I look fine," she insisted. "It's not like Ford is going to notice anyway."

Her friend made one last adjustment to the hair comb covered in ceramic flowers that rested in the side of her hair with a huff. "You're better than fine, you're absolutely gorgeous. And this isn't for him, it's for you. You want to look good for your pictures, don't you?"

"Pictures?" Millie groaned. "I didn't sign up for pictures." Though it might be nice to have something to look back on when she was alone again in a year's time. Maybe she could pretend that the whole marriage was real and had a happy ending like one of her novels while she drifted off to sleep in her empty bed.

"Well, you're getting them," Jo commanded from her other side. She was wearing one of her navy pantsuits that made her look like the girlboss she was. Jo and Archer's new sports marketing firm was getting off the ground, and Millie was glad that her friend had finally been able to get out of her toxic workplace and create an environment that was safe and welcoming to everyone. "Besides, you'll need pictures of you two around the house if you're not going public with the whole sham marriage deal."

Millie hated the designation, but it was something she needed to hear. It would be so easy for her to pretend that this was real, that the thing she had wanted for half her life was actually hers, but it wasn't. As much as hearing that caused pain to slice through her chest, it had to be said to keep her from getting too caught up in a fantasy.

"Fine, we can have pictures, but not too many," she acquiesced.

"I don't know." Gigi crossed her arms. Millie

could tell her friend was still not happy with her going through with this whole scheme, but luckily she had stopped saying as much and was at least trying to act supportive. "Ford's house is huge, so you might need a lot of pictures."

Ford's house was big. Of course, Millie had never been inside it before, only in the backyard when Gigi would steal his gate key and they would use his pool while he was at work. It was a nice pool. There was nothing better than a swim when it was hot out. Now she would get to swim as often as she liked. After their meeting on Wednesday to go over her requests, he'd called her with their appointment time with the judge to get married that Friday. While they were on the phone, they talked about the logistics of their marriage.

Ford had a huge house and Millie had an apartment the size of a shipping container, so it made more sense for her to move in with him. Millie was able to find someone to sublet it starting a week from now, so they agreed that after they got married, they could move all her stuff in with him. His house was fully furnished, with a guest room all ready for her to settle into, so she would mostly just be bringing her clothes, books, and baking supplies. At least the move would be pretty easy. It would only take a couple of trips in Ford's car to move all the boxes and her bike.

Millie thought of Eleanor with a sigh. Ford lived too far from the library for her to be able to bike there and back, so she was going to have to start taking the bus. Ford would offer to drive her, but he was already helping her out by introducing her to some wealthy, connected people, so she didn't want to ask for anything else. Millie was getting the better part of the deal anyway. She would get to help fund her library outreach program and spend a whole year with the man she loved. Sure, he didn't love her back and likely never would, but she would get to help him realize his dreams. That was enough for her. Millie would rather have one year as his fake bride, getting to know him better and seeing his smiling face every day than spend another fifty as nothing more than a friend, watching from the sidelines as he toiled away at his father's firm.

"I know I promised I wouldn't ask again, but I feel like I have to." Gigi's cautious voice interrupted her thoughts. Millie knew what she was going to ask, but waved her question forward anyway. "Are you sure you want to do this?"

Millie's eyes moved over to Jo, who had been less vocal about her objections, but was now just as concerned as Gigi. *Am I sure?* Millie was sure that she loved Ford and wanted him to get everything he wanted out of life, even though she would never be one of those things. At that moment, the door to the small government building opened. Ford strode inside wearing a dark blue tuxedo complete with a white rose as his boutonniere. His hair was neatly styled and he still sported his four-day stubble, but it looked neat and tidy. In short, Ford's handsomeness was dialed up to eleven. Now that she could see his face, she knew with absolute certainty that this wasn't a mistake. Making his dreams come true would never be a mistake.

"I'm sure," she told her friends with conviction.

When Ford finally got to the three of them, his eyes widened in surprise as he took in her gown. "Wow, Millie," he marveled, his jade eyes moving up and down her body. "You look lovely."

"Thanks, so do you," she squeaked, her cheeks flushing. "Handsome, that is. You look very handsome." Ford always looked handsome but even she wasn't silly enough to blurt that out.

Ford beamed at her, adjusting his bow tie. "Why thank you. I figured if you were wearing a wedding dress, I could spruce myself up a bit as well."

Millie couldn't help but smile at his thoughtfulness. He may not love her, but at least he was making an effort to have the day feel as real to her as possible. "Well, you did good," she told him, linking her arm with his. "Shall we?"

Ford nodded, turning over to his sister and Jo. "Thank you both for being here to act as witnesses." He smiled at his sister and her friend.

"Of course." Gigi grinned over at Millie. "We wanted to support the two of you. Even if one of you didn't loop me in on his little predicament at all." She glared at her bother for a moment, but before he could protest or apologize, the court clerk called them forward.

After filling out a bit of paperwork with the clerk, Millie and Ford were finally in front of the judge. Gigi and Jo stood off to the side, Gigi dabbing at her eyes with a tissue and Jo snapping pictures with her phone while she and Ford recited the rote vows that the judge instructed them to repeat, slipping the simple silver bands he had procured for them on their fingers. They agreed to simple jewelry and to just use whatever vows the court had available, but the night before, Millie had actually taken out a piece of paper from her stationary to write the vows that were in her heart, folding it up and putting it in one of her favorite romance novels for safekeeping. Any book by Julia Quinn was never in danger of getting sold or lost with her, and that was where those vows would stay forever unless she ever got the courage to give them to Ford. Knowing herself as well as she did, Millie realized that would probably never happen, but it was the thought that counted.

"You may now kiss," the judge declared.

The words caught Millie so unawares that she almost started laughing, but when she looked up at Ford who was smiling and leaning toward her, laughter was the last thing on her mind. Her gaze flicked to his juicy lips and she found herself automatically rising up on her toes to reach him. The kiss the other day in his office had been brief, but wonderful. It was easily the best kiss she had ever had. Millie knew it was the best because she had been waiting to kiss Ford for so long, and it had been everything she'd ever dreamed it would be. She wanted more.

The moment Ford's lips met hers, she sighed happily and gripped his forearms to steady herself. Feeling emboldened by the day, she opened her mouth slightly and kissed his upper lip, then his lower before planting a final, firm kiss on both and returning her heels to the floor. When she opened her eyes, she noted his curious expression. Was his heart racing as hers was, or was it something else? Before she could study him further, that face disappeared as the officiant congratulated them and broke whatever spell they had found themselves under.

Ford turned to the judge and shook the woman's hand. "Thank you for doing this," he told her with a polite smile.

"Of course," the white-haired woman replied. "Have a happy life."

"Thanks," Millie answered wistfully.

Her life would be happy, for the next year anyway, and then it would go back to being lonely again. At least she would have memories to take with her and her library program would be funded. Ford already mentioned hosting a barbeque at his house, *their house*, that weekend to introduce Millie to some people from society circles she hadn't been privy too yet, and then there was a party for his mother's charity coming up that they would also attend. It would be like going on a date except for the fact that this whole thing was a business arrangement, but she could push that to the back of her mind while she enjoyed his company.

Ford escorted her out of the building. At Gigi's insistence, they posed for a few pictures in front of the courthouse. Smiling up at Ford like she was madly in love with him wasn't difficult for her because she'd been doing it forever, but Ford must have taken drama courses while he was at Duke or something because he looked almost as infatuated with her as she was with him. Millie thought she remembered reading about lawyers sometimes taking acting classes to help them in the courtroom and decided that must be the reason he had such a beatific expression. Well, Ford should get an Oscar for this performance because the look in his eyes was making her weak in the knees.

"Okay, got it," Jo called, drawing Millie's attention away from her husband. Millie couldn't believe she was married to the man of her dreams and for the next year she was going to call him her husband as often as she could.

Ford loosened his bow tie and smiled at her. "You ready to get all settled in to your new home?"

Millie nodded and turned to her friends, giving each a large hug, thanking them for their support, not just for today, but pretty much every day since they'd all become friends. "I'll see you guys at the barbeque, right?"

"Wouldn't miss it," Jo chirped. "Archer and I can't pass up the opportunity to rub elbows with society darlings who might have connections we need."

Millie chuckled and turned to Gigi. Her friend sighed and nodded. "Coop and I will be there, but I expect there to be at least one batch of brownies with my name on it," she demanded with a smile.

"Of course," Millie told her friend. "See you guys then." She waved to her friends as they walked to their cars and turned to Ford. "Ready?"

"Yup." He bit his lip nervously.

Two hours, one wardrobe change each, and four trips back and forth between her apartment and his house later, Ford was giving her the grand tour of his place. *Their place.* She would never get used to thinking that. "Welcome to our humble abode." He spread his arm out as they walked into the house from the garage. She had already been inside a bit to drop off some boxes, but this was the first time she was getting a good look at the place.

"Wow," she gushed, scanning the area and spotting large windows that opened up to the expansive, grass covered backyard complete with crystal blue pool. The inside consisted of pale yellow walls lined with white shelves, a stone backed fireplace as the centerpiece of the family room, sleek furniture, and state of the art kitchen. Millie's eyes widened at the large marble counters and stainless steel appliances. She was going to have so much fun baking in that kitchen. "This place is fantastic."

"You don't think it's too showy?" Ford seemed a little unsure of himself, something Millie wasn't used to seeing. He always seemed so confident in both himself and his surroundings, seeing him slightly vulnerable was jarring, but also charming in a way. Millie liked this new vulnerable side to him, and she hoped he would trust her enough to show it to her more often.

"It's not showy at all." Millie stopped walking and placed her hand on his forearm. Her touch seemed to relax him because his shoulders had come down from up by his ears. "It's very you," she explained, taking in the large, open spaces.

Ford looked around for a moment before focusing on Millie again, smiling sadly. "Big, boring, and empty?" It sounded like a joke, but she knew that people often did that to mask their emotions. Millie had never been very good at it, but she witnessed it enough in others to recognize it for what it was: fear of rejection. Having experienced enough of that for a lifetime, Millie wasn't going to do that to him.

"No." Millie gripped his wrist and dragged him to the center of the connected rooms. "Look at the stone wall behind the fireplace and the big wooden beams in the ceiling, the huge windows and bright paint, and the plants and art on the walls."

"One painting is hardly a lot of art," he sighed, shrugging and shaking his head. "I guess I don't get it."

"Ford," she whined, tugging on his wrist a few times. "Don't you see? There's strength." She pointed to the wood and stone. "Lightness." Millie waved arm at the windows and walls. "And beauty." She pointed to the plants that lined the windows in the kitchen and the single painting that was displayed on the wall of the family room. Turning back to him, she smiled brightly, trying to convey all the wonderful things about him that were reflected in his home. "All very you."

Ford exhaled shakily, his eyes slightly shiny. "Thanks, Millie," he told her quietly before taking a deep breath. "Uh, how about I show you the rest of the house and you can get your room set up?"

Millie released her hold on his wrist, disappointed that whatever little moment she thought they were sharing was over. "Sure." She followed him through the downstairs as he pointed out the home gym, the large TV room with long, cushy couch that she was already thinking would make an ideal reading spot, and his home office. "Do you work from home much?"

Ford clicked his tongue. "More than I would like," he complained as they made their way up the carpeted staircase. "I mostly work in there after hours, but I'm hoping to be able to cut back on that a lot with my new firm. I want my place to afford its employees a work-life balance that's more life than work."

"I think that's amazing." Millie loved the idea that he wanted to provide law services to people while also letting his employees live their lives more freely than his father had. "I like working at the library, but I also enjoy having enough time off to do the things I love."

Ford stopped in front of the door to her room and leaned against the wall, smiling at her. "And what do you love, Millie?"

It was a good thing he said *what* and not *who* because she never wanted to lie to him, and no, she was not counting the lie of omission that was her unrequited love for him. "I love reading, baking, and doing things for the people I care about."

Ford chuckled and pushed off the wall. "All of those things sound very *you*." He pointed to the double doors that were just adjacent to her room. "That's my room and the room at the end is empty. I'll let you get settled in. Holler if you need anything." With those parting words, he drifted down the stairs and out of sight.

"I need you," she whispered to herself before heading into her room and trying to figure out what to do first. The room was nicely furnished with a large, king-sized bed with white duvet cover, and there was a sleek gray dresser for her clothes as well as a walk-in closet, but other than it was pretty bare of anything that would make the space a little warmer, cozier. Millie walked over to the box with her bedding and took out her patchwork quilt, spreading over the top of the bed. "Well, at least that's a start," she told the empty room. The whole day was the start of something. Whether it would ultimately be good or bad was yet to be seen.

Chapter Ten

~Ford~

The smell of pizza permeated the air as he and Millie sat down for their first meal as husband and wife. Ford wasn't sure he would ever get used to referring to his sister's friend as his wife, but he would have to if he was going to get his money and open his law firm. The ink on their marriage certificate had barely dried before he was scanning it and emailing it to Jonah Burgess.

With that stipulation checked off, all Ford had to do was sit and wait for his birthday to roll around, then he could finally fund the dream he'd had for a long time. The dream of his own firm was fairly recent, but it was more the dream of practicing law in a way he felt proud of and being away from the demands of his father and people like him that had been around much longer. The current work environment he was in was not the type Ford thrived in, and he was tired of merely surviving.

"I ordered your favorite while I set up my room," Millie exclaimed, her sweet voice breaking his thoughts. She proceeded to serve him a couple of slices of mushroom and bell pepper topped pizza with some dressed leafy greens on the side. Ford had no idea he even had the ingredients for a salad in his refrigerator, but he must have because Millie had been able to whip one up in no time.

Ford took the plate from her gratefully with a smile and nod of his head. "Thank you, Millie." He took a bite of the pizza and groaned, but his satisfaction dissipated as he watched Millie picking the bell peppers off her pizza. "Do you not like green peppers?"

Millie's nose scrunched up adorably as she shook

her head. "Not especially, but it's your favorite and I don't mind picking them off." With a shrug, she took a bite of her pizza and chewed methodically as she glanced around the dining room. "Would you mind if I added some of my stuff around the main rooms?" When he didn't respond immediately, she was quick to fill the silence. "It wouldn't be much. Just a couple of vases and some succulents I had around my apartment."

Ford sighed at her worrying about making herself at home with him. "Millie, unless you plan on hanging up pictures of clowns or creepy dolls, you can add whatever you like to the house. It's your house now too." It was, at least for the next year, and he wanted her to feel comfortable in it, make it her own in whatever way she saw fit. Millie was doing him an enormous favor, the least he could do was let her put up a few knickknacks.

"Okay, thanks." She nodded and took another small bite of her pizza. "Have you ever even seen clown or creepy doll artwork? I shop at thrift stores all the time and I have seen some pretty crazy stuff, but never anything like that."

Ford chuckled. "No, I guess I haven't, but if someone has thought of it, I'm sure it exists out there somewhere."

He watched Millie as she ate her pizza, her short hair still down in waves the way it had been at their wedding ceremony. She was just as pretty now in her purple t-shirt and jeans as she was in her wedding gown. Remembering just how beautiful she looked only hours ago brought a smile to his face. Ford was certain the image of Millie standing in front of him in her gorgeous floral gown, a serene smile on her face and a bright light in her eyes, would be seared into his memory for the rest of his days. He hadn't planned on wearing a tux, but when she mentioned she wanted to wear a gown, he figured he out to match her. It was a good thing he did too, because he would have looked pretty foolish if he hadn't. Even in his nicest suit, Ford didn't hold a candle to Millie.

"So, why law?" Millie asked, once again breaking Ford from his reverie. This time it was much less welcome only because he was enjoying remembering her in her wedding dress, but he could always do that again later. He probably would too, if the amount of time Millie occupied his thoughts already was any indication. "Did you always plan to go into the family business?"

Ford scoffed. "Um, well. It was always just assumed that I would be a lawyer, and I guess I just never questioned it." Ford had never gone against his parents' wishes in all the years he had been on this Earth. Well, up until that very day when he married Millie, that is. "Don't get me wrong, I love the law, but I guess I just always thought I would be more of a good guy fighting for truth and justice rather than just another suit trying to help rich people get richer."

Millie smiled sadly. "You're still a good guy, Ford. You're honest in your dealings and you don't cheat anyone out of anything. It's not your fault that the law isn't always fair or just."

"True," he huffed. "I just wish I thought a little more for myself when I was younger. Questioned things and went my own way a bit more, like Ginny." If Ford had pushed against the boundaries his parents had put in place more often as a child and teen, maybe it wouldn't have taken so long for him to carve out his own path like he was trying to do now.

Millie grinned. "Gigi did always like to make waves with your parents, but she followed along with them more often than she would have liked."

That was also true, but his sister seemed to be

done with all that now that she was with her fiancé. Cooper wasn't someone his parents would ever approve of, despite the fact that he was a decent, responsible guy, but Ginny wasn't ever going to give him up. Ford admired his sister for that. "I don't see Ginny going along with their plans for her anymore."

"No, I suppose not." Millie smiled and took a sip of her water. "Some things are just worth fighting for, I guess."

"What? Like love?" When Millie nodded, he asked the question that had been on his mind since they moved in her boxes and boxes of books. "Is that why you read nothing but romance? Are you someone who loves love?"

Millie's smile faltered, causing Ford to wonder what he had said wrong. "I don't know if I'm someone who loves love for the sake of it, but I'm someone who has felt its absence pretty acutely over the years. I guess I just like reading stories of people who get to find it and keep it forever." She smiled sadly before scooting back from the table and putting her dish into the sink. "I'm going to go put some of my books away."

Before Ford could say anything else, she walked away into the family room. *God, you are so dumb.* He thought he was asking a simple question, not realizing just how deep the loneliness of her upbringing went. Millie was a sweet girl, and because of that, it was easy to forget just how neglected she had been growing up. *Way to go, Ford.* Even though this was a fake marriage, there was no reason for him to start it off by upsetting his wife.

Pushing back from the table, he strode over to the family room, peeking around the corner to see Millie sorting through her many books, no doubt finding the perfect system for all the stories with happily-ever-afters. Ford walked over to where she was crouched on the floor and placed a hand on her shoulder. "I'm sorry, Millie."

She shook her head and patted his hand before shuffling some more books. "Thank you, but it's okay. I know you didn't mean to stir up old demons. You'd think they would be gone by now, but they're still around." She showed him a book with a happy couple on the cover as he kneeled on the floor next to her. "I guess it's just easier to escape into books than to deal with my own reality."

"Oh, I don't think you're reality is all that bad." He took the book from her hand and flipped through it. "You're married to me after all." Ford flashed his most charming smile at her and it widened when it earned him a laugh from her.

Millie smiled and took another book out of the moving box. "I suppose that does come with some perks. I mean, look at all this shelf space." She swept an arm out to showcase the place for all her books, and dissolved into giggles when he pushed her over onto the floor. "Okay, okay. You're not bad either."

"That's right," he stated, brushing some imaginary lint off his shoulder. Ford looked over at Millie and got serious again. "Though, I am sorry. I'll do better."

Millie's brow scrunched up. "What do you mean by that?"

Ford shrugged. "I don't know. I'll try not to say something dumb again." Ford didn't like that he had upset her or reminded her of her loneliness. He would make a concerted effort not to do it again.

Millie scooted over to him and stared into his eyes, studying him. Ford squirmed, feeling slightly self-conscious under the scrutiny. Finally, Millie rested her palm on his knee. "I don't expect you to be perfect, Ford. No one is. You were asking me about myself and I got a little maudlin about it. That wasn't your fault, and it wasn't mine. It just happens sometimes." Ford raised his brow at her and she smiled softly at him. "I know that you've spent most of your life with a lot of people expecting certain things from you, but there are no lofty expectations with me. I know you're a good guy, and that's all I need."

Ford struggled to swallow the lump of emotion that clogged his throat. The weight of everyone's expectations had been crushing him for so long that it sometimes felt like it was slowly killing him. To hear that he was a good guy and that's all he needed to be was a relief. Millie just removed a five hundred pound weight off his chest. He couldn't even begin to express the amount of gratitude he felt toward her in that moment, but he would try.

"Thank you," he whispered, trying not to show too much emotion as to scare her off.

"Anytime," Millie replied as she gathered her books and walked them over to the shelf.

Ford took a moment to admire the woman in front of him. Millie was not only sweet, but she was strong, and not just for herself, but for others too. The fact that he was among those she felt protective of caused a warm, fuzzy feeling in his chest. Ford hoped that the next year of his life was filled with many more moments like the one they just shared. He suspected that he would be all the better for it.

Chapter Eleven

~Ford~

Padding down the stairs of his house and finding Millie buzzing away in his kitchen wasn't something he was used to yet, but Ford had to admit that he did enjoy the sight of it. After the prior evening where they ate pizza, bonded, and unloaded the seemingly endless supply of Millie's books onto the built in shelves of his TV room, he felt a little more settled with the whole "fake marriage" thing. He'd be lying if he said he hadn't been nervous about how they would get on once they lived together, and though it had only been one night, they seemed to be doing quite well.

A smiled pulled across Ford's face as he recalled pulling one of Millie's books out of the box last night and smiling at the familiar title. *The Dastardly Duke* must be a pretty good read if the worn quality of the cover was any indication.

"Read this one a lot, do you?" he chuckled. Millie snatched it from his hands, a fierce blush overcoming her cheeks.

"I got it from a used book sale," she explained sheepishly as she placed it on the shelf. "But yes, I read it a lot."

Ford had decided not to tease her about any more of her novels, but he was tempted every time he saw a book cover with a shirtless biker or shirtless cowboy. At lot of these fellas liked to walk around without their shirts on. Ford again wondered if he was her type as he entered the kitchen. If Millie's widened eyes were any indication, she definitely had a thing for half-naked men. It was late August and almost one hundred degrees out, so he wasn't even going to bother with a shirt today. Evidently, Millie was on board with his decision.

"Good afternoon, Millie," he called, drawing her eyes up from his torso to his face. "What are you making in here?" Whatever it was, it had the whole kitchen area smelling divine.

Millie smiled shyly and spun around to open the fridge, the purple cotton cover-up she was wearing swirling around her. "Well, you said you were doing steak and chicken skewers on the grill, so I made a few sides," she explained as she pointed to various food containers in the refrigerator. "We have potato salad and coleslaw. I made a spinach dip to go with the pita chips you had in your pantry."

"*Our* pantry," he corrected with a smile. It was nice to share his house with someone, even if it was all under false pretenses. After less than twenty-four hours of her moving in, the whole place already felt much more like a home than it had in the years previous.

"Our pantry." Millie's soft voice carried over to him before she started shuffling around more food containers on the counter. "I made the brownies I promised Gigi, and some lemon bars if people want something a little more refreshing since it's so hot out. Oh, and I'm almost done with some more pecan shortbread for you."

Ford chuckled. "You don't have to always make my favorite cookie, Millie. You certainly didn't need to go to all this trouble." He swept across all her hard work. "We could have ordered all this from a caterer or the store." He didn't have his trust money just yet, but he certainly wasn't hurting for cash and could have bought out the bakery section of the grocery store if he wanted to.

Millie shrugged. "I noticed the tin I brought you

the other day was empty, so I figured it was time for a refill," she professed with a smile. "And I like making things, so you inviting some colleagues over was the perfect excuse."

Ford returned her smile, but after taking in all the information she gave him about what she made, something was troubling him a bit. "What's your favorite?"

"Hmm?" She rolled some crumbly dough in her hands.

"Which food that you made is your favorite? The lemon bars?" Ford had known Millie a long time and knew that she loved romance novels and shopped at thrift stores, but he didn't know anything about her dietary preferences.

"No, I don't like lemon," Millie admitted, biting her lower lip. She scanned the counter and pressed her lips together. "I guess I didn't make my favorite." Her brow furrowed. "I'm not sure I have a favorite."

Ford scoffed. "How can you not have a favorite food or dessert?" That sounded impossible. Then again, he told people his favorite meal was grilled salmon when it was mozzarella sticks and chicken wings, but he was always too embarrassed to admit that. Probably something drilled into him by his mother. Finger foods were not something the Davenports served in their house. "Is it a gross combination of foods that you're too afraid to tell me of?"

"No, it's not that." With a sad smile, Millie finished rolling. She placed the ball of dough on her baking tray before grabbing another handful. "You know, we didn't have a lot of food growing up. Don't think I didn't know that it was you and Gigi sneaking granola bars into my backpack every now and then." She glared at him, but there was no real heat in it. "I guess I just got so used to being grateful for whatever food I did get that I didn't think about whether or not I actually liked it. I like some foods more than others now, but I still have a budget to meet and everything, so I haven't explored it much." She sighed.

Ford was both proud of her for surviving a difficult upbringing and angry that she had to deal with it in the first place. How she retained her sweetness and light was a mystery, but he was glad she had. He wanted to do something to show her that she could leave the past behind and live a little more for herself now.

Ford placed his hand over hers, squeezing it lightly and chuckling when cookie dough oozed into his fingers. "Thank you for sharing that with me, Millie." He smiled as he wiped his hands on the tea towel she handed him. "But you don't have to worry about a food budget anymore, so I want you to get all the recipes you've been wanting to try that weren't in your price range and we're going to make one every night until we figure out which is your favorite."

Millie twisted her fingers together for a minute. "I don't want to take advantage…"

"You're not," he insisted, rounding the island to stand next to her. He wiped a spot of flour off her cheek with his thumb and smiled. "You're doing so much for me. Let me do something for you. Please?"

Millie nodded. Her eyes were so bright and happy that he felt ten feet tall. All he did was tell her to do something for herself, but she gazed at him like he handed her the world. "Will you do it with me?"

"Hmm?" he asked, having gotten momentarily lost in her eyes. "Oh, yes. We can try all sort of new things together."

Millie blushed again. He realized where her mind went. Suddenly, his mind joined hers there. Trying new things with Millie in the kitchen suddenly took on a new meaning. Now he was fantasizing about laying her out on his kitchen island and dining on her sweet pussy, his mouth already watering at the thought. The sound of his doorbell ringing almost caused Ford to nearly jump out of his skin, but the interruption was a welcome one. He shouldn't be thinking about his wife that way. The absurdity of that statement was not lost on him, but he didn't have time to ponder it further when the door opened.

His sister pushed her way inside, followed closely by her fiancé Cooper, Jo, and her boyfriend Archer. Ford had hung out with Cooper several times since he and Gigi got engaged. He'd met Archer once and found him friendly enough. He supposed he would have to get used to them all being around more often now that Millie lived with him.

"Come on in," Ford called his sister, sarcasm dripping from his voice. "Our home is your home, apparently."

"That's what happens when you give me a key," she sang, jangling said key from her hand. "Now, did we beat the stiff squad or are they out back boring one another to death?"

"Gigi," Millie scolded his sister, but he saw the corners of her mouth twitch with the desire to smile. "You guys are the first ones here, so if you want you can help get everything set up."

"Yay," Jo said with an unenthusiastic wave, but she dutifully helped Millie in the kitchen, dragging her boyfriend along with her while he showed Ginny and Cooper where they could leave the beer and hard ciders they had brought with them.

A half hour later, everyone had arrived for the barbeque. Ford had introduced Millie to a fair number of his colleagues and their significant others, beaming with pride as she happily talked about her library program and solicited donations in way that was polite and understated as well as effective if the thick stack of business cards she was holding was any indication.

There was still one colleague that Ford knew was a big fish and could get her to her goal faster, so he placed his hand on the small of Millie's back and walked her over to Brian Atwater, the grandson of the other founding partner of their law firm and a fairly respected lawyer. Ford had never cared for the man personally, but he had deep pockets, and he'd promised Millie he would help her out as best he could. He intended to keep that promise.

"Brian," Ford called as they approached and shook the man's hand. "Glad you could make it. I would like to introduce you to my wife, Millie." The words "wife" and "Millie" were getting easier and easier for him to utter together. They became music to his ears.

Brian looked down at Millie with his trademark grin, but Ford didn't like the look in his eye as he took in the rest of her. "Lovely to meet you, Millie," he purred, taking her hand and lifting it to his mouth for a kiss. Ford definitely didn't like that, but he was there to help Millie make connections, not act like a caveman every time another man touched her.

"Thank you," Millie replied, her voice just as engaging and friendly as it was with everyone she met. "I've heard a lot about you."

"Well, that's interesting because I have heard absolutely nothing about you," Atwater chortled as he continued to leer at Millie. Meanwhile, Ford was doing his level best to not deck him in the face, his fist clenched so tight his nails dug into his palm. "Though if I had a girl as pretty as you, I suppose I would keep her all to myself just like Davenport here did."

"Oh," Millie replied, caught off-guard. "Thank you?" It sounded more like a question than a statement. Ford could understand why. Atwater was being a bit of a dick and a creep. Ford would happily toss him out of his house if it weren't for the promise he made to the woman next to him.

"What do you do for a living, Millie?" Atwater asked. Like the smart cookie she was, Millie transitioned seamlessly into her work at the library and the need for her outreach program.

Ford smiled down at her and watched her eyes light up when she spoke about reading being a lifeline to the community, especially to those that society had seemingly forgotten like the poor and elderly, and she didn't twist her hands together at all as she spoke. Evidently, her belief in the program overcame her nerves. Witnessing Millie talk so passionately about books was almost like a drug, one he could easily become addicted to.

"Well," Atwater said, impressed when Millie finished her pitch. "That sounds like the type of program that anyone here would be happy to help fund. You call me sometime and we'll chat more about a donation." He pulled a business card out of his wallet and handed it to her. Leave it to a group of lawyers to always have a card on them, even when they were in swim attire. "If you'll both excuse me."

Atwater went to mingle with some of their coworkers. Ford turned to beam down at his wife. "You were fantastic, Millie," he exclaimed before hauling her into his arms for a hug. The cover-up she was wearing was thin and he could feel her soft curves against his body, causing him to thicken in his trunks. He leaned back slightly and beheld her pink cheeks. Maybe it was from the heat, or maybe she was just as affected by him as he was her.

The sound of his sister squealing in delight broke his concentration on his wife, and he peered over to see Ginny's fiancé flipping her over his shoulder. Ford laughed because anytime his sister got dunked on was a good time. It was even better now as it distracted him from the strange reaction his body continued to have where Millie was concerned.

When his sister finally came up for some air, she called over to the woman next to him. "Mills, come on. You can't live in a house with a pool this gorgeous and stay out on the deck."

Millie looked up at him with a smile before turning to her friend. "I'm not a big swimmer," she called over to Gigi as she tugged at her hooded cover-up, pulling it further down her legs.

Suddenly Millie swimming sounded like the best idea in the word. Or the worst, seeing as how he couldn't stop getting aroused just about every time he looked at her, but Millie dressed fairly conservatively most of the time, so he never got a peek at what was hidden underneath all of her tweed skirts and fluttery blouses. Ford found that the temptation to see that outweighed his desire to tamp down his growing attraction toward her.

"C'mon, Mills," Jo begged, splashing some water their way. "I want to see the swimsuit I made you buy at the beginning of summer."

Millie turned to Ford. "Go ahead." He backed toward the grill. "I need to get the food going anyhow."

With a smile, Millie turned to the pool and shook her head. "Fine," she called over to her friends. "Give me a minute though because I need some sunscreen."

She walked over to one of the high top chairs at the outdoor bar and reached into her bag, pulling out a small bottle. Time seemed to slow as Ford watched her reach up to the top of her cover-up and tug on the zipper, slowly bringing it down all the way to the bottom before her hands were sliding up and parting both sides of the fabric. He closed his eyes and he took a deep breath for a second before opening them once again just in time to see her cover-up fall away from her body. Ford nearly passed out at the sight.

Millie stood not ten feet from where he did, wearing nothing but a white, string bikini that showcased her amazing body. Full, heavy breasts were barely covered by the small triangles of fabric. His eyes lingered there for a moment before wandering south over the planes of her soft, slightly rounded stomach down to her, thick juicy thighs and smooth legs. She was all soft curves, and when she turned around and displayed a good amount of ass, he almost lost it with the need to grip her hips and pull her body into his.

"Fuck," he whispered to himself, thankful that the grill blocked anyone's view of his erection. When she started to rub lotion all over her hot little body, Ford imagined her hands were his and he nearly shot into his swim trunks.

"Your fire's out," someone gruffly told him.

"Seems pretty hot to me," he murmured as he watched Millie continue to rub sunscreen all over the body that was made perfectly just for him.

Someone chuckled next to him, and Ford turned around. It was Cooper, Gigi's fiancé, standing there dripping pool water and sporting a very amused expression. He pointed to the grill. "I was talking about the grill," he said with a smirk.

Ford glanced down to see that he still hadn't turned the gas on. "Whoops," he mumbled, his arousal gone in an instant as he tried to focus on the task at hand.

He reached under the grill and turned the knobs to get the pilot going and get everything heated up.

Cooper clapped his shoulder and gave it a shake. "No one can blame you for getting distracted." The man glanced over at Gigi. She was currently laying out on a pool float and sipping one of the hard seltzers she brought with her. Coop had a bright smile on his face as he watched his fiancée enjoying herself. "I'm finding it hard to stay focused myself."

Ford snorted. "Dude, that's my sister!" He shook his head, but the other man just laughed and raised his hands in supplication.

"Sorry, sorry. I'll try to refrain from ogling Gigi while we're at your house," he replied.

"It's the least you could do," Ford insisted haughtily, grabbing the meat from the small fridge next to the grill. He glanced up to see Millie gingerly stepping into the water, her nose scrunching up at the temperature, before climbing down another step.

"Just dive in," Jo called from the arms of her boyfriend. "It's not cold once you get used to it."

"No way. I'm acclimating slowly." Millie continued her leisurely descent until she was finally waist deep, smiling as her hands skimmed over the surface of the water. "This isn't too bad." Millie glanced over at Ford and waved. He couldn't help but smile and nod at her before turning his attention back to the grill.

"Oh man. You've got it bad," Cooper whispered, cracking open one of the beers he grabbed from a large bucket of ice.

"I don't know what you're talking about." Ford played dumb, finding the grill extremely fascinating all of a sudden. He didn't want to look at Cooper because the man was surprisingly astute.

Ford had always thought Millie was cute, but the

close interactions they'd shared over the last couple of weeks and that amazing body she had been hiding away had him looking at her a little differently. Now she was less "cute librarian who helped you find the book you were looking for" and more "sexy librarian who dragged you into the stacks for a quick fuck against the bookshelves." *Great.* Now that image was in his brain. Erasing that little fantasy would be no easy task, and he wasn't sure he would actually even bother. It sounded pretty hot.

Coop snorted and drank from his beer bottle. "If that's how you want to play it, fine, but you might want to mop up the bit of drool on your face," he jibbed, pointing at the corner of Ford's mouth.

Ford swiped at his mouth, but it was dry. He glared at his soon-to-be brother-in-law before knocking him with his shoulder. "Dick," he muttered.

Cooper smiled slowly and laughed. "You know you love me, bro," he said before walking over to the side of the pool and crouching down to give Gigi a kiss.

Ford watched his sister drag her fiancé into the water, laughing and splashing him while he chased her around the pool. He turned to Millie, who was swimming off by herself while her friends and some of his colleagues laughed and played with their partners. He wanted so badly to jump in and join her, haul her into his arms for a wet kiss, and drag her around the pool with her legs wrapped around him, but that wasn't what their arrangement was about. With that little reminder to himself, he turned back to the grill and added the meat skewers.

"Food's ready," he called about twenty minutes later.

Ford glanced over the grill and watched as Millie got out of the pool. Then he searched for a towel. She was sopping wet and shivering as she padded over to him, her stunning body all wet and on display. Her hands shook as she pushed her wet hair out of her face, and he finally snapped out of his trance long enough to grab a towel and open it up for her. She smiled and walked in automatically, and he felt a great sense of accomplishment and having been able to do even that small thing to take care of her. Millie was always taking care of everyone else. She deserved more than a little of that for herself.

Once she was wrapped up, Millie faced him and beamed. "Thanks. I guess I forgot a towel," she said, rolling her eyes at herself.

"Always happy to give you what you need, Millie," he confessed, reaching up and rubbing her arms to help her warm up. He hadn't even thought about doing it. It just happened automatically. Now that his hands were on her, he didn't want to take them off.

Millie's body swayed closer to him. He caught her blushing as she looked down at his bare chest again which made him smile. Millie's head tilted up and she licked her bottom lip, the same lip he desperately wanted to drag between his teeth before licking the sting away with his tongue. "Ford," she whispered, her voice low and sultry, and he found himself leaning his head down to meet her. Ford wasn't sure where this seemingly sudden attraction to her had come from, but it was one he couldn't resist.

"These brownies are amazing," Gigi chimed in, practically parking her body between the two of theirs.

"Thanks," Millie said, blinking the haze from her eyes. "Oh shoot. I think I forgot to put out the fruit salad." She put her cover-up back on and scurried into the house.

When Ford turned to his sister, Gigi gave him a

death glare, the same one she used to give him when he would give her boyfriends a hard time whenever she brought them home. "What?" he asked, wanting to go chase after his wife and show her just how much he appreciated all her hard work in the kitchen, preferably with lots of kissing and touching.

"Don't mess with her, Ford," she warned. "Millie is a sweetheart and this is just business for you, so don't do anything stupid to hurt her. Please."

"I won't," he promised his sister for the hundredth time. The last thing he ever wanted to do was hurt anyone, especially someone as kind and generous as Millie. When his sister didn't look convinced, he placed his palm over his heart. "I won't hurt her, Ginny. I swear it."

"Okay," Gigi huffed, turning toward the house. "If you do, I am having Cooper grill your ass on his engine."

Ford chuckled and nodded. "Threat noted."

With a curt bob of her head, his sister stalked off into his house to help Millie in the kitchen. As he watched his sister and wife gather more plates and food, he tried to steel himself and bury his attraction to Millie. They might be married, but Ginny was right. It was just business. Though, the more time he spent with his thoughtful, adorable wife, the less that statement seemed to be true.

Chapter Twelve

~Millie~

Thursdays at the library were Storytime days. Millie's absolute favorite duty as a librarian was reading books and singing songs with the children who attended. The sound of their laughter and seeing the kids eyes go wide as they went on an adventure with her through the books they read was probably the best way to fill her happiness bucket every day. Millie longed to have children of her own to read to, but that would have to wait at least another year and probably much longer than that. She would be entering the dating scene again in one year as an almost thirty-year-old divorced virgin. Not exactly the thing that would have guys lining up around the block, though it wasn't as if they had been doing that anyway.

Millie ran her thumb over the smooth metal of her wedding band and smiled. At least she had Ford. There were small moments when it seemed he might want her just as much as she wanted him, but it was probably just wishful thinking. They had almost kissed at the barbeque, but in the week since then, she hadn't seen Ford much at all. He worked late most nights, and other than spotting him on his way out to the office some mornings, she hadn't seen him nearly as much as she had hoped she would.

"How are you today, Miss Millie?" someone interrupted. Millie looked down to see one of the many small children who attended storytime with her, so she stopped packing up the books that needed to be reshelved to give him all her attention.

Millie smiled at the boy's mother, who was

watching them from across the room while she chatted with a few of the other parents, before she crouched down to the little boy's eye level. "I'm pretty okay, Bobby. Thank you so much for asking. How are you today?" She smiled at the blond-haired boy who attended pretty much every storytime the library held.

His bright blue eyes widened with delight. "You know my name?" Bobby asked, his small voice full of wonder.

Millie chuckled and tussled his shaggy hair. "Of course I know you're name, Bobby. You are always the first person to come into storytime and the last one to leave, and you help remind the other kids to be quiet while I'm reading." Millie was especially grateful for that last part. Keeping a large group of preschool-aged children in check was no easy task. "You're a library VIP."

"What's VIP?" His tiny brow furrowed in confusion. Millie didn't know his exact age, but she would guess four or five based on the books he liked to borrow.

"VIP means a very important person," she explained. "I don't know what I would do if I came in to do storytime and you weren't here. It would throw off my whole day."

Bobby spun around and ran to his mother, grabbed her arm, and pulled her back over to Millie. "Mom! Miss Millie knows my name and says I'm library wee IP."

Millie chuckled. "VIP, but yes, I did tell him that," she explained to his mother. "He's our most loyal participant and we appreciate you bringing him every couple of days." Millie loved all the regulars at the library and was happy to have such loyal attendees to storytime. It was just one of many things she adored about her job.

The boy's mother smiled. "Oh, it's no problem. He loves it and I'm happy to get even the small half hour break." The mother's gaze followed her son as he ran off to play with some friends on the other side of the room. "I think you just made his whole year by remembering his name. Bobby absolutely adores you. I bet your own kids feel lucky to have you as their mother."

Millie's smile faltered slightly, but she tried to play it off. "Oh, I don't have kids of my own, but that's part of what makes doing storytime so fun for me. I get to meet so many different children it's like having a hundred of my own without having had to change a single diaper."

She ignored the pain in her chest at the thought of having her own little baby to care and change diapers for. Millie knew there were options for her to have a baby on her own, but she didn't want to bring a child into this world just to fill her loneliness. A kid deserved more than what she could give them as a single parent on a lower income, but maybe someday if she ever met the right man, it could happen.

"Well, skipping all the dirty diapers does sound like a good time," the woman chuckled. "Thanks for storytime, Miss Millie. You have a good day."

"You too." Millie watched as the other woman walked away and the rest of the kids and their parents filed out of the room as well. When she was finally alone, she sighed. "Back to work, I suppose."

The next four hours dragged by, giving Millie way too much time to think about things, like the masquerade party she was going to with Ford on Saturday night. Millie was nervous about being on his arm in front of his parents, but it had to be done. Only a couple of weeks remained for her to raise some more money for the library program, and while a good amount of the people she talked too at the barbeque had donated to the cause, she needed at least a half dozen more to tip the scales.

She thought about dipping into her savings if it came right down to it, but the idea of doing that brought a familiar, panicky feeling into her chest and her fingers started to twist automatically at the thought of not having as big of a financial safety net for herself. Lingering financial anxiety was probably one of the worst parts about growing up poor. Though she was sure Ford would step in to save her, she needed to do this on her own. Millie never owned much of anything, but she wanted to own this. This program was hers. She would be the one to make it happen or not.

After finishing her afternoon tasks, Millie popped by the main office to let Marsha know she was headed out for the day. The woman smiled when she spotted her and waved her in. "Millie," she sang. "I just got another parent email letting me know how wonderful storytime was. Keep up the good work."

Millie returned her smile and made a mental note to bring cookies to the next session as a thank you to all the parents. "That's great." Millie was genuinely pleased with herself. She put so much of her energy into her work that it was nice to have someone else notice. "Storytime is probably my favorite part of the job."

"It was always mine too," Marsha said wistfully. "Much more exciting than dealing with order forms and budgets. Speaking of which, how is the fundraising going?"

Millie ducked for a moment before answering, "It's going pretty well. I'm going to a party with Ford this weekend. Hopefully, I can scrounge up the last few donors there."

Her boss gasped. "I still can't believe you're married. We didn't even know you were dating anyone," she admitted.

"We're private people, but I'm happy and that's all that matters," Millie said, trying to deflect from any potential questions about their courtship. It helped that Millie had never been much of a gossip and her boss always liked to keep things professional, so her not having mentioned Ford before wasn't as big a shock as it could have been.

"Well, I am happy that you're happy. I'm proud of all your hard work on the outreach program. I wish the city gave us more funding, but you know how it is." The woman shook her head sadly.

Millie simply nodded because she did know. Libraries were so important, but the city had limited funds and they were always last on the list when it came to public services. "Yeah, it's okay though. I'm confident I'll find the money," she answered. At the very least, she was confident in her husband's connections that she had access to. "I'm actually headed home for the day. I'll see you tomorrow. "

Marsha smiled. "Sounds good." The woman turned back to her computer, essentially dismissing Millie. "Have a good evening."

"Thanks, Marsha. You too." Millie grabbed her bag from her desk and headed outside, turning to the bike rack for a moment before remembering that she took the bus now. She was surprised she was able to forget it since she had to take two different busses in order to get home. At least the weather was milder today. A cool breeze came along every now and then as she walked to the bus stop, making the trek much more bearable.

Forty five minutes later, Millie was strolling down the sidewalk toward her new home, glancing around at the other fancy houses that lined the streets. It wasn't the type of neighborhood she ever saw herself living in. The whole thing still felt a little surreal. She had only been married for just under two weeks, but she had hoped to feel differently after she and Ford had said "I do." Sadly, she still felt like the same old Millie. Maybe it was because her husband seemed to be avoiding her or because they slept in separate rooms, but Millie didn't feel the least bit different. Her sleep had gotten better since she now had a cloudlike mattress to crawl onto at night. *At least I have that.*

"Millie?" someone called from the road. Millie turned to see Ford in his SUV crawling alongside her. "What are you doing out here?" he asked, bewildered.

"Oh, I'm just walking home from the bus stop," she explained with a smile as she continued to stroll toward their home.

The car halted abruptly and she looked over to see Ford frowning at her. "Why are you taking the bus?"

"The library is too far to ride to on my bike, silly" she chortled. "I don't want to arrive at work covered in sweat. I do not think that would endear me to the community."

Ford sighed and hopped out of his now parked car. He looked good in his brown slacks and white button down as he strode over to her. Millie tilted her head back to meet his beautiful green eyes that were a little turned down in the corner. "I'm sorry, Millie."

Her eyes widened. "What are you sorry for?" As far as she knew he hadn't done anything wrong. Sure, she wished he spent more time at home, but she knew what she was signing up for when they got married, so he didn't even owe her that.

Ford shook his head, his light brown hair falling into his eyes a little bit as he did. "I'm not being a very good husband," he sighed, wrapping his arms around her and pulling her into a hug. Millie's body melted into his as if it knew exactly where it was supposed to be, like he was her home. It was a fanciful thought, but one she couldn't help thinking when their bodies seemed to fit so well together, like two perfectly interlocking puzzle pieces. "Do you forgive me?" he asked, his breath blowing against the top of her head and his presence warming her heart.

"I don't think you need any forgiveness, Ford." Millie leaned back and gazed upon his handsome face. "You've already helped me so much with introducing me to so many important people. I don't need anything else from you."

That last part wasn't strictly true. She could tell herself she only *wanted* more from him, not *needed* it, but most days it did feel like she needed everything from him. Millie was so sure in her heart that Ford Davenport was the only man who would ever be able to give her the love she needed, but unless she was willing to come right out and ask for it, it would probably never happen. Even then, he could always reject her. That wasn't something she thought she could come back from, so she stayed silent.

His brow furrowed. "Introducing you to people is the least I could do," he countered, escorting her over to the side of his car and depositing her inside. Once he was back and driving them home, he turned to her, his expression determined. "I'm going to do better. Starting with getting you a car."

"Ford," she exclaimed. "I don't need a car. The bus is perfectly fine. I'm not buying a car and I'm not letting you buy me one either." She crossed her arms over her chest, annoyed at his insistence to do things for her while being deeply touched by it at the same time.

Millie's eyes peeked over at him to see him smirking. "You can't stop me from buying a car, Millie," he challenged, his expression mischievous.

"Well, even if you do buy one, I don't have to drive it," she huffed as they pulled into the garage.

Ford shut off the car and turned to her. This time, his eyes were filled with concern instead of provocation. "Please, let me do this for you, Millie."

"I already told you, you don't owe me..." she started, but Ford stopped her with a finger on her lips. She blinked at him in surprise. Ford appeared to be just as bewildered by his own behavior.

"Millie," he whispered. "I want you to be safe, and while I am certain that the bus is a fine mode of transportation, if I can do better for you, I will." Millie opened her mouth to protest again, but the pleading in his eyes stopped her. "Please, sweet girl?"

It could have been the soothing sound of his voice or the lingering feel of his touch, but Millie was pretty sure it was the endearment he used that got her nodding in agreement. "Okay," she whispered, and smiled when his expression lightened and he looked pleased. She wondered if she should be mad at herself for how easily she always caved to him, but she couldn't muster the strength to care. Ford wanted to take care of her. Millie was a little tired of having to always do it for herself, so why shouldn't she let him?

"Thank you," Ford said, getting out of the car and opening her door for her while she had been gathering up her bag. "We can go car shopping Saturday morning and test it out on the drive to the party Saturday night."

Millie groaned internally. Car shopping followed by a masquerade ball did not sound like her idea of a fun day off, but she would do it for him and for her library program. "Sounds good." She walked into the mudroom that connected the garage and the rest of the house. "I made pizza dough the other day and was thinking of trying a new chicken pesto recipe for the toppings. Are you eating with me or do you have to work some more?"

Millie peeked over her shoulder to see Ford watching her with a shy smile on his face. "Pizza sounds good," he agreed, removing his jacket and rolling up his shirt sleeves to reveal the corded muscles of his forearms. Millie turned away and exhaled slowly. Surviving the next year with all his hotness on display was going to be rough. Maybe she should invest in a new toy to help take the edge off.

"Afterward, I can work on something for my new firm while you read. What do you think?"

"I think I have the perfect book already picked out." Millie reached into her purse, pulling it back out to reveal a brand new novel she checked out from the library. It was a romance, obviously, about a Scottish highlander and an English princess who ran away together. Millie needed a guaranteed page-turner too keep her mind off her husband, hopefully this would do the trick.

"Hmmm," he said, taking the book from her and grinning at the cover. "A shirtless guy in a kilt, huh?"

Millie blushed and shrugged. "What can I say? It's a good look." The cover model was pretty yummy, though she was certain the look would be even yummier on her husband.

"I'll have to keep that in mind come Halloween. I wonder where I could find a kilt." Ford winked at her before turning and walking into their home.

What did that mean? The idea of Ford wearing nothing but a kilt for Halloween was definitely the kind of treat she would like to enjoy for the holiday. Now it was all she could picture. Millie was definitely going to need to invest in a new toy. Otherwise, she might just go ahead and do something dumb like try to seduce her husband.

Chapter Thirteen

~Millie~

It was Saturday night, and the masquerade ball was in full swing. Millie and Ford had already made a lap around the room, their arms linked as they chatted up donors, spoke with some of his colleagues and clients, and had a surprisingly wonderful time. When she had been getting ready earlier in the evening, Millie felt a little silly in her black lace gown and matching mask, but as she descended the staircase and spotted Ford at the bottom in a black tux and gold mask, she felt like she was living her very own fairytale and decided to lean into it.

Millie knew that it wasn't real, but it was hard to ignore his affectionate expression or the way he treated her. Like when they went car shopping that morning and he held her hand as they walked the lot until she settled on a compact SUV, or the night before when he was working on his laptop and reached over, pulled her feet to rest on his leg while he typed and she read. Millie knew all of that wasn't real. Ford was probably just slipping into the husband role, but she was giving herself this one night to play into the fantasy a little for herself as well.

Millie and Ford had just finished chatting with Mr. Mapplethorpe and his lovely wife, and were making their way to the bar for a drink when a hand on Ford's arm caught her attention.

"Ford Davenport. Is that you?" someone asked in a nasally voice.

Millie turned to see a statuesque, raven haired woman smiling at over at Ford, her expression one of keen interest. Millie's jealousy was strong and instantaneous, but then she remembered that Ford wasn't hers and tried to reel it in. The fact that Ford looked like he had just swallowed a mouthful of angry bees soothed her.

"Presley. So good to see you," he told the woman with a tight smile. He lightly removed the woman's hand from his arm before slipping his own around Millie's waist and pulling her closer to him. Millie felt a bit like a human shield, but she was happy to play the part. She recognized the name as Ford's ex-girlfriend from long ago, but the woman's obvious interest made Millie wonder if Ford's discomfort was one-sided.

"I'd hoped I would see you here tonight," the woman purred as swept her long hair over a bare shoulder, blatantly ignoring Millie. "It's been too long. We should go out and catch up sometime."

Even behind his mask, Millie could see Ford's eyes widen with panic. Millie shouldn't be enjoying his discomfort as much as she was, but his obvious lack of interest in his ex-girlfriend made her feel a little better about their current situation. Ford would never love her, but at least he didn't squirm at her like he did at the other woman.

"How rude of me," Ford began, pulling Millie closer. She tried not to get lost in the feel of his warm body against hers, but it was difficult to concentrate on anything else when she was plastered to his side. "Presley, this is Millie. My wife."

Millie stuck her hand out to the woman, who stared at it like it was a cold fish before she finally shook it. "Pleased to meet you, Presley," Millie told the woman. It wasn't exactly a pleasure, but it was turning out to be a lot more fun than she thought it might.

The woman cleared her throat. "It's Presley. With a *zee* sound, not an *s* sound," she huffed with a roll of her eyes. Millie could have sworn Ford's mouth twitched in the corners.

"Anyway. Ford, I didn't know you were married." Presley gave Millie a once-over before turning back to Ford. "Congratulations. I guess there is a pot for every lid." With that, the woman spun on her stiletto heels and left the two of them alone again.

Millie glanced up at Ford. "Sorry about that," he muttered. "I would say I'm surprised that she was so rude, but…"

"It's fine, Ford." Millie gave his chest a reassuring pat, loving the feel of hard muscle beneath his shirt. "I've dealt with rude people before. If anything, my mind is still stuck on which of us is the pot and which is the lid."

Ford chuckled, transforming his smile from saddened to amused. "Your guess is as good as mine, Millie." Notes from the band starting to play reached their ears, and they watched as people went out to the floor to dance. Ford held his hand out to her. "Would you like to dance, Mrs. Davenport?"

Millie smiled. She hadn't legally changed her name and didn't intend to. Why bother when it would be back to Legare in a year? But she enjoyed hearing it all the same. "I would love to, Mr. Davenport," she proclaimed, giggling at their goofiness.

Ford strode onto the dancefloor and spun her around once before pulling her into his arms, one hand on her hip and the other still clasping hers as they swayed to the band playing a cover of Elvis's "Can't Help Falling in Love with You." Millie sighed and rested her head against his chest as they danced, enjoying the steady beat of his heart and the feel of her small hand in his larger, stronger one.

"This is nice," she admitted, her breathing steady and sure as she leaned against him.

"It is," he replied breathily. Millie noticed an uptick in his heart beat.

Millie pulled her head back. "Is everything okay?"

"I don't know," he told her. "I think so." His gaze flicked to her lips and she gazed upon his. Ford leaned down toward her and she tilted her face up to meet him. Millie had been wanting another kiss since their wedding day. Although she knew this was just for show, she didn't care. She needed his lips on hers more than she needed her next breath.

"There you are, Davenports," someone boomed, breaking the spell they were under and causing their heads to swivel toward the sound. "I've been looking all over for you."

Millie shook herself free of the romance-filled haze and tried focus on the words of the man in front of them. It was Brian Atwater, the man Ford had introduced her to at their barbeque. She wasn't the biggest fan of the man, but she put on her polite smile anyway. Millie noticed a beautiful blonde woman on his arm and recognized her as the mayor's daughter.

"Good evening," she said.

"Yes, nice to see you again," Ford told the pair. "And what can we do for you, Atwater?"

"Oh, it's what *I* can do for *you*," the man replied, gesturing to his date. "Sara, this is Ford and his lovely wife Millie. She wants to put together the program I told you about." He turned to Millie and smiled. "Sara loved the idea and would like to donate."

"That's right," the woman said with a smile. She pulled out a check and handed it to Millie. "I hope that will be enough."

Millie tried hard not to gawk at the check or the woman who handed it to her, but that was difficult when it was written out for six thousand dollars. "Um," Millie mumbled, swallowing down her excitement and nerves as best she could. "This is more than enough and entirely too generous of you. Are you sure you want to donate this amount?"

The blonde smiled at her and patted her shoulder. "Absolutely sure. Now, you two enjoy your evening." Then she dragged Atwater toward the bar.

"Oh my god." Millie gasped, the check shaking in her hand slightly. She showed it to Ford, who simply beamed down at her. "Oh my god." Her voice grew a little louder, the reality of her program getting more than enough money finally hitting her and causing joy to spread out her chest and body. "This is amazing."

"You did it, sweet girl," Ford gushed.

"Thank you. Thank you, thank you, thank you." Millie leapt up to wrap her arms around his neck and pulled him to her for a kiss. She hadn't planned on it, but how else was she supposed to show the man she loved how grateful she was for all of this help in making one of her dreams come true.

Her lips explored his, relishing them as she ran her fingers into his soft hair. Ford licked her lower lip and she parted for him, letting his tongue explore the inside of her mouth. He tasted like the bourbon and orange peel he had drank earlier. It was a combination she didn't think she would enjoy but found she couldn't get enough of because it was from him. Millie wanted more, but a cough from behind them broke their kiss.

"Well, if it isn't the happy couple," Ford's father drawled. While the man appeared polite enough, she could spot the contempt for her underneath the façade. "We haven't had a chance to congratulate you."

"Yes," Ford's mother added snidely. "We're sorry we couldn't be at the ceremony, but you know…" The woman waved as if that would explain their absence.

Millie knew the real reason. The Davenports had never liked her, thinking her less than reputable since she had no money and lived in the trailer park. She would always be grateful for them in some small way, because if they didn't exist, neither would her best friend or the man she loved.

"You were missed," Millie told them, a friendly smile on her face. "Hopefully, we can get together in the future." She doubted that would be the case, but she could make an effort for her husband.

"Certainly," his mother replied, her smile not reaching her eyes. "We can also just wait and see. One never knows that the future holds." There was no missing the implication that Ford's mother was making. She didn't think the marriage would last long, and unfortunately for Millie, she was right.

"Perhaps we can gather for Ford's birthday," his father cut in. "I know it is an important year for you."

Ford's brow furrowed slightly, but he wrapped his arm around Millie and squeezed her shoulder. "It is because I'm married now and have a wonderful life with Millie to look forward to." He peered down at her lovingly. She wished so badly that it was real and not just a show for his parents.

"Well, if you'll excuse us." Ford's mother grabbed her husband's arm and dragged him to the bar even though they had both been holding a full glass of champagne.

Millie glanced over at Ford's thoughtful expression as he watched his parents depart. "That wasn't so bad," she admitted, hoping to clear his away whatever was bothering him.

He only hummed as he turned to her with a sad smile. "Shall we go? You can get in some more practice with that new car of yours by driving the two of us to Daisy Cow's Creamy for a milkshake on the way home."

Millie nodded. A break from the constant barrage of people sounded nice, so she let him steer her out of the venue. Ford dropped his arm from her shoulder the moment they stepped outside, and she wondered if he was upset about the kiss they shared. "I'm sorry for kissing you," she lied. She wasn't sorry, but she didn't want him to be mad at her. "I wasn't trying to complicate things."

"It's fine," he replied as he opened the door for her. "I know you didn't mean it."

Millie sighed, wanting to tell him that she did mean it. She would always mean everything that happened between the two of them, but she wasn't sure he meant it, and she was too much of a coward to risk her getting to spend the next year with him to speak up. Millie kept her thoughts to herself the whole ride to grab a milkshake, and the ride home, and as they walked up the stairs. Millie had been swallowing her love for him for so long, but it felt like it was going to gush out of her if she didn't say something soon.

"Ford," she called as he walked toward his room. This was it, she was finally going to tell him, but when she saw his tired expression, any confidence she had at confessing her feelings disappeared instantly. The night had been a lot, and she didn't want to add to it.

"Yes?" he asked.

"Goodnight." Millie didn't want to upset whatever balance they had come to in the time since they had kissed. Ford nodded and walked toward his room, shutting the door behind him, and Millie stuffed all of her feelings for him back into the closet of her heart. The more time she spent with Ford, the more she worried that the door on her feelings wouldn't stay shut anymore, not fully anyway, and the ticking clock on her marriage just sped up.

Chapter Fourteen

~Ford~

With his thirty second birthday finally here, the stipulations of his trust fund having all been met, and Jonah Burgess just having called to inform him that his trust money would hit his account in forty-eight hours, Ford drove toward his house with a wide smile on his face. In the time since the masquerade ball, Ford had been worried that his father was up to something, but every day at work came and went without incident, so he was confident that it had all been in his head. His father was always good at playing mind games. Ford wouldn't put it past the man to pull out those tricks with his own children, so he tried to push it to the back of his mind. For the most part, he had been successful.

What had been less successful was pushing away thoughts of the most recent kiss between him and Millie. Every time he closed his eyes, he sensed her soft lips on his, her hands in his hair, and her body crushed against his own. Ford replayed the kiss over and over every night as he tried to fall asleep. Every night, he was only able to finally slip into unconsciousness after he had pleasured himself, Millie on his mind and her name whispering across his lips as he came. It wasn't satisfying, but it was enough to take the edge off. For now at least.

Ford was convinced he was going to lose his mind if he couldn't have her soon, both from a lack of any gratification from physical release and from the total mind fuck that was him slowly falling in love with his wife. *Your fake wife*, he reminded himself, but nothing about their arrangement felt fake. Millie had apologized for the kiss, and maybe she regretted it, but Ford did not.

That kiss was the most real thing he had experienced in a long while, and he wanted more. The desire to taste her again was almost unbearable, as was the need to care for her like she deserved.

They had found themselves in a routine of sorts over the last few weeks. Ford would wake, start the coffee maker, and put some of the breakfast pastries Millie spent her evenings making in the oven. Then he would go get ready for work just as she was coming down the stairs already dressed in one of her cute librarian outfits to finish breakfast and prep their coffee. They would chat about their upcoming day while they dined together, and he would give her a kiss on the cheek as they both went off to work.

The evenings went similarly with Ford coming home to find Millie prepping one of her fancy new recipes. He would wash up and join her, and they would make dinner together before sharing how their days went over a nice meal. He was pleased to observe what Millie's cooking revealed about what she liked. Her go-to meals of pizza and pot roast were just as warm and cozy as she was, and she kept a batch of pecan shortbread on hand at all times just for him. She was always so considerate, and trying to keep things strictly platonic in the face of all her thoughtfulness and care for him was getting difficult.

His excitement at being able to see his wife soon amplified with each minute as he approached their home on his drive from work. It was a real home now that she was there. Millie had added more than just her books, a few knickknacks, and her colorful throw pillows to his house. She had added vitality. Her sweetness and light filled the black hole that had existed in his heart.

Ford pulled his car into the garage and shut it off, smiling at his romantic thoughts. Millie was rubbing off on him. He grabbed his briefcase and left the car, pausing when he saw the door to the house. A large wreath made entirely out of deflated balloons hung from it with a sign in the middle that read, "Happy Birthday!" He smiled at his wife's kindness and pushed in.

Ford walked through the mudroom, seeing a few red, yellow, and purple balloons through the doorway that led to the living room. He chuckled as he hung up his jacket and dropped his briefcase before walking through the door, peeking around the corner and into the kitchen to see Millie dancing along to some country music that was playing on her phone. Her wide hips shimmied and swayed, and she tapped on the tile to the beat as she worked on whatever project was in front of her, the tiny little bun on her head bobbing as she did. She was dressed a little more casually in denim shorts and a tank top, but she was as beautiful as always.

Ford took another step toward her, taking in the rest of the room. She had gone all out with the birthday decorations. Balloons and streamers hung from every corner of the rooms and there were two giant Mylar balloons in the shape of a three and a two tied to one of the dining room chairs. There was even a "Happy Birthday" banner hanging above the fireplace. Millie's thoughtfulness knew no bounds, and his infatuation with her grew because of it. Ford had never known anyone as purely selfless as she was. Being around that kind of rare person was intoxicating.

"Millie," he called when he finally got to the kitchen island.

Millie jumped and grabbed at her chest, the action drawing his attention to the ample cleavage on display in her top. "Ford, you scared me." Millie quickly wiped her hands on her blue apron. "I was going to surprise you with all this."

Ford smirked. "Well, I am pleasantly surprised," he told her, and he was, both by her kindness toward him and how good she looked in her short shorts and tiny top. Ford tried to focus his attention elsewhere, but it was difficult because her breasts were, quite simply, spectacular.

Millie rolled her eyes at him and shook her head. "Well, now that the cat's out of the bag," she replied, turning and grabbing something behind her. "Happy birthday!" In her hands was a cake plate that held a large, round cake covered in white frosting with swirls of every color of the rainbow on it and a comically large candle in the middle. "I didn't know if you would want vanilla or chocolate cake, so I made red velvet. I hope that's okay."

Ford rounded the island and pulled the cake from her hands, gently setting it on the counter before hauling her into his arms for a hug. "It's more than okay, sweet girl. It's amazing." Ford inhaled, breathing in her milk and cookies scent. Despite working in a library filled with dusty books, Millie always smelled as sweet as the goodies she loved to bake. It gave him more comfort than he thought possible from something as simple as a smell. "Thank you."

"You're welcome." Millie sighed against his chest. "Oh, and I made your favorite for dinner."

"Millie," he started to scold, wanting to remind her that she should be thinking about herself more, but when she stepped back and smiled at him, he stopped dead in his tracks. It was impossible to be upset with someone so incredibly thoughtful, especially when she beamed at him.

"It's okay," she explained, opening the refrigerator to reveal not only mozzarella sticks and chicken wings prepped and ready for the fryer, but a platter filled with pigs in a blanket. "I made my favorite too."

Ford looked at her, amused that after all the fancy recipes she tried, she settled on hot dogs in a roll. "Pigs in a blanket are your favorite?"

Millie scrunched up her nose at him. "Don't judge. Besides, I elevated the recipe. These are sausages with Gouda cheese and apple wrapped in puff pastry. Pretty fancy pigs if you ask me."

"You're right, and there's no judgement from me." Ford raised his hands in surrender. "Clearly, I am all about the bar food." He pulled out the platters she'd made for him, his mouth already watering at the thought of eating all that deliciously greasy food. As he pulled the cling wrap off the dishes, he glanced over at Millie. "How did you know these were my favorite foods?"

Millie lifted her shoulder nonchalantly, but she ducked a bit to hide from him. "I just noticed that you enjoy yourself when you're eating them," she confessed softly. "It was more of a guess than anything else."

Ford didn't believe for one second that it was a lucky guess. Millie clearly took care in observing those around her so she could better take care of them, and he counted himself lucky that he was one of those people. "It wasn't a lucky guess, and I appreciate you thinking about me." He tossed the cling wrap and stepped over to her. "I'm glad you also thought about yourself a little."

"Well, I needed something to eat since I figured you'd hog all the wings and cheese sticks," she quipped, poking him in the belly. "I know how you don't like to share food."

"It's like that is it?" he asked. At her nod, he pinched her side. When she shrieked in reply, he went all in and started to tickle her, enjoying the sound of her laughter and the feel of her in his arms. Her back was to him, and his face was right next to hers. It would be the perfect moment to try and plant a kiss on her, but the doorbell ringing had him setting that thought aside. "Are you expecting someone?"

Millie peeked over her shoulder at him and nodded. "I invited your sister and Cooper for dinner. Gigi mentioned that your parents never made a big deal of your birthdays, so I thought it might be fun for both of you." While he could once again appreciate her kindness for both him and his sister, he was a little put off because he had been looking forward to spending the evening with just her.

"I'll go get the door." He kissed the top of her head and turned to leave, adjusting his pants along the way. Ford couldn't have a woman like Millie squirming against his body and go unaffected, and now he had to put those thoughts aside to greet his sister and her fiancé. Ford tried to put on his best welcome to my home face when it really said *Fuck off so I can seduce my wife* as he opened the door. "Ginny. Cooper. Come on in."

After a series of hugs and handshakes, they all made their way over to the kitchen, where Millie was still busying herself with dinner. She pulled out another platter from the fridge with some food for their new arrivals. When she looked over to greet the new guests, she almost looked as put out about the interruption as he did. That couldn't be the case though because she invited them, but the idea that it could be was a small consolation. Gigi started helping Millie with the food while Cooper started asking him about his plans for his law firm. With a heavy sigh, Ford resigned himself to spending another evening not getting to be alone with his wife.

****

The ceiling fan's low hum was the only sound that accompanied Ford as he lifted weights in his home gym, but that was fine. He had already tried playing music to drown out the thoughts of Millie, but all it did was irritate him further. Ford had turned it off and tried to focus on the steady rhythm of his heart and breathing instead of the rhythm of Millie's hips swaying while she had danced in the kitchen last night, or the smile on her face when she gave him his present, a leather-bound copy of *Black's Law Dictionary*.

"For the law library at your new firm," she had explained with a shy smile.

Ford's tongue had felt thick as he thanked her, overwhelmed once again by just how considerate and gracious she was. Millie did so much to make his birthday special. It was the best one he'd ever had. If his sister and her fiancé hadn't been there, he would have hauled her into his lap and kissed her, but they stayed late into the night, so he put his need for Millie on hold. *Again.*

It was that need that was driving him to work out early that morning. Normally he would try to sleep in on a Saturday, but he couldn't stand being in his bed one moment longer, not without Millie there next to him. Ford had never felt his loneliness as acutely as he did when she was in the same house, but not in the same room. His normally comfortable bed felt too large. Millie was the only woman he wanted to fill the empty space next to him, especially since she had already started to fill in the empty space in his heart. Now he was working off the sexual frustration and tension in his body the only way he could: exercise.

The room was getting hotter by the second. Sweat dripped down his back, making his t-shirt cling to his skin. The dampness bothered him, and his fuse was so short he practically ripped it off and tossed it in the corner. Ford dragged a towel down his face to mop up the moisture before hitting the weights again. If this didn't work, Ford wasn't sure what he would do to keep his control from snapping when it came to his wife. If only she could be less thoughtful, less beautiful, less perfect, then he might be able to resist her, but she was so wonderful that he was kicking himself for never having noticed it enough before. Then he could have courted her properly instead of being stuck in a weird limbo where things were supposed to be all business, but he wanted them to be anything but.

The door to the gym opened, and Millie stepped inside. Her eyes widened and filled with heat when she looked at him, her eyes roaming over his body like a soft caress. Ford wanted her hands on him, not just her eyes. While she was dumbstruck by the sight of his naked except for gym shorts body, he took a look at hers.

Millie's waves were tucked behind her ears and her face looked freshly washed, but it was her body that had his attention and caused a stirring low in his belly. It seemed her modesty ended at the door to the library because today she was dressed sinfully. The inseam of her biker shorts was so small that it looked like she was wearing underwear and the straps of her tight tank top were so thin that they strained to contain her ample chest. One good tug would cause them to snap, and he was so very tempted to give in to his urge to do just that. Instead, he started reciting law principles in his head and took a deep breath.

"Good morning, sweet girl," he called over to her. He'd been using the endearment more and more because that was who she was to him, his sweet girl.

Millie stepped closer, a shy smile on her face. "Good morning." She fidgeted a bit but appeared to be less nervous around him than she used to be. "I didn't think you'd be up yet, and I don't want to interrupt your workout, but would it be okay if I did some yoga in here? I was telling Gigi that my back was hurting and she gave me a couple of poses to try."

"That's fine," he gritted. Maybe he would go take a cold shower to calm himself down. He walked over to his water bottle to grab a drink and had every intention of leaving to go get that shower, but he stopped when he caught Millie's reflection in the mirrors lining the wall.

With her yoga mat all spread out, she took a deep breath before bending down to touch her toes, showing off her juicy ass. Then she stepped her feet to the end of the mat and stretched her body into the pose he knew as "downward-facing dog," but was already renaming "The Tempting Miss Millie" because that was what she was. Moving her body this way and that, her shorts hiking higher with each movement and her tank riding lower as gravity threatened to expose her breasts to him. His cock lengthened in his shorts and he dragged a hand down his face. Ford couldn't take it anymore, the longing, and the fire burning its way through his veins anytime he caught a glimpse of her.

"Fuck," he said to himself, or maybe not so much when he saw Millie moving to stand and come over to him.

"Is everything okay?" she asked concerned, touching his forearm. His arm tingled on the spot, and that was it. Out of everything else, it was that small touch that ended up being the straw that broke the camel's back.

"No. No everything is not okay," Ford told her just before he grabbed the back of her neck and crashed his mouth down over hers.

It took Millie no time at all to get on board with what was happening because as soon as they were kissing, her hands were sliding up his chest and circling his neck. He slipped his other hand up to cup her cheek while he used his tongue to lick her lower lip, and when she whimpered and parted for him, he drove his tongue inside as he backed her up into the wall.

A soft "oomph," followed by a moan slipped from her mouth when her back hit the wall, but she recovered quickly, sliding her tongue against his until he could taste the mint of her toothpaste. All the pent-up desire he had for her was pouring out of him, and the same must be true for her too. He groaned as he tilted her head to deepen the kiss, and he pushed his aching cock against her until it was digging into her stomach.

Millie moved her hands to his shoulders and gripped onto him, and when she bucked her hips into his, Ford dropped his hands to her round ass and lifted her higher so their bodies were slotted together exactly where they needed to be to grind against one another. Sparks of pleasure shot up and down his spine as his hard cock rubbed against her warm center, and when she ground her hips down against him, he thought he just might come in his shorts.

A few more frenzied moments passed when Ford realized he wasn't the only one that was close. He could hear Millie's breathing speed up as she whimpered against his mouth. Suddenly, she arched her back, breaking the kiss as she let out a shout. Ford held her close, watching the rapture play across her face. Her eyes were slammed shut but her mouth opened in another silent scream as her legs shook around his waist. Ford loved the sight of her giving in to pleasure and was already eager to get her there again. He hadn't made a woman come from dry humping since his senior year of high school, and he kind of liked that he was able to get her off with such little effort.

As she came down from her high, Millie opened

her eyes wide with wonder, but after a minute she shuddered and appeared slightly embarrassed. "I-I'm sorry," she huffed, shifting in his arms until he took the hint and gently placed her back down to the ground.

"You don't have anything to be sorry for. I like that you're so responsive," Ford told her. Millie wouldn't look at him, so he tucked his finger under her chin and tilted her gaze to his. "Hey. What's the matter?" Maybe she regretted their actions. He sure as hell didn't, but they hadn't gone into this marriage planning to take their physical relationship so far, so he could see why she might feel uncomfortable.

"That was just unexpected was all," Millie explained as she caught her breath. "I-I thought you wanted to keep things businesslike."

Ford nodded. He had wanted that, but that went out the window almost the moment she agreed to be his wife and he kissed her on the couch in his office. There was just something about this woman that beckoned him on an almost molecular level that he couldn't resist. "I had wanted that, but now I want more." He moved his hand to the back of her neck and ran his thumb along her jaw. "I want you."

Millie's eyes watered. He was afraid he had upset her to the point of crying. "You do?" she sniffed. He thought about backtracking to spare her feelings, but there was no way he could deny it, not after what they just shared. Now he was thinking of how to keep her in his life forever, not just one year.

"Yes, sweet girl, I do." Ford leaned down and kissed her again, dragging his teeth along her lip and nipping at it. Millie leaned into the kiss and they were hot and heavy once more, her hands in his hair, his hands on her arm and neck until he ventured south to cup her large breast. Millie pulled back on a gasp and he dropped his hand to his side at her distraught expression. "Was that too much?" She seemed pretty into everything they were doing, but he didn't want to push.

"No," Millie blurted, but then shut her eyes. "Yes, or maybe. I don't know." Her face collapsed into her hands and he pulled her over to the bench to take a seat.

Ford rubbed her back in soothing circles. "It's okay to take things slow," he told her. While he wanted to hit the "fast forward" button and drag her upstairs caveman style, he would happily press pause and do things at her pace.

"I know," she mumbled into her hands before dropping them and giving him a pitying look. "I'm just afraid you won't want to do anything after what I have to tell you."

Unsure of what she could possibly say to make him want her any less, Ford urged her on. "You can tell me and it won't change the way I feel about you."

"How do you feel?" she asked, her fingers twitching in her lap.

Ford covered her hands with one of his and looked deep into her soulful brown eyes. "I think I'm falling in love with you, Millie," he confessed with a smile.

"Really?" The fact that she was shocked someone could fall for her pissed him off a little bit. Didn't she know how amazing, how special she was? If not, he would just have to spend the rest of his life telling her until she believed it.

"How could I not? You're smart, beautiful, caring, and you always make my favorite cookies for me." He winked, tucking a strand of hair behind her head. "Now, what did you want to tell me?"

Millie took a deep breath and exhaled shakily. "Um," she started, her eyes darting around the room nervously before settling on him again. "I'm kind of, sort of…well not kind of actually, but anyway, I am definitely um, a bit of a virgin."

Ford stared at her dumbly for a second before repeating what she just told him. "A virgin?"

Millie nodded and bit her lower lip. Ford tried to process that information and while such a beautiful, amazing woman was unlikely to be a virgin, he played the last fifteen years back in his mind. As far as he could remember, she'd never had a boyfriend and hadn't dated much, and there was no way a romantic woman like Millie was into hookups, so yeah, it all added up.

"Wow." He tilted his head up to the ceiling to try and gather his thoughts. "Wow." It was apparently the wrong thing to say because Millie hid her face again. Luckily he caught her before she disappeared completely and held her hands in his, giving her a squeeze for comfort. "Thank you for telling me."

Millie nodded and twisted her lips together for a moment. "Does that change your mind? I mean, I would get it if it did. I won't know what I'm doing and I probably won't be very good at it…" she suggested, closing her eyes tightly as if it could shut out the conversation they were having.

Ford leaned down and rested his forehead against hers until her eyes opened and found his again. "It does not change my mind," he told her firmly. "It does change my strategy a little bit though."

"Strategy?" she asked. He sensed her brow raise against his and smiled.

"Yes, strategy." Ford wrapped his arms around her, and when her arms did the same, he felt relaxed enough to continue. "So instead of throwing you over my shoulder and carrying you upstairs like those alpha male book heroes you love so much, I'll go slow and ease you into things a little bit. Does that sound good to you?"

Millie was blushing. "The first way sounds like more fun, but I'm probably better equipped for the second," she admitted.

Ford chuckled. "It's good to know ourselves, but hey, if you ever feel more equipped for the alpha male style, you let me know." He would happily throw her over his shoulder and take her upstairs anytime she felt ready for it.

"Oh, I definitely will," she giggled.

They both stood and walked to the door, her a little easier than him because even after their conversation, or perhaps because of it, he was still very ready to go. "I'm going to go take a shower," Ford told her as he opened the door to the hallway. It would be cold and he would probably need to rub one out, but Millie didn't need those details.

"Okay. I can get started on breakfast. Is there something in particular you're hungry for?" she asked, peaking at him over her shoulder.

"Yes, but it's not on the menu yet," Ford said, sweeping his eyes up and down her body before turning to the stairs. "I'll settle for whatever you're having instead." When he saw Millie's cheeks turn pink, he smirked and climbed the stairs for what would likely be the first of many icy showers.

Chapter Fifteen

~*Millie*~

Six days. It had been six glorious days since Ford admitted that he wanted her and they shared a kiss that set her whole body alight. The whole thing took her by surprise, but what a wonderful surprise it was. The feel of Ford's hands on her body, cupping her rear as he lifted her up and ground himself into her center. It all felt so very good and she got so lost in her pleasure so quickly, not realizing she was coming until her legs were shaking as the tremors flowed through her body demanding more.

Millie wanted more, but she had been so embarrassed at coming from the little they had done together that she hid herself away. It was something she was used to doing, hiding what she wanted or what she needed. Her needs had always come secondary while she was growing up. Hearing Ford tell her he liked how responsive she was and that the fact that she was so inexperienced didn't change his mind about her made it easier to stop shying away from what she wanted.

Their physical relationship hadn't progressed much further than kissing, though that was something they did every morning before they left for work and every evening when they came home. Millie would read on the couch while Ford secured offices for his firm and ordered furniture and whatever else he might need to fill the space. He told her he was starting small at first. It would be him, his assistant Kevin, and a couple of paralegals and admins from his current firm, not to mention others he had worked with in the past. It was all coming together for him, his dream, and she felt wonderful that she had been able to play a small part in it and witness it happening for the man she loved.

Millie's own dream was coming together nicely as well. Now that she had secured funding, the library outreach program was coming along nicely. She had been tasked with getting the library systems web administrator to set up features for people to be able to reserve and renew books online and buying another van for volunteers to be able to drive to and from those people's homes to pick up and deliver books. Millie hoped that, eventually, she would be able to get enough permanent funding to hire a part-time worker to do the outreach program instead of relying on volunteers, but she was trying to leave that for a later day and enjoy her moment of victory.

As for her other dream, the one that involved a certain lawyer falling in love with her, well, that was going well too. The kissing was good, and some nights while they sat on the couch and relaxed with a good book, her with a romance, him with a thriller, they would catch the other person staring. The next thing she knew, they would be kissing and touching each other until she felt like she was going to explode. Millie wanted to take things a little further, but she was so unsure of herself in this area that she didn't know how to ask for what she wanted.

Her romance novels were a good guide, and there was always the Internet. Yet both of those only took her so far. She needed real, helpful input from a reliable source, which is why she called Jo over to the house an hour earlier than their girl's night was supposed to start. Ford had already taken off to meet Cooper and Archer for a beer at The Taphouse Bar, so she was all alone when Jo finally knocked on the door.

Swinging the front door open and smiling at her friend, Millie swept her arm to the side in a motion for Jo to enter. "Come in, and thank you for getting here early," she greeted as the woman strode in past her.

Jo wore jeans and a faded baseball tee, her curls that were up in a ponytail bobbed as she walked. The look reminded Millie of when Jo came to Willow Creek in second grade, looking and acting every bit the tomboy, and while she dressed similarly now, she was definitely not a tomboy when it came to certain bedroom activities. It was that expertise that Millie was hoping to tap into right now.

"No problem." Jo deposited the bottle of white wine she brought onto the counter before she spun on her heel to face Millie. "So, what's with the early call time?"

Millie smiled and took a seat on a stool on the kitchen counter, sliding a platter of freshly baked cowboy cookies over to Jo. They were her friend's favorite, and Millie was not above using every tool in her arsenal to get her to cooperate. "Cookie?"

"Always," Jo said as she rolled her eyes at Millie, grabbing a cookie and nibbling on the edge. "I know you didn't bring me here for cookies though, so spill it. Why am I here and not Gigi?"

Suddenly Millie was looking everywhere except at the one person who was speaking to her, and she picked at the corner of one of the cookies, focusing on it instead of her friend. This would be much easier to talk about if she couldn't see Jo's face. "I wanted to ask your advice about, um…about sex."

Jo's cookie dropped to the counter and she clasped Millie's shoulders. "My baby is all grown up," she crowed as she pulled her into a hug.

"Shut up," Millie chuckled, shoving Jo off of her and seeing a wide smile on her friend's face. "I was always grown up, just a little shy about things."

"If the blush on your cheeks is any indication,

you're still shy about things," Jo chortled, picking up her cookie again and taking a huge bite. "Who's the guy?" she asked through a mouthful of her treat.

Millie gulped. "Um, Ford," she admitted and had to grab a bottle of water for Jo because the woman immediately started choking.

Millie rubbed Jo's back and lifted her arms in the air, trying to recall her Heimlich maneuver training in case she needed it, but her friend finally stopped choking. "Did you say *Ford*?" Jo coughed, wiping a tear from the corner of her eye.

"I did," Millie repeated. At seeing Jo's eyes widen again, she pushed the water at her and sighed. "Well, who else did you think it would be?"

"Who knows?" Jo shrugged. "I thought this was a business arrangement and maybe you had an open marriage or something." Her nails tapped on the marble countertop and her head nodded. "Ah, now I know why I'm here instead of Gigi. I'm guessing you didn't want to ask her for sex tips to try and use to bone her bother."

Millie scrunched her nose. "Can we not say bone? It sounds so…"

"Animalistic?" Jo offered, waggling her eyebrows. "Come on, Mills. I've seen the smut you read. Hell, I've borrowed some of it and it is wild, girl." She shoved Millie's shoulder lightly with a laugh. "You're going to have to get over your fear of talking about sex if you plan on having it."

"I know," she insisted, irritated when her face flushed. Stupid visual cues to her discomfort. "That's why you're here. I need to get comfortable with some things because I want to try and move mine and Ford's physical relationship forward a little." She shook her head in frustration and placed her clenched fists on either side. "Urgh, I don't know what to do. I can think a thousand dirty things, but when it comes to saying them out loud or acting them out, I'm too worried about looking stupid."

"Girl, just flash him those big ole titties of yours, and he won't care if you come at him wearing a pair of clown shoes. He'll be too focused on your bazongas to notice anything else," Jo told her with a smile.

Millie huffed a laugh and slapped her friend on the leg. "Come on, Jo. I'm serious." She asked the woman here for advice, not to make jokes at her expense.

"So am I," Jo argued, crossing her arms. "I would kill for your boobs and you can't tell me that you haven't caught Ford checking them out."

Millie's shoulders relaxed a little. She had noticed her husband looking at her cleavage every now and then, and when they would kiss, his hands would find their way to her ribs and he would run his thumbs under her breasts, but he hadn't tried more than that since that morning in the exercise room.

Jo pointed to her face. "Ah ha! See? I bet twenty bucks that he is dying to motorboat those bad boys."

Millie rolled her eyes but laughed at Jo's words. "Okay, let's say that's true. How do I go from knowing he wants to…?" Jo whipped her head back and forth and made a motor sound, forcing another laugh out of Millie before she continued. "How do I go from 'knowing what he wants and knowing what I want' to 'making it actually happen'?"

Jo stopped her head movement and smiled. "You want to know how to seduce your husband?" When Millie nodded, Jo's smile widened. "You've come to the right place my friend because I am a seduction guru." Jo cracked her neck and shook out her arms. "Okay, are you ready for my big words of wisdom?"

Millie pulled over the notepad and pen she had

brought out to take notes. Yes, she was that girl who would write down instructions and even draw a diagram if necessary. "Hit me," she commanded, ready to jot down every single word her friend said.

"Okay, here it comes. To get your man to do what you want him to do, all you need is this one word: communication." Jo sat back with a smug smile on her face, either oblivious to or purposefully ignoring Millie's irritated expression.

"What?" One word and she was basically just telling Millie to talk to Ford. That was what was difficult though. She was hoping for some kind of trick or move she could do to push things forward. Talking about sex always brought out her awkwardness, or exacerbated the existing awkwardness because let's face it, Millie was not smooth when it came to just about anything, especially men. "What does that even mean?" she asked shrilly.

Jo placed a firm hand on her shoulder. "It means that if you want to take things further, you tell him. If you want him to go down on you, you ask him to. If you want to jerk him off, you ask if he's cool with that, and each and every time you're together, you talk about what you want, what feels good, and what doesn't until you know each other's bodies so well that when you come together, it's like an orchestra playing the sweetest symphony." Jo smiled wistfully, probably thinking about sex with Archer before her eyes met Millie's again. "Even then, you're always talking because preferences change. People want to try new things sometimes and what worked once might not work a second time."

Millie tried to process everything she just heard and sighed. "That sounds complicated." Why couldn't things be as easy as they were in her novels?

Jo moved her head from side to side, a couple of curls escaping her ponytail in the process. "Yes and no.

Sex can be pretty easy, but that tends to only be the case if you're leaving emotions out of it or you've been together for a while." She smiled sadly at Millie. "I know sex in your romance novels is all, 'Oh, I'm a virgin and have never seen or touched a penis, yet I am giving you the best blow job you've ever had,' but that's not real life, Mills."

"Well, that sucks," Millie fumed. "I was hoping that I could just twitch my hips or something and not have to use words."

Jo rolled her eyes but smiled at Millie. "Mills, you are the smartest person I know and have read more books than the library you work at can hold. You already have all the words you need. Now, you just have to figure out how to use them."

Millie nodded, taking that all in and wondering if she would ever find the confidence to use the words she longed to say. "You know," she told her friend with a smirk. "You're pretty wise about relationships for someone who didn't have one until two months ago."

"Right?" Jo said, looking mighty pleased with herself. "I would take all the credit, but honestly, all lot of that is Archer. He brings out the best in me."

Millie leaned over and hugged her friend. "I think you bring out the best in you, but we can give him a little credit if you want."

Jo chuckled and gave Millie a squeeze. "Sounds good to me," she said, pulling back and brushing her hand over Millie's head. "I know you're in love with Ford, and I'm happy that he has finally taken his head out of his ass long enough to see what a catch you are, but don't rush into anything you aren't ready for, okay?"

"I won't," Millie promised, knowing that while she may not be ready to go all the way, she was ready to maybe try and take a few steps forward. All she had to do was look inward and find the words to tell her husband about it.

****

The ceiling in their house had never been particularly interesting, but it was what Millie focused on while she waited for Ford to get home from his night out with the guys. Jo and Gigi left after they had dinner and shared a glass of wine, but Ford was out a little later, having texted her that he and the boys had moved from The Taphouse over to another sports bar to watch a baseball game. Millie replied with a thumbs up, too nervous for anything else before she hopped in the shower to freshen up before her husband got home.

After slipping on her pajama romper that was covered in donuts, she padded down the living room and laid down on the couch, staring up at the ceiling and counting the exposed beams that ran along the length of the combined living room and kitchen. That is where she had been for the last twenty minutes, and it had crossed her mind to give up entirely on Operation: Fool Around with Ford, but the sound of the garage door opening had her dedication to her plan renewing rapidly.

Millie sat up and glanced over to the mudroom. She caught Ford ambling in. He wore distressed jeans and a worn t-shirt, but she knew that both probably cost more than her entire wardrobe. It didn't matter if they cost one dollar or one thousand because they looked darn good on him, and the way his pants molded to his muscular thighs and how the sleeves of his shirt strained at the bicep had her libido perked up and ready to put her plan into action.

"Hey, sweet girl," he said when he spotted her. "I thought for sure you would be asleep already." Ford leaned over the back of the couch and brushed his lips against hers. He tasted like beer, and she wondered how much he had to drink. Obviously, it couldn't have been too much or he wouldn't have driven home, but she didn't want to mess around if his judgement was even a little impaired. Millie wanted all of his focus tonight.

"Hey. I wanted to wait up for you," she disclosed, kneeling up on the couch to face him. "Did you have a good time?"

A slow smile spread across his face. "I did." Ford leaned his arms on the couch so he was face-to-face with her. "Cooper is always fun, and Archer is actually chill too. I think I found myself a nice little group of friends."

"That's great." She was truly happy that he found some people to hang out with. Ford worked too hard and needed to have a group of friends he could let off some steam with. Speaking of letting off a little steam, Millie gathered her courage and leaned toward him a little. "Did you have a lot to drink?"

Ford shook his head. "Nah. I had one beer and called it a night." He patted his flat stomach. "I did eat my fair share of wings though."

Millie giggled and licked her lips while she searched for her words. "I'm glad you had a good time," she told him, running her hand up his arm and into his hair. "Do you think you'd want to continue that good time with me?"

Ford's eyes darkened as he looked at her, and he gulped, his throat bobbing in a way that shouldn't be sexy but was. Millie followed the movement of his Adam's apple and tried not to whimper. "What are you asking me, Millie?"

She shakily cupped his cheek with her other hand. Letting the solid feel of Ford ground her, she leaned up to whisper in his ear. Millie had her words, but saying them was still a little tough. She took a deep breath and let the feel of him beneath her hands ground her. "I was hoping that maybe you… that you would lick my pussy until you make me come and then I could try and suck your cock to return the favor," she heaved, proud of herself for asking for what she wanted, but still nervous that he would say no.

"Fuck," he said, rubbing her jaw and tilting her face so that he could stare into her eyes. "Who knew my sweet girl had such a filthy mouth?" Before she had a chance to say anything about his remark or backpedal on what she'd said, he was kissing her, running his thumbs along her jaw and down to her shoulders. He nipped at her lip, causing a little sting that she found pleasurable before he pulled back and smirked. "Lay down for me."

"Here?" she squeaked. There were so many large windows, and while she knew he had no neighbors behind him and a pretty tall fence, she wasn't sure she was comfortable being watched.

Ford rounded the couch and kneeled in front of her. "We can move to the bedroom if you like, but it's completely private out here," he vowed, raising her hand to his mouth to kiss it. "Trust me, Millie. I would never risk letting anyone else see what's mine." At his words of assurance as well as the possessive declaration that she was his, Millie nodded and lay back on the soft micro suede of the sofa. Ford's face hovered above hers, his eyes searching until, finally, an encouraging smile came across his face. "Relax for me, baby."

Millie nodded, though relaxing was easier said than done. She had never put herself in such a vulnerable position before. What if she squirmed too much? What if she smelled or tasted weird? What if...? Her spiraling anxiety disappeared the moment Ford's lips touched hers in a searing kiss, and she let herself get lost in the feel of him, reveling in finally getting the man she always loved to do the things she had always wanted to do but had been too afraid to try before. She wasn't afraid to try it with him though because she trusted Ford and knew he would take care of her, just as she would always do her best to take care of him.

While he kissed her, she laced her hands in the soft strands of his hair, and it wasn't until cool air breezed across her skin that she realized he had undone the ties at her shoulder and slipped her romper down past her chest. Her nipples pebbled tightly, and the next thing she knew his mouth was no longer on hers but suckling at her breast. Ford's large hands pushed her tits together and he massaged her as he lapped at her rosy peaks, causing a shock of awareness to go straight to her center. She writhed beneath him, mewling and gasping for breath as he worked her into a tizzy. Millie was already close and he hadn't even touched her anywhere else yet.

She squeezed her legs together to create some friction, but Ford reached down and pushed them apart. "Nuh-uh, sweet girl," he said when he popped off her breasts and licked his lips. "You asked for something specific. Don't settle for less."

"But I-I need more," she whined, trying not to sound as desperate for an orgasm as she was. Millie needed to come, and while she wanted to try oral with him, she also wanted her orgasm a little bit more.

"Then I'll give you more." With one swift movement, he pulled her romper down her body and over her feet, tossing it behind him.

Ford's eyes roamed over the body that was laid out before him. It was all for him she thought to herself as she struggled to not cover up the parts of her she was more self-conscious about. Her hips, her soft rounded stomach, her thighs striped with stretch marks, even her breasts that he had already proven that he liked were things she had always thought were too large, too squishy for anyone to find appealing, but the fire burning in his eyes told her he found them more than tempting. Ford wanted her, and he lifted his hands to touch her, running them lightly over every exposed surface until he was parting her legs and settling himself in between them.

"So beautiful," he whispered, and whether he was talking about all of her or just the part he was staring at, she didn't know and she didn't much care.

Ford's thumbs rubbed her inner thighs in relaxing circles until he brought them up to the heart of her and parted her folds. Millie rolled her eyes up to the ceiling, not sure if she could watch him while he did what she had asked. It wasn't until he placed one of his hands over hers that she realized she had started nervously twisting her fingers together. Her eyes met his and they were jade pools of tranquility and reassurance. He lifted her fingers to his mouth to kiss them before placing them in his hair.

"If you need to twist something, you twist and pull my hair while I lick your sweet pussy," he commanded, leaning back down to do just that.

A sharp intake of breath accompanied the first long lick from her center to her clit, her fingers tightening in his hair as he repeated the action over and over. He rubbed his thumb over the small bud at the top, sending sparks up her spine until she was coming already. Lightning started appearing behind her eyelids while she moaned and writhed under him. Once she was able to form words again, she told him, "T-thank you," but he was already shaking his head no at her.

"Don't thank me yet, sweet girl. I'm not done." He dove back down to center and started licking and sucking at her again, running his hands over the tops of her thighs for a moment before one hand found her clit and the other slipped down to her hole where he slipped a finger inside her.

A cry of pleasure left Millie's mouth as he

worked his finger in deeper and deeper, his other rubbing her pearl while he lapped at the juices spilling out of her. Another finger slipped its way in, and the stretch felt so amazing that she couldn't wait until it was him inside her, filling her up. Goosebumps broke out over her skin and when he moved his mouth over her clit and sucked on it, she exploded again, noises she'd never heard herself make coming out of her mouth while he worked her over and over.

Millie gripped his hair until her knuckles were white, but he didn't stop or complain. Ford kept going and going until he drove her to the point of no return. Her hands fell from his head and every muscle in her body tensed just before Millie's back bowed off the couch, and she came harder than she ever thought possible, her eyes rolling into the back of her head and her mind seeming to go offline. Her body was in charge now, and it was all about sensation. No thoughts needed here.

Minutes later, when her body stopped trembling with aftershocks and she finally came back to herself, her eyes blinked open and she looked down to see Ford smiling at her as he licked her release from his lips. "You taste just as sweet as I thought you would," he revealed, moving until he was hovering above her. "Do you want to see what you taste like?"

Millie hadn't thought about it before, but now she was curious. Her head bobbed and he leaned down to kiss her, driving his tongue into her mouth until she could taste herself. It was sweet, a little tangy, and not at all unpleasant like she had worried it might be. Ford pulled back, smiling at her softly while he brushed a hand over her hair.

"I want to taste you now," she demanded, pulling herself up to sit. She was surprised at how comfortable she was being completely naked, but after what he had just done to her, there was no real reason to be shy now.

Ford's brow furrowed. "Are you su—" Millie nodded before he could even finish his sentence. With a chuckle, he sat up on the couch and unbuckled his belt. "Whatever the lady wants."

Feeling the slightest bit emboldened, she reached over and pushed his hands aside, taking over and undoing the button of his jeans with a pop before pulling the zipper down. "That's right," she told him. "And right now the lady wants you to shove your cock in her mouth until she's choking on it."

"Damn, Millie," Ford said as he shifted on the couch, his erection tenting the dark blue briefs he was wearing. "Love hearing you talk like that."

Her hand hovered over his briefs as her eyes shot up to his. "You do?" Millie liked reading all the dirty talk in her books, finding that the filthy words turned her on about as much as anything else did, but she never thought someone would like hearing those words come from her.

"Fuck yes," Ford said, reaching to cup her neck and kissing her deeply for a brief moment. "I want all your words, the sweet and the filthy." He looked at her with a smirk. "I think you want that for yourself too. Am I right?"

Millie blushed and nodded. "I do." There was something about hearing about all the wild things that were going to happen that worked for her. She blamed her love of books for why she needed dirty talk so badly, but at the end of the day, she couldn't be mad about it. Who knew the English language could be so much fun?

"Then pull out my fat cock and suck on it until I'm screaming your name," he commanded. Millie's eyes widened and Ford winced and peaked at her. "Too much?" he asked sheepishly.

Millie's head shook quickly. "No, I think I almost

came again just from hearing you say that," she confessed.

When he smiled and flicked his gaze down to his pants, she shivered. With a shaky hand, she reached into his briefs and gripped him, enjoying the silky feel of his skin that covered the steel pipe that was his cock. Millie pulled him free from the cotton prison and marveled at the look of it. She had seen plenty of penis' before because duh, Internet and the male propensity to photograph their junk, but she'd never seen one in person and held the weight of it in her hands as her mouth watered with the need to warp her lips around it.

Millie licked her lips and looked at Ford while she pumped her fist up and down his thick length. "Let me know if I'm doing something wrong, or something right," she said, licking her lips again and diving in before she could lose her nerve.

Millie took her first taste of him and moaned. Ford was salty, and he smelled musky, but in a way that signaled he was all man. It drove her need further. She went to put her mouth over the top, licking the precum that dripped there before she did and engulfed him as well as she could, stopping before she triggered her gag reflex. He rested heavily on her tongue as she licked and sucked on him, hoping that she was doing something right and pleading with the sex gods to not let her mess anything up. Ford's fingers slipped into her hair and he stroked it gently.

"That's it, sweet girl. You're taking me in so well, that sexy mouth of yours feels like heaven," he moaned, using his other hand to take hers and wrap her fist around his base. He guided her to stroke him up and down and when she got the rhythm and strength he wanted, he let go and relaxed against the couch. "Fuck, Millie. You feel so good. Every time I look at this couch I'm going to picture your pussy in my face and your mouth on my cock."

Millie groaned, continuing to work him as his words drove her close to another cliff, but words alone wouldn't get her there this time. As if he could read her mind, or maybe her body, Ford slid his fingers from her hair, moving them down her back and gripping her ass for a moment before he drove them inside her once again. Millie whimpered and moaned, her mouth and center both being filled by him. She pushed herself back against his hand to get the angle she needed, and she felt Ford harden even more in her mouth.

"Using my hand to get yourself off. So fucking sexy," he groaned, and Millie sped up her movements to get him as close as she was feeling. Ford moved his fingers and found the spot inside her that drove her insane. Her muffled cry filled the room as she came with him in her mouth, and she hollowed her cheeks and sucked like her life depended on it. "Shit, baby. You're making me come," he mumbled before she felt him swell and empty into her mouth. Millie swallowed every drop and kept going until she felt him shudder beneath her and he pulled her hand away.

With one last swallow, she licked her lips and raised to sitting, watching as Ford sat against the couch, his head toward the ceiling, and his chest rising and falling with rapid breaths. "Was....was that okay?" she asked. Obviously, he came, so there was that, but that could just be a natural reaction to stimulus. Millie wanted to know if she did a good job.

A quick breath huffed from his lungs and he turned to her, cupping her cheek. "Better than okay," Ford told her, a slow smile coming across his face. "Fairly certain I saw God for a moment."

A smile pulled at her lips and she rested on her

heels. "Same," she replied, tiny bumps breaking out over her skin from the cold of the room. Millie looked around for her romper, but before she could, Ford grabbed a throw from the back of the couch and wrapped her up in it.

"Here you go, sweet girl," Ford said, kissing her on the lips and leaning back to tuck himself back into his briefs. He peeked over at her and smirked. "So that happened."

Millie chuckled lightly, enjoying the feel of the soft fabric of the blanket against her skin. "It did," she replied, remembering what Jo said about asking for what she wanted. It already paid off in spades, but she wanted to keep her momentum going. "Do you think it could happen again?"

Ford laughed and wrapped his arm around her. "Millie. What we just did can happen as often as you'd like. I am at your beck and call twenty-four seven," he stated firmly, kissing the top of her head. "This is the kind of night I will remember for the rest of my life."

"Me too," Millie confessed.

As they snuggled, she wondered if it would be for the same reasons, and would the rest of his life include her, or was this just something to pass the time while they waited out the clock. He mentioned falling in love with her, but *falling* and *fallen* were two different things. Ford's breathing evened out and she realized he was asleep. Instead of continuing down her spiral of anxiety, she rested against him and closed her eyes. If this was all she would get, she was going to try and turn off her brain and enjoy it.

Chapter Sixteen

~Ford~

The sun was hidden behind a bevy of gray storm clouds, thunder boomed overhead, shaking the windows of his office, and the sky opened up, the heavens weeping large drops of rain down on Willow Creek. All in all, it was a bleak day, but Ford was happy as a clam as he strolled into his office. Life was good and getting better by the minute. He had an amazing, thoughtful wife at home who was an expert in the kitchen and in the bedroom. After their first rendezvous on the living room sofa last week, they had come together to explore each other's bodies every day since. They traded oral favors or hand jobs at least once a day, sometimes more if his wife was amenable, which she always was.

Now that Millie had a taste of what it could be like to be intimate with another person, she couldn't get enough. Ford was here for it. Day, night, or Sunday before dinner, all she had to do was bite her lower lip and look at him with her bedroom eyes and he was dropping to his knees for her. He thought of what they had done not one hour ago and smiled wickedly. She'd been bending over the island to grab for something, and he spun her around and shoved his hand into her pants, fingering her until she screamed his name.

Damn, Ford was getting hard again just thinking about it, so he went through his mental checklist of tasks to complete that day to cool himself off. No one wanted to see him sporting a boner as he walked the halls of Davenport and Atwater. He hoped it would be one of the last days he would have to walk these halls at all.

Ford spent most of the free time he had available

getting off with Millie, reveling in each filthy word that came from her sweet mouth while they brought each other to the edge of bliss and toppling over together. The rest was spent putting together his law firm, Davenport and Associates. Some might accuse him of trading on his family name, using the reputation that his grandfather and father had built, but it was his name too and he had worked damn hard for a long time to build an honorable reputation for himself. Ford wasn't going to throw all that away just to thumb his nose at his lineage.

Everything was in place for him to make his move in the next week, all he had to do was survive until then and he would be golden. The office space he rented was right near the library, a place he'd originally chosen because of price and central location, but he almost wondered if his subconscious hadn't been pushing him toward it for another reason, a reason that had the most beautiful mocha eyes he'd ever seen and a smile that lit up his whole world.

"Someone's having a good morning," his assistant Kevin said as he rose from his desk and handed him his coffee.

"Yes, someone is," he replied with a smile, blowing on the steaming liquid before taking a sip. "This is delicious, Kevin. Thank you."

His assistant's eyes widened. "Wow, um. You're welcome." His voice was high and sounded surprised.

"What? Do I not thank you enough?" That didn't seem true, but Ford wanted to make sure he wasn't taking advantage of his assistant. Kevin was the best and Ford was counting on him to jump ship over to his new law firm next week.

Kevin shook his head, blond waves flopping into his eyes. He brushed them back smoothly and smiled. "No, you thank me every morning. It's just that it's normally sort of offhand or automatic. I don't think I've seen you this happy, I mean, you look almost ebullient," he explained, tapping his lip. "Usually you come here looking like you're carrying a fifty-pound weight on your shoulders, but not anymore. It's nice."

"It is nice," Ford replied, walking into his office.

Everything seemed better now that he had Millie in his life. He was definitely falling in love with her if he wasn't there already, and while he felt bad that she had spent so much of her life alone, wanting love and never finding it, he was happy to be the one to finally give it to her and accept her love in return. At least, he thought she loved him. Millie hadn't said anything, but she looked at him like he was the greatest man on the planet. It was a lot to live up to, but he would face that challenge head-on just to keep that dreamy expression when she gazed at him.

Ford smiled and sat at his desk, adjusting the frame that held a picture of the two of them on their wedding day. Millie gave it to him soon after they were wed, telling him it was for show, but it didn't feel like a show anymore. If he was honest with himself, he wasn't sure it ever felt like that. Their relationship felt more like this strange culmination of feelings that he might have always had but never looked too closely at. Millie had always been someone he admired and cared for, so maybe his marriage scheme was just the excuse he needed to explore them. Either way, their relationship felt more real than anything he'd ever had in the past and when he thought of his future, she was there with him.

Ford checked his calendar for the day, noting that he didn't have any meetings past three o'clock, and an idea started forming in his mind. He wanted to surprise Millie at the library and take her out on a date. They had gone to events for his current firm or his mother's charity, and every night at home making dinner together was nice, but he hadn't taken her out on an actual date yet. Ford wanted to do something that was just for the two of them and no one else. *Where should I take her?* He could afford to go anywhere in town, but he wanted her to be comfortable and Millie never loved big displays of wealth.

When Ford had bought her a car, she chose the most modest one, waving away the salesman's offer to include more bells and whistles. The man smelled money on Ford, but he hadn't seen Millie coming with her practical ways and desire to keep things simple. She was a marvel, and he wanted to do something special for her. After spending a good amount of time on the internet researching, Ford finally came up with the perfect place to take his wife. It was simple, but she would love it and he couldn't help but feel pleased with himself when he thought about the smile that would come across her face when they arrived. With his plan in place, he tried to focus on work, but his mind kept drifting to thoughts of the evening he would get to spend with his beautiful bride.

****

The workday had dragged on, but Ford was finally free and racing through the rain up to the Willow Creek Library to surprise Millie. He left work a little early in hopes of intercepting her before she left for the day. After shaking out his umbrella, he walked into the main entrance. The circulation desk was where he normally found her, but today it was occupied by her boss, Marsha. Ford had met her once before, but only in passing, and hadn't seen her since he and Millie got married.

"Good afternoon, Marsha." Ford gave the woman his most polite smile and rested his hand on the desk.

"Could I trouble you for the location of my wife?"

The older woman grinned and pointed to a small room at the main entrance. "She's just finishing up afternoon storytime right now," she told him. "I'm so happy that Millie finally has someone in her life to take care of her. She is just the most precious girl I have ever known."

"Yes, she is. I'm lucky to have her," Ford agreed, rapping his knuckles on the desk and sneaking into the back of the small room to watch Millie work.

"...The ogre, having had a change of heart, decided that he couldn't harm the princess like her evil uncle had wanted. Instead, he became her friend and most loyal protector. When they returned to her palace, the ogre put her uncle in the dungeon and the princess ruled over the land with kindness and courage, and the entire kingdom lived happily ever after," Millie read to the small group of kids, her eyes and smile soft. A little boy's hand shot up into the air. "Yes, Bobby?"

"Miss Millie, how come the ogre changed his heart? I thought he was a bad guy too," the boy asked with a lisp in his voice.

Millie smiled kindly at him. "Well, I don't think anyone is all good or all bad. Sometimes it's just a matter of someone treating them differently to change how they act," she explained, flipping through the book. "See here? The townspeople treated the ogre terribly, so he behaved terribly, but as soon as the princess was nice to him, he started acting better. So what do you think the lesson of the story is?"

A little girl raised her hand when Millie nodded at her, she stood and spoke. "It's that you should be nice to everyone so that they act like nice people."

"Exactly, Bethany," Millie said. "It's a good lesson and one I know all of you will practice every day because you have listened and behaved so well for me this afternoon. Now, let's sing our goodbye song."

After clapping and singing along with her, the children stood and wandered over to Millie, giving her hugs before they ran over to their parents. Ford already knew she was magical, but witnessing her with the kids proved it once more. She was amazing with them, listening to their questions so patiently and answering with a calm voice and a small smile for each one. Millie was going to be an amazing mother, and imagining her being so sweet with their kids had him swallowing thickly, his chest swelling with so much happiness at the thought of having a family with her that he didn't know what to do with it.

Once all the kids had said their goodbyes and left the room, Millie finally spotted him and smiled widely, walking over and stepping into his waiting arms. "Hey, you. What are you doing here?"

Ford kissed the top of her head and swayed her from side to side. "I came here for storytime, but I was only able to catch the end. Think you can read me that ogre/princess book before bed tonight?"

Millie snorted and smacked his back, tilting her head up to look at him. "I can if you want," she said, her expression looking a little sultrier than before. "There are other books I can read that might be of more interest to you though."

"That so," he replied, his voice low as he leaned down to caress her cheeks with his lips. "And what books would those be?"

"Oh, just a couple I thought could be fun to read aloud. There is one that has a princess and the man is a bit of an ogre, but only in the bedroom," she purred, sliding her hand under his jacket to grip his bottom. It was a good thing all those kids left because what he was feeling was definitely not G-rated.

A low growl came from him as he kissed her cheek, but he remembered his plans and backed away. "You are a temptress, Miss Millie."

Ford shifted his jacket to cover the erection that had sprouted up. Millie smiled the kind of smile that said she enjoyed the effect she had on him, and Ford was pleased to see her new confidence. He liked that she was embracing the parts of her she'd shied away from or kept hidden. Her bright light needed to be on display for the whole world to see. For now, he would happily bask in her glow himself.

Ford looked out the window, seeing that the rain had finally stopped. Perfect timing. "I know you aren't technically off for another fifteen minutes, but do you think I can spring you early? I want to take you somewhere."

"I think we can swing that," Millie told him, taking his hand and lacing their fingers together. "Let me just go tell Marsha."

They walked hand in hand over to the circulation desk to her boss who smiled when she noticed the two of them. "Well, hello lovebirds."

Millie blushed at the term and smiled at the woman. "Hey, Marsha. Do you think I could head out a little early?"

The woman smiled at the two of them and nodded. "Go enjoy the break in the weather while you can. I'll see you tomorrow."

"Thanks," Millie said, and after a quick trip to her office to grab her things, they strolled out to his car to get ready for their adventure. Her head turned to him as he opened the passenger door for her. "Where are we going?"

"That, my sweet girl, is a surprise." He bopped

her nose, kissed her lips briefly, and helped her inside.

"I like surprises," she said just before he shut the door, and he made a mental note to surprise her more often. Millie deserved to get everything she ever wanted, and he wanted to do his best to give it to her.

The car ride to the nearby town of Pinkerton wasn't long, and Ford enjoyed their easy conversation and the feel of her hand in his as he drove down the country roads to the small town. When he pulled up to their destination, Millie glanced out the window, taking in the old brick building before looking over at him curiously. "Pages and Pans?" she asked, reading the name of the store to him.

Ford smiled and nodded, turning in his seat to look at her fully. "Okay, hear me out. I wanted to take you somewhere special, but I didn't think you'd want to go to a fancy restaurant." At her scrunched-up nose, he had his confirmation of that thought and barreled onward. "When I found this place online, I knew I had to bring you." Ford was so excited for her to see the unique store that he was practically bouncing in his seat. He couldn't wait to see the smile on her face when she stepped inside.

"What is it?" She glanced out the window again, her brow furrowed in confusion.

Ford grinned. "It's a thrift store that specializes in books and antique baking equipment," he revealed, and when her eyes bugged and her jaw dropped, he knew he made the right decision in bringing her there.

"That's a thing?" Millie asked, her hand already on the door handle so she could sprint from the vehicle. Ford chuckled at her excitement and hopped out of the car just in time to see the green hem of her skirt disappear into the store. Her head peaked back out of the door a moment later. "Aren't you coming?"

"Wouldn't miss it," he told her, grabbing her hand

and letting her pull him inside. He wouldn't miss another second with her ever again if he could help it.

The interior of the store was surprisingly well-kept and clean for what was essentially an antique shop. An elderly gentleman sat behind the register reading the newspaper. He tipped his head up in greeting before diving back into whatever story gripped him, not paying mind to the customers in front of him for more than those few seconds.

Millie looked up at Ford and beamed. "This place is so amazing," she gushed, her hands brushing over copper Bundt pans and rolling pins covered in strange patterns.

"What are those for?" he asked, pointing at a rolling pin that was covered in a leaf pattern. Ford knew very little about baking, but he knew how much Millie loved it and if it was important to her, he wanted to know more about it.

"Those are for rolling onto sugar or gingerbread cookies. The pattern transfers onto the dough and stays there after you bake it," she explained, stopping to pick up an old book and riffle through the pages before smelling the binding. "I love the smell of books."

Ford leaned down to smell the pages, inhaling a little dust. He shook his head before leaning down to rub his nose behind her ear. "Mmm," he hummed as he inhaled her increasingly comforting sugary scent. "I think I like the way you smell better."

Millie shivered next to him. "I'm glad you like it," she sighed, her body leaning closer to his.

A throat clearing from behind the counter had him smirking. "I think we better move on before we get tossed out of here for indecency."

Millie giggled and started walking through the thrift shop, touching everything she thought was interesting with more respect than the beat-up items probably deserved, smelling dusty books with weathered leather bindings. When they reached a section of cookie cutters, the reverence dissipated and she squealed in delight, rushing over to the shelf. After digging through what had to be at least a hundred cookie cutters, Millie gasped and pulled up a small, flat box. Ford joined her and gazed down at what had her reacting with such glee. In her hands was a set of Christmas cookie cutters in the shapes of a tree, a bell, a gingerbread person, and a star.

"What'd you find, sweet girl?"

When she looked up to Ford and her eyes met his, the cocoa brown pools shined with moisture. "I've been looking for these for ages," she spoke in hushed tones, holding the box in her hands like it was the most precious treasure she had ever encountered. Her fingers lightly smoothed away the dust on the box, her hands shaking slightly as she did. "My parents," she began before swallowing thickly and looking away for a moment. "I mean, my aunt and uncle had a set of these, and I always wanted to use them to make cookies at Christmas time, but we never had enough money for the ingredients and the oven in the trailer didn't always work. Christmas in our house wasn't anything special, and I would dream about a time when I was older and could go all out at Christmas, baking as many cookies as I wanted for all of my family and friends."

Millie sniffed and blinked her eyes rapidly to quell her sadness, so Ford wrapped his arm around her shoulder, hoping his comfort would give her the strength to continue. As her gracious smile met his, she took a deep breath, Ford simply standing there like a silent guardian, giving her all the time she needed to feel brave enough to finish her story.

"Anyway, I asked my aunt if I could have them,

and she said not until I graduated. I asked her to save them for me and she agreed. The day we graduated high school, the first thing I did that morning was ask for those cookie cutters, but she didn't have them anymore. She said she threw them out to make room for other things."

A tear escaped from her eyes and she reached up to wipe it away, but Ford beat her to it, gathering it up on his thumb and continuing to hold her close while she felt all that pain from her past. Ford's parents were never going to win any awards for being understanding, but he was grateful for the financial stability and safety they provided him when he was younger. He couldn't imagine growing up with next to nothing with no one giving you any kind of love like Millie did and remaining as incredibly warmhearted as she had.

"I'm sorry that happened to you, honey," he told her, rubbing her arm. Millie's marathon baking at Christmas made a lot more sense to him now. She would show up at people's houses or offices with tins filled with at least a dozen different kinds of cookies, but never the ones she had always wanted to make. At least, not until now. "I have an idea," he announced, a smile spreading across his face.

Millie's eyes met his, and while they still held the sadness from her past, they also seemed to shine with the potential happiness of their future. "What's your idea?"

Ford smiled. "This Christmas, how about we invite everyone over to our house and we can all make and decorate Christmas cookies together? Would you like that?"

She giggled. "I would love that. I love...I would love that, Ford. Thank you."

Ford smiled and nodded, steering Millie around the rest of the shop to see if there was anything else she might want. The whole time his mind was stuck on her words. *Was she going to tell me she loved me?* The thought brought him so much joy, and the desire to hear those words coming from her mouth burned deeply inside his heart. Not just because he loved her, which of course he did.

Ford now knew that he loved Millie more than he loved anything in his life. More than getting his own firm and more than every dollar he had in his bank account. He loved her and he wanted her to return his feelings because earning the love of someone as special and good-hearted as her would make him feel like he had actually done something right in life. Being worthy of Millie's love would mean more than any college degree or any accolade he would ever receive for his law practice, and he wanted it so badly he could taste it.

After two full laps around the store, Millie had settled on her cookie cutters, a vintage copy of Jane Austen's *Pride and Prejudice*, and an antique cake display. After paying a whopping twenty dollars for all three, they headed back out to the car. While he drove home, he would glance over to Millie every now and then to see her staring down at her cookie cutters with a sad smile on her face.

"Hey, I have another idea," Ford said, changing lanes so that they could hit the grocery store before they went home.

Her eyes lit up at his words. "What's your idea?"

"We're going to make cookies tonight. I don't see a need to wait until Christmas, do you?" He wanted to give her the memory she was never able to have when she was younger. Even though December was only a few months away, he didn't want to have to wait to see the happiness on her face.

Millie stared at him for a long moment. "That sounds amazing. I love it," she replied with a smile, turning to watch the trees and wildflowers that lined the sides of the road.

"Me too," Ford told her, though it wasn't the idea he loved so much as it was the woman next to him, and while he didn't see a need to wait for the cookies, he wasn't so sure he was ready to tell her how he felt.

Oddly enough, it was the fact that they were already married that was holding him back. Ford knew his feelings went far beyond gratitude for her helping him get his own firm, but he wasn't sure she would see it that way. Things were going so well, he didn't want to upset the balance, even if it was with something as wonderful as declaring his love for her.

Millie didn't have a lot of experience with sex, but until her, he hadn't had any with love, and he was unsure of how to proceed. A caution sign flashed in the corner of his eye just before he made a sharp turn, and Ford took the sign literally and figuratively. Losing Millie wasn't something he was willing to risk, so proceeding with caution was exactly what he had to do.

Chapter Seventeen

~Millie~

Last night had been the best night of Millie's life so far. Ford taking her out on an adventure to a store he knew she would love touched her heart in ways she couldn't begin to describe, and then he went and outdid himself by taking her grocery shopping and spending the evening baking and decorating Christmas cookies with her. Finding the vintage cutters had been a dream come true. They were the only thing from her past besides her books that she had ever wanted to hold onto, and she never thought she would see them again. It was like fate knew that making the cookies with Ford would be more meaningful, and that's why she hadn't ever found them again until last night.

It had been one of the most magical nights of Millie's life, and it was nothing more than a thrift store trip and baking. She and Ford made the dough and rolled it out, snacking on cheese and crackers for dinner while they worked. After cutting and baking the cookies, she whipped up some buttercream frosting and they decorated and added sprinkles on a few because that was how Ford liked them. Then they took their dessert over to the couch for sampling. The cookies were sweet, but the man with her was much sweeter.

Ford was so attentive to her emotional needs, soothing her when she was upset and cheering her on when she was happy. Later, when he swiped a bit of frosting off her cheek and sucked it off his thumb, he was attentive to her physical needs as well, pushing her back on the couch and lifting her skirt up to sample her, telling her how she tasted like sugar before making her come. When it was her turn, she took him into her mouth again, needing less guidance the more she did it and bringing him to a climax within a couple of minutes. Millie was ready to try more, and she felt confident enough to talk to Ford about it soon, but at the moment, she did not feel well enough to even leave the bed.

A small knock on the door caused her to stir in her sheets. She and Ford still had their own rooms, though they traded off whose bed they slept in based on wherever they ended up fooling around that night. "Millie?" Ford asked, walking in carrying a cup of coffee and wearing nothing but a pair of sweatpants slung low on his hips. The fact that her libido barely stirred at the sight of his chiseled torso spoke to just how garbage she felt.

"Good morning," she rasped, her throat feeling like she gargled with broken glass.

"Oh no." Ford padded over to the side of the bed, placing his coffee on the nightstand and sitting down next to her. The back of his hand rested against her forehead, and the coolness of his skin felt so refreshing. "You're burning up, sweet girl. I think you're going to need to call in today."

"M'kay." The words were barely audible, Millie not wanting to speak more than she had to because her throat hurt too much. She scrubbed her face and reached over to the nightstand to grab her glasses. After putting them on, the world seemed a little less fuzzy and she gazed at her husband adoringly. Ford smiled at her and leaned down to kiss her. "I'm sick," she protested, but her husband was undeterred.

"Don't care," Ford muttered just before his lips brushed against hers. His lips felt cool too and she wanted him to brush them all over her feverish body, though that would only make her want things she definitely did not have the energy for. When he pulled back, he brushed a hand over her damp hair. "I'm going to call in too and then I'll take care of you." She opened her mouth to protest, but he was already shaking his head no at her. "Nothing doing, honey. You always take such good care of me, let me take care of you now." Millie smiled shyly and watched her husband walk out the door of her bedroom.

With her arms over her head, she tried for a stretch and winced when every muscle in her body ached. A warm bath sounded heavenly, but she knew she needed a cool shower to help bring the fever down. Millie tossed her quilts off her body and made her way over to the bathroom. After taking care of business and brushing her teeth, she turned on the shower to cold and started to strip off her pajama shorts and top. The water felt freezing to the touch of her fingers, but if it would help bring down her fever, she would deal with it.

Millie was used to doing whatever she needed to in order to get better quickly the few times in her life she had been sick. Missed school meant missed homework and lower grades which affected her chances of getting and keeping a scholarship. Missed work meant money missing from her bank account when it came time to pay for tuition or her bills. Even though she was in a much more secure place financially, she never felt relaxed enough to just lay back and recover.

Millie plopped her glasses on the counter and stepped around the low wall of the open shower, squeaking when the icy water hit her scorching skin. It felt horrible and yet, she stayed under it to get the fever to go down. The sound of the door opening drew her attention to see Ford stepping inside, giving her an exasperated look. "Millie. What the hell are you doing?"

"B-b-bringing th-the f-ff-fever d-dd-down," Millie stuttered, holding her arms over her chest to try and warm up a little. It wasn't at all out of shyness or shame. They had spent a good amount of their time together without clothes on, and Ford was probably the only person besides herself she was comfortable being naked in front of.

Ford walked over to the shower and reached over to turn the handle to a warmer temperature. "You'll make yourself even more sick doing that," he scolded, stripping off his sweats and revealing his glorious body to her. She knew he slept either with briefs only or naked because she was right there next to him every night, but the sight of all of his muscles and golden skin always took her breath away.

Ford stepped into the shower behind her, his body going slightly rigged at the still not quite warm enough to be comfortable water. "W-what are y-you doing?" she asked, her teeth chattering.

"I'm helping you out, sweet girl," Ford said, grabbing her body wash and creating some suds before running his hands up and down her arms and back. "You're barely strong enough to stand and you're shivering so much your body looks like it will vibrate over into another dimension." Millie chuckled at his joke before it turned into a ragged cough, and Ford held her until the fit was over. After washing her body, he shampooed her hair and massaged conditioner into her scalp, creating a lovely tingling all over her body. A shiver wracked her body, but not from the fever.

"You still cold?" he asked. Millie shook her head, looking at him with hooded eyes. "Ah," he said, leaning over to her ear. "You getting a little heated, honey?"

Millie nodded and Ford smirked in reply. He helped lean her head back under the spray to rinse the conditioner from her hair before he shut the water off and grabbed two towels. He wrapped his around his waist,

Millie catching a glimpse of his hardness before he was completely covered. Ford then dried her hair and her body as best he could with the towel before sweeping her naked body up in his arms and carrying her back to the bed. After laying her down, he handed her some meds and a glass of water. She took both gratefully and drank it all down, handing the cup back to him and lying down on the bed.

Ford placed his hand next to her side and leaned over her body. "What do you need, Millie? I want to take care of you."

God, she loved this man. If her throat were feeling better, she might even tell him, but she didn't want such a gross confession to be etched in his memory, what with her face resembling a puffer fish and her nose running, her words sounding like they came from someone who smoked four packs a day for sixty years. No, it could wait, but her desire for him could not. Maybe it was the fever talking, but her whole body felt engulfed in flames and only Ford could extinguish them. She went to talk, but it hurt too badly. She pat her throat and he nodded.

"You don't have your words, huh?" Millie shook her head, and he smirked. "Well, how about I use mine and you can tell me whether or not you like them. Sound good?" Millie nodded and smiled, adoring him more with each word he spoke. "I'm going to take it easy on you today since you aren't feeling well, but once you're all better we'll get back to business as usual."

Ford leaned down closer to her to whisper in her ear. "I'm going to rub my hands over your luscious body, working out the aches and tension that you're feeling. I'm going to play with these amazing breasts, licking and sucking at the rosy peaks of your nipples until you're panting and writhing beneath me," he said, running the tip of his finger over one nipple and then the other, making her wet for him. "When you can't wait a minute longer, I'm going to shove my fingers into your pussy and drive you higher and higher until you break for me, silently screaming my name until you're so spent you sleep for half the morning while I make you some soup."

Millie's head whipped to the side, her mouth twitching into a smile "What? I told you I was going to take care of you, and that includes soup." He kissed her lips and then started to rub her body, fulfilling every dirty promise he had made to her. When he was finished, Millie rolled over on her side and drifted off to sleep, a sappy smile on her face, her husband on her mind, and nothing but love in her heart.

****

The smell of garlic and onions drifted into her room and brought Millie back from unconsciousness. She swallowed tentatively to check the state of her throat, and while it was still sore, it felt marginally better. The sheets weren't soaked with sweat and she didn't feel overheated, so her fever must have broken as well. Apparently, a combination of medicine and orgasms was just what the doctor ordered. The mid-day sun shined through her window and she greeted it with a smile, rolling toward the side of the bed. Her body still ached, but she needed to move. After putting on her glasses, she padded over to her dresser and threw on a pair of comfy pajamas. Sick days called for pajamas.

As she left her room and approached the stairs, laughter drifted up toward her. When she finally made it to the kitchen, the source of the laughter was revealed to be Gigi and Ford, smiling while he ladled soup into a bowl. Her husband caught a glimpse of her, quickly put the bowl down on the counter, and rushed over to her. "What are you doing out of bed? I was just going to bring lunch up to you." Ford wrapped a strong arm around her

197

waist to help steady her. His voice sounded slightly concerned, but his expression betrayed the fact that he was happy to see her. Millie was happy to see him too, just as she always was.

"I needed to stretch my legs," she explained, her voice still slightly hoarse from whatever bug she was fighting off. It was probably something she picked up from storytime. As much as Millie loved children, they were germ factories and the storytime room may as well be a petri dish. The scent of the soup he made wafted over and she inhaled happily. "The soup smells amazing. Thank you, Ford."

"I promised you soup, and I don't break my promises. Not to you, sweet girl." His lips brushed the top of her head as he walked her over to one of the soft chairs at the dining table. "You sit and relax. Do you want bread or crackers with your soup?"

Millie beamed up at how attentive he was being. "Can I get both?"

"Whatever the lady wants," he promised, leaning over to kiss her cheek before heading back to the kitchen. Gigi leaned against the counter, her auburn hair in a high ponytail that swung back and forth as her head pinged between Millie and Ford. Millie waved her over and she finally came and sat down at the table.

"Hey, I was texting Ford and he told me you were sick so I came over on my lunch hour to see you," Gigi explained looking back at her brother in the kitchen. "I thought you might need something, but it looks like you're being well taken care of?" She raised a brow and Millie wondered if she was asking about more than just Ford making her soup.

"Thanks for stopping by," Millie said softly, and not because her throat hurt. She felt a little bad about keeping the progress of her relationship with Ford a secret from Gigi, but her friend had advised Millie to give up her crush and wasn't exactly on board with the marriage thing, so Millie figured she was saving her the worry. Now it felt more like she was lying to her very best friend. "I appreciate it." Expressing her gratitude didn't assuage her guilt in the least, and she realized she needed to come clean.

"Here you go," Ford said, dropping a large bowl of what looked to be chicken noodle soup in front of her as well as a plate with a thick slice of white bread and oyster crackers. "Eat up. We need you at full strength." He winked at her and Millie blushed, both of which did not go unnoticed by his sister. "I'm going to go check up on a few things at work. I'll be in the office, but if you need anything holler at me and I'll come running."

"I will. Thank you," Millie said, surprised when Ford leaned down and brushed his lips against hers for a brief kiss before straightening up and walking away.

Millie's eyes were wide when they met Gigi's gaze. Her friend had a knowing expression. The jig was definitely up, and it was time for her to do some explaining. "It seems like you're being taken care of in more ways than one," Gigi chided. Her friend was smiling, but Millie could see the hurt in her eyes. "When did that happen?"

"Um," Millie started, her knees knocking together nervously. "A couple of weeks ago?"

"Weeks?" Gigi asked. "Why didn't you tell me?"

Millie sighed and rubbed her head. She was starting to get a headache and wasn't up for this conversation, but it needed to happen. Millie made sure to keep her voice low so Ford wouldn't overhear. "Well, you know I've been in love with him for ages, but you told me to stop wasting my time and get over it." She slumped. "I guess I thought I was saving you the worry, but I also thought you might be mad that I didn't take your advice. I tried dating other people, but it never went well. Even if I wasn't horrible at dating, no one else ever stood a chance because I was always comparing them to him. Ford's always been it for me." There was never a man she had looked at the way she looked at him. Ford was the end-all and be-all for her, and if he didn't end up feeling the same way, it would ruin her.

Gigi nodded, taking in everything Millie had just told her. Her brow furrowed and she looked down in her lap for a minute. When her eyes raised to Millie's again, they were watery like she might cry. Millie panicked. She hadn't thought Gigi would be that upset that she didn't tell her, but that was the case. "I'm sorry I didn't tell you…" she started, but Gigi batted away her words with a hand.

"That's not why I'm sad," Gigi sniffed, pulling a handkerchief out of her purse and dabbing at her wet eyes. "I'm sad because I have been a horrible friend."

Millie leaned back. Gigi was her best friend. Always had been and always would be. "You haven't. You're the greatest."

Gigi shook her head sadly. "I'm not, and I am so, so sorry, Mills. I should never have told you to get over your feelings," she fretted, glancing over her shoulder in the direction of the office before facing Millie again. "I've never seen Ford be so attentive to someone else nor have I seen him so happy. He looks like he's walking around on cloud nine."

Millie shrugged. "Well, he's wanted his own firm for a long time and he's finally getting it. Why wouldn't he be happy?" Ford was finally going to be able to break free of his father and help people like he had always wanted. Getting her outreach program up and running gave her a similar sense of satisfaction, so she understood how he was feeling.

Gigi shook her head. "That's not what I'm talking about." Her friend reached over to pat Millie's hand. "I'm sure he's happy about his career path, but you're the one putting that big smile on his face."

Millie smiled despite the small doubt that lingered. She never believed someone like Ford could love her, but the more time they spent together, the more they shared emotionally and physically, the smaller that doubt was. "Do you think so?"

"I know so," Gigi insisted. "Now, I want to be able to share relationship gossip with you and all, but I may need you to keep a lot of the details to yourself. He is my brother after all." Her face pulled back in disgust and her whole body shuddered, eliciting a raspy laugh from Millie.

"I'll keep it vague," she promised. "We haven't gone all the way yet, but we have done some stuff."

Gigi winced. "That may not be vague enough, but I'll work on my tolerance level," she vowed, leaning over to give Millie a hug. "In the meantime, I'm sure Jo would love to hear all the details." Millie laughed because Jo did love getting all the details and Millie had already given her a couple, but she kept a lot of things to herself. What she had with Ford was special and not for everyone. "I have to get back to work, but I'll call later and see how you're feeling."

"Thanks for coming and for being understanding about stuff," Millie said, nodding toward the office.

"Same to you, Millie. I'm happy for you." Gigi smiled widely and hugged Millie again. "I'm happy for both of you." She walked toward the front door, shouted goodbye to her brother, and left with one last smile in Millie's direction.

Having cleared the air with her friend made Millie

feel loads better mentally, but physically she was wearing down again, and fast. She tucked into the soup, enjoying the feel of the warm broth on her throat, the robust flavor as it hit her tongue, and the texture of the noodles and veggies as she chewed. She dunked a piece of her bread in the broth and ate it as Ford was walking back out, holding his laptop.

He smiled widely and sat next to her. "I figured since Ginny left I could work out here and keep you company."

Millie smiled at her husband. He was a wonderful man and her love for him grew exponentially every day. "I would love that." With a nod, Ford opened his laptop and started working while she finished her soup. When she was done, they moved to the family room couch and she read under a blanket while he worked for a while longer, eventually stopping and giving her the most amazing foot rub. Millie hummed happily as he rubbed her aching feet. "I could get used to this," she mumbled, talking about much more than the foot rub.

"Me too, sweet girl. Me too." Ford's words meant more to her than she could ever know, but she wanted to tell him. He needed to know, but was now the right time? Millie had loved him for so long and the idea of telling him had been so daunting that it got built up into this almost impossible task, but it didn't seem quite so impossible anymore. With Ford, everything was possible. As soon as she was feeling better, she would tell him exactly how she felt about him.

Chapter Eighteen

~*Ford*~

The sun was shining, birds were singing, and Ford was walking into his father's law firm for the very last time. Of course, only he and a few key individuals knew it was the very last time, but knowing that couldn't keep the smile off his face. It had taken a little longer than he would have liked, but his own firm was finally ready to go.

The office was set up with furniture for everyone and the few people from his firm he had asked to join him in this new endeavor agreed and were ready to start the following day, a few clients he had signed were already calling for meetings, and a list of potential clients was already in his briefcase. Most were small business owners in the area looking for better representation when it came to fighting off corporate buy-outs or rent hikes, and Ford was excited to be able to help people keep their dreams alive. He was finally getting his after all, so why not spread the love?

The word "love" had Ford thinking of his wife and how much he loved her. Ford certainly hadn't entered their marriage expecting to fall in love with Millicent Legare, but it happened, and now he wanted nothing more than to tell her how much he loved her and wanted their marriage to be a real one. It had never truly felt fake anyway, nothing with her ever had.

From the moment she entered his life as a young girl to the moment just this morning when she popped up on her heels and kissed him goodbye as they left for work, every interaction with her had been real because she was real. Millie was the most genuine, authentic person he knew. She wasn't loud about it or out there for everyone to see, but those she chose to let close got a glimpse of a caring, loving, generous person. Everyone deserved a Millie in their life, and he couldn't be happier that she was in his.

The elevator dinged and he stepped off, smiling at the receptionist as he walked further inside the office. A few odd glances were pointed his way, but he ignored them. Ford would be gone by the end of the day anyway, so he wasn't going to expend too much time or energy thinking about it. When he approached his assistant's desk, his steps faltered slightly as he took in Kevin's appearance. His normally impeccable-looking assistant had wide eyes and his hair looked like he had been pulling at the ends of it. Kevin seemed skittish. A sinking feeling took root in Ford's stomach when he glanced inside his office and saw his father standing there, staring out the window.

Kevin walked up to him, no coffee in his hands today. "Your father is in the office," he whispered, glancing nervously behind him. "He didn't even speak to me, just unlocked your office and strolled inside like it was any other day. Do you think he knows?"

"That I'm leaving and taking a good chunk of people with me? I don't know how, but there's a reason he has a reputation for being a shark. The man is sharp and slick." Ford gulped but pushed down the slight bit of fear that was coursing through his veins. He wasn't a little boy anymore, clamoring for Daddy's approval. Ford had his own approval and the approval of the woman he loved. That was all he needed. With a gentle pat on Kevin's shoulder, he walked into his office with an easy smile. "Good morning, Dad."

His father kept his back to Ford. "Is it? I don't know if I would call the morning my son's betrayal became final a good one," he reproached, his tone lofty and his body language stiff.

So his father knew. On the one hand, it was bad because he could try to call around and dent Ford's reputation a bit. Loyalty was revered among lawyers. Even though many of them left to start their own businesses, they were always viewed as a bit treasonous, no matter how unfounded that view was. On the other hand, it saved Ford from having to talk to his father later that day and maybe now at least he could stop by the library and have lunch with Millie. That was definitely a bonus.

Ford took a deep breath, readying himself to address the elephant in the room that his father just called out with a shot to the face. "It's not a betrayal, Dad. I'm just ready to go out on my own, make a name for myself in a different way than you and Grandpa did," he explained calmly.

Clifford Davenport the second finally turned to his son. His face was surprisingly serene for the emotions he was espousing, a fact that unsettled Ford to his very core. If his face was this peaceful, he was either hiding his anger, or he was plotting something. "Well, I suppose I can't fault you for that. Everyone is entitled to go their own way. Isn't that how the song goes?"

This was not the way his father normally spoke. He was never this calm and Ford was certain he hadn't listened to Fleetwood Mac a day in his life, so he must be gearing up to drop the hammer. "I think it's something like that," he replied, trying to think of a way to salvage his working relationship with his father. While he knew it was a possibility that he would have no other choice, Ford didn't want to burn the bridge if he didn't have to. "Listen, Dad. I appreciate everything you and Mom have done for me and the start of my career. I just want to do something a little different now. It's still law, just a different kind of law."

His father nodded, sticking one of his hands in his pocket. The man looked far too relaxed for their conversation and Ford wished his father would just kick him out already. "I understand that. There was a time when I wanted to do something a little differently with my life, but my father showed me the error of my ways and I walked the path I was meant to." He stepped forward and clasped Ford's shoulder. "You can change your mind. There's nothing that you've done that cannot be undone."

Ford's brow furrowed in confusion. "Dad, I love you and admire your skills as a lawyer, but I'm doing this." Starting his own firm was a dream he wasn't willing to give up, especially if it meant continuing at a job he didn't enjoy.

The man's hand dropped from his shoulder and he sighed, shaking his head. "I didn't want to have to do this Ford, but you've forced my hand," he said, reaching into his breast pocket and producing a thick set of papers, handing them over to Ford.

As he unfurled the papers, he had a moment to wonder what it might be. Was his father suing him for breach of contract? Ford had gone over his contract with the law firm with a fine-toothed comb, and there was nothing about a non-compete or anything like that. When he finally got a look at the words on the top page, he scoffed. They were papers to start divorce proceedings between him and Millie.

"What the hell is this?"

His father's expression was furtive, looking like the cat that caught the canary. "I had a very interesting discussion with Jonah Burgess the other day," he revealed ominously. "I had wrongly assumed that my father made your trust in the same manner he made your sister's. I figured you already had the money, so I didn't think about it much because it was my father's business and he made a point never to involve me in his dealings." He walked around Ford's desk and picked up the picture of him and Millie. The urge to snatch it from his father's cold grasp was incessant, but he had to keep his cool to keep the upper hand in this interaction, if that was still possible. "Then you announced your marriage, and to Mildred no less."

Anger burned in Ford's veins and his fists curled at his side. "Her name is Millie and you will respect my wife by remembering her name," he spat.

His father's eyes widened. Maybe because he figured the marriage was for show or maybe because it was the first time Ford had ever spoken to him in anger. Either way, Ford had no more fucks to give as far as his father was concerned. He was ready to leave, but he needed to stay and listen to the rest of his father's bullshit because whatever he was up to would surely affect either his personal or professional life.

"Her name doesn't matter because you won't be married much longer. You have two choices, Ford. The first one involves you keeping the little law firm you've worked so hard to create, and the second involves keeping your wife."

Ford pinched the bridge of his nose. "Can you fast forward to the part I might actually give a shit about? This evil villain monologue is running a little long, and I have an important lunch later." Ford had already decided he was leaving as soon as his father was finished. He just wished the man would spit it out already so he could go spend time with his wife.

"Very well. Your mother and I were willing to indulge your sister's little romance, knowing that you would keep the family relatively scandal-free, but you had to go and marry some piece of trailer…"

Ford stepped closer to his father, glaring at him as menacingly as possible. "Watch your next words or they may just be your last, old man," Ford snarled. He could withstand a lot of things, but his father referring to Millie as trailer trash was not one of them.

"You had to go and marry someone of a lower class," his father said, rolling his eyes at Ford's behavior. That alone made the need to punch his father greater, but there was a reason he was a lawyer and not a boxer. Ford hated violence, but no one brought out the threat of it like his father. "And leave the family business? That we can't allow. So you can either keep your firm and divorce, keeping the family dignity at least somewhat intact, or you can keep your wife and lose your firm."

"You have no control over my firm. Even if I was willing to entertain the idea of divorcing Millie, which I sure as hell am *not*, I have to be married for a year to anyone or I have to repay the money to my trust," he explained. He would think a lawyer would have read all the fine print.

His father waved as if everything Ford had just said didn't matter in the slightest. "You don't have the connections I have, son. I could have that one-year stipulation tossed out in five minutes." Ford's breath caught. That…that could actually be true, but he meant what he said. There was no way he was divorcing Millie. "As far as having no control over your firm, that's technically correct, but as I said, you don't have the connections I have. I can tank your reputation like that." He snapped his fingers, the sound foreboding. "I already told as much to the other few associates from the firm that were going with you, and unsurprisingly, they've all had a change of heart. Well, all but your assistant. At least someone around here has a sense of loyalty."

The thought that Kevin stuck by him wasn't much of a surprise and almost made Ford want to smile, but the others staying put was a definite setback. It would mean long days and late nights until he was able to replenish the workforce he was losing, but that might not take too long. The threat to his reputation? That was the real kicker.

No one was going to go to a lawyer whose own father didn't trust him, and despite the cartoon villainy he was displaying at the moment, his father was extremely well-respected and influential in both the local community and the state law community as a whole. One bad word from his father would guarantee an end to his firm. His eyes ran over Millie's name as it was printed on the page. Millicent Louise Legare. Ford stared at it for a good minute, considering his options, and at the end of that time, all he could think about was how she needed to change her last name to Davenport.

A smile came across Ford's face and he handed the divorce papers back to his father. "I choose option three," he said, moving to grab an empty banker's box from the side of his desk and gathering up his personal items, starting with his wedding photo. "I'm keeping my firm and my wife. I don't think you're willing to risk a public feud with your son. It's bad for business, after all, but even if you are, I don't care. You can tank my firm and I'll just do something else. I'll go teach at the community college, or I'll work at the legal aid office for whatever they can afford to give me. Hell, I'll even go work at the local Piggly Wiggly if needs must. It doesn't matter what I do, but it does matter who I'm with. I'm with Millie and I love her, so you can take those papers and shove them up your ass."

Ford grabbed a few other items from around his

office. There were some books that were his, a couple of plants Kevin insisted he needed in his office to make him seem "less like a robot," and a tin of cookies Millie always kept full for him because she knew he needed that two o'clock sugar fix to keep him going. Ford smiled as he placed it in the box and straightened up to look at his father, whose expression was a delightful mixture of shock and offense.

"Good talk," Ford jibed, pushing past his father.

"You're making a mistake," his father thundered.

Ford looked back at him and smiled sadly. "I'm sorry you think that, but I'm not making a mistake. I hope you and Mom come around. You know, Ginny and I are pretty awesome people and so are our partners. Maybe you'll take the time to get to know the real us sometime." With a nod, he walked out of his office and stopped at Kevin's desk. "Ready to get the hell out of here?"

"I've been packed and ready for days," his assistant exclaimed with a wide smile. He stood and grabbed his things, walking next to Ford as they left their old lives and headed toward a new one.

While they waited for the elevator, Ford leaned over and bumped his assistant with his shoulder. "Hey. Thanks for sticking with me even though Harvey Dent went full-on Two-Face back there," he quipped.

Kevin's eyes lit up. "Does that make you Batman and me Robin? I look amazing in tights, so I could see it."

Ford laughed, thankful for the levity after such an intense confrontation. He was a little nervous that his father might go through with his threat and tank his reputation, but Ford meant what he said. It didn't matter if he could no longer practice law as he once had. As long as he had Millie with him, nothing else mattered. Having his own firm was his old dream, but a life with her was his new one.

Later that night, as he unpacked the banker's box in his home office, he saw his father had slipped the divorce papers inside when he wasn't paying attention. "What a dick," he said, shaking his head.

"Are you talking about someone or are you offering?" Millie asked, leaning against the doorframe, with a sultry expression as she raked her eyes up and down his body.

Ford shoved the papers into a desk drawer to shred later on. He wouldn't be needing them. Not now, not ever. "For you, sweet girl, it's always on offer."

Millie smiled and stepped into the room. "Good," she said, biting her lower lip while she unzipped the swimsuit cover-up from top to bottom to reveal the body that was not wearing one stitch of clothing underneath. "I was thinking of going for a dip in the Jacuzzi. Want to join me?"

"Honey, you couldn't stop me," Ford said, loosening his tie and pulling his shirt from his trousers as he followed her out of the office and into the backyard.

Ford watched her gorgeous body disappear into the water while he finished stripping off the rest of his clothes, and when he joined her, their bodies slipping and sliding against one another as they snuggled in the warm water, he knew that even if it cost him the dream of his own firm, being with Millie was one decision he would never regret because she was the dream he hadn't known he wanted, but was so happy had become a reality.

Chapter Nineteen

~Millie~

The table was set with white linens, the tall candles that served as the centerpiece were lit and already dripping wax, and the boeuf bourguignon was staying warm on the stove. Everything was set up for a romantic evening, the only thing missing was Millie's husband. Ford was at his new office today, working hard to get everything up and running. He had told her last night that a few people who were going to leave with him from his father's firm decided to stay, so he would be working long hours at the beginning. It was too bad that things wouldn't be as easy for him as he thought they would be, but she was happy that he was getting out on his own.

Ford had always been a better man than his father, and it was nice to see him forging his own path. Millie wanted to do something nice for him, so she put together a great dinner and planned to tell him how she felt about him before taking their physical relationship to that next level. She had been ready to sleep with him for a while, but she held back, wanting to express her feelings for him before they made love for the first time. She hoped it would be the first of many times together, and she squealed a little inside as she thought of spending the rest of her life with her crush, her husband, her love.

The clock on the wall read a quarter past seven, so Millie slipped her phone out to check her messages. The last text from Ford was still up on her screen, and she smiled as she read it again.

Ford: **Can't wait to come home to you, sweet girl. I'll see you around seven or so. xx**

After setting her phone down on the kitchen counter, Millie did one more check of the dinner, giving it a stir and inhaling the wine and herb mixture. It was a dish she'd only made once before for herself, so she hoped Ford would like it. The door to the garage opened, the sound causing her to flit around nervously as she quickly fluffed the waves in her hair and smoothed down the light pink dress she was wearing. She had taken an hour off from work to get everything ready for that night and spent a good amount of that time trying to look her best. With one last adjustment to her glasses, Millie stepped around the island and waited for her husband. When her fingers started to twist, she clasped them together behind her back to keep herself from fidgeting.

Ford emerged from the mudroom looking a little tired after his long day, but he perked up when he saw Millie, and her heart swelled when she saw the bouquet of red roses in his hands. His eyes darted to the right and widened at the sight of the dining table. "What's all this?"

Millie stepped over to him and reached up to kiss his cheek. "I wanted to do something special to celebrate your first day," she told him, pride for how hard he worked to get where he wanted to be filling her chest. Her eyes moved down to the flowers. "Are those for me?"

The dreamy expression he had on his face changed to amusement and he handed the bouquet to her. "Yes, these are for you." Millie stuck her nose in the flowers to get a hit of the rosy aroma.

"Any particular reason for them?" Millie asked, walking over to the kitchen and grabbing a vase. Once it was filled with water, she arranged the roses inside and placed them in the center of the island where she would be sure to always see them.

"Actually, I've been wanting to give you flowers for a while." Ford rubbed the back of his neck and peeked over at her. "I thought tonight would be a good night to give them to you since I had something to talk to you about." Ford seemed a little nervous, a rare occurrence indeed and she hoped that everything was okay. Her concern pushed aside her need to express her feelings, and she swallowed them as he led her over to the dining table to sit down.

Millie took her seat and Ford paced back and forth for a moment before finally grabbing a chair and sitting directly across from her. His knees bracketed hers and he held both of her hands, eyes shining like jade stones as he looked at her meaningfully. The Adam's apple on his neck bobbed up and down as he swallowed and took a deep breath. Millie was trying not to freak out, but whatever he had to say was clearly something important. She hoped it was a good kind of important and not a bad one.

"Millie, I came into this marriage thinking that it would be an easy fix to a ridiculous problem, and when it was over we would part ways as friends, or maybe just a little closer than we had been before." Millie nodded, still unsure of where this was going, but she didn't want to interrupt Ford since he seemed so apprehensive. She gave his hand an encouraging squeeze and a small smile to help him along. He returned the smile and laced their fingers together. "I didn't expect to feel more than friendship and I didn't expect...." he huffed. "Fuck it. I love you, Millie. I do. I love you and I am tired of not telling you. I know you might not feel—"

Ford never got a chance to finish that last sentence because Millie had launched herself off the chair and into his arms. *He loved her.* Ford Davenport loved her and the knowledge of that felt better than she ever imagined it could. Millie felt lighter than air, like she could float away at any moment if she didn't ground herself on something, so she chose to use him. Her hands slipped behind his neck and she crashed their lips together while she sat in his lap. His hands went to her waist and gripped her tightly as he held her close. It wasn't close enough. If it were possible, Millie would want to crawl inside him and live in his heart forever.

"I love you too," she confessed after breaking their kiss. "I've loved you my whole life."

Ford looked shocked at that last bit and Millie wondered for a split second if maybe she should have held that little nugget of truth back a little, but he chuckled and shook his head. "Why didn't you ever say anything?"

Millie shrugged. "I didn't think you would ever love me back, so I kept it to myself." She was done with that now though. Millie would tell him she loved him every day for the rest of eternity if he would let her.

Their foreheads met. Ford rubbed her back. "You sweet girl. How could I not? You're amazing, Millie." He kissed the tip of her nose. "I'm sorry it took me so long to see it."

Millie sniffed, tears of joy gathering in her eyes. "That's okay. I got pretty good at making myself invisible, but I'm just glad you finally did." She reached over to the table and slipped the folded piece of paper she had kept since the night before their wedding out from under her placemat. "Can I read something to you?"

Ford nodded and smiled. "You can do whatever you want, love."

Bolstered by his declaration and the new endearment, Millie glanced down at the stationary she had written her vows on before looking back up to Ford. "I wrote these the night before we got married." Ford kissed her lips briefly, his eyes filled with so much love that Millie was no longer afraid to say what had been in her heart for so many years. She dropped the paper, no longer needing it because the words were tattooed on her heart and always would be. "Ford, I love you. I have loved you from the moment you held my hand to help me across the street when I was seven and didn't know any better. I loved you from the time when I was thirteen and you showed me how to slow dance before my eighth-grade promotion, and I loved you when you would hold my big stack of books while I piled them into my locker in high school. I have loved you for so long that I can't remember a time when I didn't, and that love for you has only grown with each passing day. You are the kindest, smartest, most generous man I have ever met, and I feel like the luckiest woman on the planet to be able to call you my husband. I love you so much, Ford Davenport, and I always will."

Millie stared into Ford's green eyes that were brimming with moisture. "That was beautiful, Millie." He gathered her in his arms and held her tightly. "Thank you for loving me, sweet girl. I'm the luckiest man in the world to be able to call you my wife, something I plan on doing for a very long time." Ford leaned his head down and took her mouth with his. The kiss was gentle, but the longer it went on, the hotter it became.

Now that they had declared their love, Millie was ready to declare something else. "I want you," she spoke quietly, not wanting to interrupt the reverence of the moment.

Ford's tongue peeked out and ran over his lower lip. "How do you want me?"

Millie shifted so that she was straddling his lap and rolled her hips over his growing hardness. "I want you inside me." She kissed his cheek and nibbled his earlobe. "I want you so deep that I feel the stamp of you on my soul forever."

Ford nodded shakily and his hands squeezed her hips once more. "What about dinner?"

Millie leaned over, blew out the candles, and tossed her eyeglasses on the table. "It'll keep," she told him, standing from his lap and holding out her hand. Ford took it immediately and she led them upstairs into her bedroom. She had been anticipating this all day, so she made sure to clean her room and even changed out the light bulb in her lamp so that when she flicked the switch, a warm glow was cast over the space.

"I like the mood lighting." Ford smiled down at her and she stifled a laugh.

Spinning to face him, Millie backed away and started to undo the buttons on the front of her dress. "If you like the lighting, I think you'll get a kick out of this." She reached the last button and parted the two sides of her dress to reveal a white lace teddy and matching thong. Her body confidence had climbed steadily higher ever since they had started fooling around a few weeks ago, but it went into the stratosphere when she saw the raw hunger in Ford's gaze as he took in her new outfit.

"Damn," Ford whispered, stepping closer and cupping one of her large breasts. He ran his thumb over the peak and she gasped, the pressure already building in her core. He repeated the action on the other side, and soon he was rubbing her and pushing her toward the bed at the same time.

When the backs of her knees hit the bed, Millie sat and tilted her head to look up at him. Her eyes narrowed. "You're wearing too many clothes," she commented, grabbing at his belt, flicking it open, and whipping it off in record time.

A low chuckle sounded overhead. "Why do I get the feeling that you're in a hurry?"

Millie smiled up at her husband. "In a hurry to

start, not necessarily in a hurry to finish," she admitted, unzipping his pants and shoving them down to his knees.

"How about I lend a hand." Ford slowly unbuttoned his shirt, and Millie decided to find a way to occupy herself while she waited, reaching into his trunks and freeing him. "Fuck, Millie," he growled, reaching down and cupping her face.

Millie smiled as she gripped him and gave his thickness a few hard pumps. "You were taking too long," she pouted before she licked a stripe up the center of his length and bobbed her head over the top.

Ford panted and bucked his hips. "God your mouth feels so good, sweet girl." He stroked the side of her face and pulled her off him. "As much as I always love that, I want to be inside you." He backed up a step and quickly removed the rest of his clothing while Millie laid back on the soft sheets of her bed. Once all his clothing was removed, Ford crawled up her body until his face was hovering above hers, his eyes searching. "Don't worry, love. I'll take care of you."

His lips were on hers for a brief moment before they trailed over her cheek and down her neck until she felt the fabric of her teddy tugged down and his warm mouth engulfing her nipple. Millie's fingers laced into his soft strands as she held him to her, enjoying the feel of his tongue as it teased her peaks into hard buds.

"More," Millie panted, pushing on his head with a little pressure as her body writhing underneath him.

"Whatever the lady wishes," Ford said with a chuckle as he kissed the tops of her breasts and slid down her body, pushing the fabric of her teddy up to kiss her soft stomach while he slid her panties down and off her legs. Then he was back and diving into her center, licking, sucking, and moaning as he drove her further and further toward oblivion. When he added a couple of fingers and curled them to hit just the right spot, her climax slammed into her, a guttural moan coming from her throat as waves of pleasure rolled through her body.

Millie's eyes blinked back open, seeing Ford above her again with her release glistening on his lips. "You ready for more?" A lump formed in her throat. After all the years of waiting, she was ready, and the significance of it being Ford who she was finally giving herself to hit her full force, a tear escaping from the corner of her eye. "What's wrong? Did I hurt you?"

Millie's head shook and she smiled. "I'm just so happy it's you," she confessed, cupping his face with both hands and kissing him. "I love you so much."

Ford's smile was blinding, his love for her apparent in the happiness that was etched on his face. "I love you too, sweet girl." He pushed her teddy up and off her body and leaned down to kiss her before popping up quickly again. "Condom?" he asked, and with a wince, Millie shook her head. Of course, she was so caught up in the romance of it all that she forgot the most practical thing. His brow furrowed before his eyes lit up. "Be right back," he promised before rushing out of the room. The sounds of cabinets and draws opening and shutting came from the other room until he reappeared holding a box, a grin on his face. "I knew I had some around here somewhere." He slapped the box on the nightstand and pulled out a little silver wrapper, ripping it open and sliding the condom on with surprising speed.

"Now who's in a hurry?" Millie was in a hurry too, but while she waited the view of him walking around naked wasn't half bad.

The question got a wry smile from her husband before he was on top of her again, pushing his body between her legs. "I'm definitely in a hurry. I've been dreaming of having you since we kissed on the couch in my office," he admitted, and her eyes widened at the information.

"Then have me." Millie reached up and wrapped her arms around his neck and her legs around his waist, helping line herself up to him. "Make me yours."

Ford exhaled sharply. "You've always been mine, Millie. It just took me a while to realize it," he said as he pushed forward. The first few inches of him entered her, and she stiffened at the foreign sensation, the stretch causing a slight burning, but it wasn't entirely unpleasant. "Relax for me, honey. I'll take care of you. I'll always take care of you." The vow came before another deep kiss, his mouth driving into her mouth while his hardness drove into her center. The final push caused a sharp sting and she whimpered against his lips, but the pain faded quickly, morphing into a wonderful sense of completeness. "How does that feel?"

A sigh left her lungs and Millie smiled up at him. "Good. It's like I can feel you everywhere." She rubbed his back and he shivered in her arms, the movement causing her insides to flutter in response. Millie hummed her satisfaction and Ford smiled, rolling his hips against hers until her hum turned into a moan.

"Do you need my words, sweet girl? Do you need me to tell you what I'm going to do to you?" The question preceded another hip roll and Millie felt her eyes fluttering closed.

"The only words I needed were the three you gave me at the dining table," she panted, raising her hips up to meet his next thrust and sliding her hands down to grab his firm behind so she could pull him even closer than before. Millie wanted them so close that she could no longer tell where she ended and he began. "Now stop asking questions and make love to me."

Ford smirked and bucked his hips, hitting a spot

inside her she didn't know existed until then. When she grunted and dug her nails into him, he repeated the action. "Not so bossy now are we?"

Millie shook her head and he chuckled before grinding his hips against hers. When they finally found their rhythm, any and all laughing stopped, and they lost themselves in one another. Their bodies slotted together perfectly, like two puzzle pieces that completed the picture that was their future. Ford pushed into her over and over until he was grunting and moaning along with her, the base of his cock grinding against her clit until her whole body was tensing and she felt like she was robbed of breath. Another orgasm took over, her body feeling like it had splintered into a thousand points of light that burned brighter than anything she had ever seen. Ford swelled inside her and his body shook as he followed her over the cliff, breathing hard and slowing to a stop until, finally, he was collapsing over her.

A brief kiss to the lips came and went, followed by Ford tying off and disposing of the condom in the bathroom before crawling back into bed beside her. He rested on his side and brushed a hand over her dampened hair. "How are you, my love?"

Millie smiled at him and stroked her thumb along his jaw. "I'm wonderful. Thank you." She leaned over and kissed him before resting her head back down on the fluffy pillow.

"Thank you," Ford said, his eyes shining with adoration. "For everything."

Millie sighed contentedly and rolled to face him. "I love you," she told him again, staring at her husband with the love she had tried to keep hidden for so long. It felt so good to finally have freed it, and his expression told her it was worth the risk she took to do it.

"Love you too, sweet girl." He kissed her

forehead and they snuggled down into the covers, enjoying the first of what would be many nights spent together, expressing their love in any way they knew how.

Chapter Twenty

~Ford~

Ford whistled as he closed the manila folder for his latest client. Alfred Humphries owned a local flower shop and his landlord was trying to hike the rental rate beyond what was fair and reasonable for the area in an attempt to drive Humphries out of business so he could sell the building to a developer. With his legal knowledge and a determination to make things right, Ford was able to locate a clause in the rental agreement that required ninety days' notice for all rent hikes and a buyout option for the building itself. The threat of a lawsuit for violating the agreement had the landlord selling the building to his tenant instead, allowing Humphries Floral and Garden to operate for the foreseeable future with no more intrusion from a greedy landowner. A sense of satisfaction and pride filled him as he placed the folder into his closed case file, leaning back in his chair to take it all in once again.

In the time since Ford left his father's firm, he had successfully called the old man's bluff. The employees that didn't end up leaving with him took a few weeks to replace, but now Davenport and Associates was operating with a full staff and everything seemed to be humming along quite nicely. Sure his current office wasn't as big as the old one and the view wasn't as great, but the sense of accomplishment he felt at the end of the day was worth making less money and having less prestige. Every now and then he would bump into a former colleague or a friend of his parents, and he would get pitying looks from them as if this hadn't been his choice, but the decision to leave had been his and it was the best one he had ever made, barring his marriage to Millie.

Ford and Millie's marriage was also on more solid ground than it ever had been. They spent their days working and their nights together, making dinner, making love, and making plans for the future. They also spent a good amount of time with her friends and even had a couple of double dates with Kevin and his boyfriend. The dates coupled with Millie bringing Kevin a tin of cookies every week had his assistant finally feeling comfortable enough to address him by his first name. The new dynamic was nice, and Ford liked that his firm was casual enough that everyone felt comfortable on a first-name basis and there wasn't an atmosphere of fear like there had been at his father's firm.

The intercom buzzed before Kevin's dulcet tones sounded through the speaker. "Ford, you're twelve o'clock is here," he called before the door pushed open to reveal his wife passing another tin over to his assistant before stepping inside.

Ford and Millie had a standing lunch appointment at least once a week so that they could see each other and catch up in the middle of the day. He lived for these lunches and any moment he could get with his wife. One thing he didn't live for was the cooler temperatures they were now experiencing, but not for the reasons one might think. Now that it was fall and nearing the end of October, Millie was wearing more clothing, a fact he resented at the moment. When he remembered that later on he could peel off her wool skirt, blouse, and sweater to see more of her, a smile pulled across his face.

Millie shot him a wry grin as she shut his office door. "What's that smile for?"

"That smile is because I am happy to see you and I can't want to get you all to myself later," Ford said, spinning in his chair and opening his arms for her. Millie entered automatically, sitting sideways in his lap and leaning over to give him a kiss. Ford leaned back and looked at her gorgeous face. "How has your day been?"

"Not bad," Millie said, wrapping her arms around his neck. "We've almost got the website for the outreach program fully set up, and Marsha said we could think about doing a test run in December to make sure it's ready to launch after the beginning of the year." Her smile widened and she was positively glowing. "I'm so excited to get books to more people. It's going to be great."

"It absolutely will be." Ford kissed her lips and rubbed her back. "So proud of you, love."

"Thanks." Millie smiled at him shyly. One day she would get used to all the praise he heaped on her because he had no plans of stopping anytime soon. "I'm proud of you too. The office was buzzing with activity out there. I'm so happy your dream finally came true."

Ford started to tell her that she was his dream, but before he could, she was standing up and walking toward the windows to shut the blinds. She moved from one to the next, and as she twisted the rod for the last one, he finally had to ask what she was doing. "Too bright in here for you?"

Millie shook her head and walked over to the door to his office, locking it before moving back to him. She leaned down to grip the arms of his chair and put her face directly in front of his. "No, just not private enough," she explained, coming to the side of his face and sucking at the skin under his jaw before she nibbled her way up to his ear.

Ford was rock hard in seconds, his fingers digging into the chair until he was sure he scratched the leather. "What are you doing to me, sweet girl?"

Millie hummed quietly, the vibration against his

skin causing him to break out in goosebumps. "I need you, Ford." Her voice was low and husky, her hands slipping down the front of his shirt to his belt buckle. She had that and his pants open in seconds before she was palming the front of his trunks, and his hips bucked into her hand automatically. "I don't know why, but I just can't get enough lately. It's like my need for you just won't stop growing. I want you inside me all the time."

Ford gasped when she gripped him through the cotton of his underwear. She had been pretty insatiable lately. From the moment they started fooling around on the couch, Millie had been wanting sex at least once a day, with rare exceptions. Yet in the last week or so, her cravings had been so strong she was asking for it in the morning and at night, sometimes even waking him up at two in the morning for another round. It wasn't as if he minded it in the least as she was basically beating him to the punch since Ford wanted her all the time too. Her desire was spilling over into the daytime hours now as well. Like the dutiful husband he tried to be, Ford was more than happy to oblige.

"I need you too," he finally admitted, reaching behind her neck to pull her down into a passionate kiss. They worked their mouths over one another and slid their tongues together until they were both panting. Ford pulled her head back and stared into her eyes. "Turn around, love," he commanded.

Millie followed his instructions and he stood from the chair, reaching into his wallet for a condom and wrapping himself up quickly. He placed both of her hands on the edge of his desk and pushed on her back until she was bent over for him. After flipping her skirt up onto her back and sliding her panties to the side, Ford leaned over to her ear and whispered in her ear. "Think you can be quiet for me? I want to give you what you need, but we can't be causing a scandal in here." Ford felt her head nod next to him and he smiled. "Want my words in your ear while I do it?" Her body shuddered and she nodded again.

How much Millie loved dirty talk in the bedroom was probably the most surprising thing about her, but then again, she loved words and it would make sense that she would sometimes need them to get her there. It wasn't always a thing with them. Sometimes they would talk dirty to one another, sometimes they would laugh and be playful, and sometimes they would stare at one another while their bodies did all the talking. It was always something different, but no matter what, it was always wonderful.

Ford ran his hands down her bottom and cupped one cheek, giving it a firm squeeze. "Love this ass of yours, honey. I could spend my days palming these juicy cheeks and never get tired of it." He reached lower, driving his fingers into her wet heat. Ford growled in her ear and another shudder racked her body. "So fucking wet for me. Only for me." He pulled his fingers out and stuck them in his mouth, sucking her sweet honey off and moaning his approval to her. "Love the taste of you. Later tonight I'm going to lay on the bed and you're going to sit on my face and ride it until your voice is hoarse from screaming my name and my chin is glazed like a donut."

Millie whimpered and he smirked. Ford hadn't been sure he had the vocabulary to keep up with all the talk she needed, but after reading a few of her books, he was good to go. "Grip that desk tight because I'm about to fuck you so hard you'll walk out of her looking like you just rode a horse for a week." Ford reached down and lined himself up to her. He drove in with one swift movement, causing Millie to cry out. He reached up and covered her mouth.

"Naughty, naughty," he told her, using his other hand to grip her hip while he pounded into her. "Do I need to teach you a lesson?"

Millie moaned into his hand and nodded, pushing herself back into him, her ass bouncing off his hips. Wet slapping sounds filled the room and Ford thanked the lord that his walls were lined with books. He hoped that would absorb some of the sound, but at this point, he had more important concerns. He slipped his hand off her mouth and cupped her breast through the thin material of her blouse. She gasped and he shushed her before his hand inched further south, slipping inside her panties until he found her most sensitive part and started rubbing.

"You feel so good. So. Fucking. Good." He grunted out between thrusts. Millie's back arched and her mouth opened in a silent scream as she came, her walls gripping Ford like a vise until he was spilling into the condom, his breaths coming fast and harsh.

After a few moments, Ford finally softened and slipped from her. After disposing of the condom, Ford reached for some tissue to wipe up any mess he and Millie made before tossing those too. Millie adjusted her skirt and spun around just in time to see him tucking himself back into his pants. She smoothed and hand down her waves and smiled as Ford reached up and pushed her glasses back up from where they had slid down her nose.

"Thanks," Millie said, her voice as sweet as ever despite the naughty things they just did.

"Anytime, sweet girl." He leaned down and kissed her mouth once more. "Are you staying for lunch? I don't know about you, but I just worked up an appetite."

Millie scrunched her nose up. "I'll sit with you while you eat, but I'm not very hungry," she said, hiking her purse up over her shoulder and walking over to the door. "A few of the kids that are normally at storytime have been out with some kind of stomach bug and I think I might be coming down with it too."

"That's no good." Ford reached out for her hand and smiled when she instantly slipped it into his. "The last time you were sick, I did have a pretty enjoyable time taking care of you."

"I liked it too," she admitted, her cheeks turning pink. "Maybe we can do that again even if I'm not feeling sick later."

Ford opened the door to his office. "Hey, Kevin. We're headed out to lunch. I'll be back soon."

"Take your time," his assistant said with a knowing smile. "Seems like you two might be a bit hungry after your, um, meeting."

Millie turned beet red and hid her face in his chest. Ford just smiled at his assistant. "Yup, talking about books will do that," he said, quickly escorting his wife toward the exit. He looked over his shoulder to see Kevin chuckling and giving him two thumbs up. Ford shook his head. They needed to be more careful. "Well, looks like Kevin's Christmas bonus just went up a few grand."

Millie chuckled and slapped his chest as they walked. "Not funny. I don't know how I'm going to face him again now that he knows we did it in your office."

Ford stopped just outside the door to the building and scratched his jaw for a moment before he looked down at his wife. "I guess we'll just have to make it happen so often that he doesn't think much of it anymore," he quipped, earning another light slap from his wife.

"You're terrible," she told him, but there was no heat in her words.

"You love it." He smiled at her and steered her

over to his vehicle.

"I do love it." She reached up and kissed his lips. "And I love you."

"I will never tire of hearing that." Ford kissed her again and helped her into his car. He never would tire of hearing the love of his life admit to loving him in return. Everything was working out so well, and normally Ford would wait for the other shoe to drop, but with no word from his father, and his professional and personal life going so well, he was pretty sure that there was nothing that could possibly disrupt his happiness.

Chapter Twenty-One
~Millie~

The library was all decked out in Halloween decorations. Cutouts of ghosts and goblins, witches and warlocks, and enough pumpkins to be considered a patch covered the walls of the lower and upper levels of the library. Millie smiled at all of them. She wasn't normally a big Halloween person. There had never been enough money for a costume when she was younger, and there were only so many years you could turn your own wardrobe into a farmer or cowboy before everyone realized you were just going as what you already were: *poor*. This year felt different though.

Ford wanted to throw a Halloween party for his firm at their house, and when he handed her his credit card and gave her permission to go all out for the bash, she took his word to heart and now their house was filled to the brim with so many skeletons, spider webs, and ghosts that it put the library to shame. Of course, Millie found most of that stuff at the thrift and discount stores, but that was because she planned on spending most of the budget on food. Her mind was already bursting with ideas on how to make some fun, creative, and delicious holiday snacks for the employees of Davenport and Associates.

In addition to food, she found the perfect costume for herself, a replica of a Regency era dress, and Millie had squealed with delight when she found it. This year she was going to look just like the heroines from her favorite romance novels. She also had Ford who was the perfect gentleman to wear on her arm to complete the look.

It was strange, being part of a couple that was

decently prominent in the community. Ford had always been influential, but Millie had thought it was mostly because of his father. It turned out that even before he opened his own firm to help small business owners, people knew Ford to be an upstanding, honest, and helpful man, now he just had more people telling him directly instead of telling his father who never bothered to pass the message down to his own son. Millie got so angry when she thought about Ford's parents and how horribly they treated both him and Gigi.

Apparently, Ford hadn't heard from either of his parents since he quit his father's law firm. When it first happened, he seemed upset about the fallout they'd had, but when she asked him about it, he said he was happy to be free of his father, so Millie didn't bring it up anymore. If Ford was happy, she was happy.

After pulling the books she would read for Halloween storytime in a couple of days, Millie walked over to her boss' office. "Hey, Marsha." She smiled, but it quickly fell off her face when she caught a whiff of the woman's tuna salad sandwich.

Quickly spinning on her heel, Millie ran to the bathroom and quickly tossed up her own lunch of peanut butter and jelly. The stomach bug she told Ford about yesterday must be hitting her harder than she thought. The stupid thing seemed to come in waves and she wished she could just get over it already. After rinsing out her mouth and washing her hands, she ambled back to the office, seeing a concerned look on Marsha's face.

"You've got it too, huh?" the woman asked. Millie nodded. "It always starts this time of year," she said, reaching over and pumping some hand sanitizer in her hands like it would ward off any germs and evil spirits in the area. "We have extra volunteers today. Why don't you head home and try to feel better?"

"Are you sure?" Millie hated missing work, but she truly felt awful all of a sudden. Even something as simple as standing up and pushing the book cart around sounded too difficult.

Marsha nodded and made a shooing motion. "Absolutely. Now go before you spread it to me."

"Sure thing," Millie replied, covering her mouth which got a chuckle from her boss.

Twenty minutes later, Millie was greeted home by the sound of a witch cackling. "Crap on a cracker," she shouted, clutching her chest. The noise startled her so much that she nearly jumped out of her skin for a moment before she remembered that the darn thing had a motion sensor.

Shaking her head at herself, Millie patted the witch's head and stepped inside, making her way up to the bedroom for a nice, long shower. After letting the warm water soothe her aching muscles and quell the nausea she had been feeling, Millie got dressed in yoga pants and a light sweatshirt before heading downstairs and into the family room. The day was cool and overcast, the kind of day that called for a good book, a warm blanket, and a nice cup of tea. Millie's stomach turned at the thought of tea, so a book and blanket would have to suffice. After scanning the bookshelves, she snagged the latest time travel romance and settled onto the couch for a read.

A short while later, the coffee table vibrated, bringing Millie out of the eighteenth century and back to the present. Grabbing the phone, she smiled at Jo's name, sliding her thumb across the screen to accept the call. "Hey, Jo. What's up?"

"Hey, girl. Sorry to bother you when you're not feeling great," her friend said, her voice slightly concerned. "I called Ford for something and he mentioned you left early. Everything okay?"

Millie chuckled at how quickly news traveled in small circles. She had only texted Ford about her leaving early a little over an hour ago and Jo already knew. "I'm fine. Just an upset stomach. Did you call just to check up on me?"

Jo scoffed. "Of course. I'm offended you even asked," she said, her voice higher than usual. "Though, since you are home and Ford mentioned he might have left the paperwork I need in his home office, maybe you can try to find it for me real quick."

"Anything for you, Jojo." Millie turned and walked into Ford's home office. She didn't spend much time there, so she was a little unfamiliar with where everything was. "Okay, what exactly am I looking for?"

"It's a draft of the complaint we're going to file," she said. Jo was suing her former workplace for sexual harassment and discrimination along with a few other women who had similar complaints. Ford was working on her case free of charge since it was a noble cause and that was kind of his thing now. Millie was so happy that the man she loved was going to help one of the friends she loved get justice. "It should say petition at the top I think? I'm not exactly sure since I don't know much about all this fancy lawyer stuff."

Millie snorted. "That's a lie. You work with contracts all the time," she said, shuffling papers around his desk and opening drawers until she came to what looked like legal documents. "Hold on. I think I see something." Millie placed her phone on the desk and put it on speaker. She reached into the drawer and grabbed the paper marked "petition" at the top. "Ah ha. I found it."

Jo replied, but Millie didn't understand a word. She was too busy holding back another wave of nausea as she read the rest of the document. The words "petition for divorce" and her full name along with Ford's were what stuck out to her the most, and she blinked to try and clear the gathering moisture from her eyes. *Divorce? Ford wants a divorce?* Millie thought they loved one another and that they would stay married for the rest of their lives. It suddenly occurred to her that he never said that. He told her he loved her, but their original agreement of one year hadn't been renegotiated. Ford already had his money and the firm, so maybe he found a way out of it early. A few tears fell on the page and she sniffled.

Finally, Jo's shouting pierced through her downward spiral. "Millie! Millie, what happened?"

"Um...um," she choked, holding her hand to her mouth to stifle the sob. "I have to go."

"Millie, what the hell happened? Why are you crying?" Jo's voice sounded panicked and the last thing Millie wanted to do was upset her friend, but she was too busy trying to figure out why her perfect world was falling apart.

"It's uh...I didn't find your papers, but I, um...I found divorce papers that Ford must have had drawn up," she sputtered, just before a sob escaped and the tears fell in earnest now.

"What the fuck?" Jo exclaimed, anger and disbelief in her tone. "It's got to be some kind of mistake, Millie. Ford loves you."

Millie nodded and then shook her head. "Maybe, but we still don't have the same room and I'm always the one making him have sex with me lately. What if he's sick of me and wants out? I knew it was too good to be true." She shook her head and grabbed her phone. Jo was still squawking at her as she walked out of the room and into the kitchen. Millie wasn't sure what to do, only that she needed time to think. "I need to go. I need to clear my head."

"Millie—" Jo said, but she hung up on her friend before she could finish.

Everything felt topsy-turvy and the room was spinning. The divorce papers didn't make sense, but then again, the marriage hadn't made sense to begin with. Ford falling in love with her didn't make sense. Millie knew that her fake marriage would always end up with her heartbroken, but she didn't imagine that she would get everything she had ever wanted only to have it ripped away so suddenly.

The rug had well and truly been pulled out from under her, and there was nothing she could do about it. Millie knew that she shouldn't jump to conclusions, but what other conclusion did divorce papers mean? Even if he didn't want the divorce anymore, he had at one point and that thought hurt too. Her mind felt so muddled she wished she could just go to Ford and have him tell her everything would be okay.

That was it. She should just talk to Ford about it. Jo said everything in sex was about communication, but that was true of everything else too. Millie sniffed and wiped her nose on the back of her sleeve as she pulled out her phone to call Ford. She was going to talk to her husband and get this all straightened out. It was a mistake. It just had to be. Millie loved him too much to let him go now, and Ford loved her too. Maybe he just lost sight of it for a moment or something, and all she would have to do was remind him.

Chapter Twenty-Two

~*Ford*~

A smile was plastered on Ford's face as he drove down the street toward his home. He had stepped out of the office a little early to run a couple of errands and even the clouds crowding out the sun in the sky couldn't damper his mood. The first errand consisted of a trip to Party Town to pick up his costume for the Halloween party he and Millie were hosting at their house. Ford couldn't wait to see the look on his wife's face when she saw him in his Scottish Highlander costume. He would wear the kilt, lace shirt, and all the trimmings for the party, and later on, he would ditch everything but the kilt so he could play romance cover model with Millie.

The second errand took him to the jewelry store to buy an engagement ring. When he spotted the dainty rose gold band with a small alexandrite gem, he knew it was the perfect one for his sweet girl. Yes, they were already married, and Ford wouldn't change the way things happened because it led them to where they were now, but he did want to give her a better ring and another ceremony. There was no way that Millie didn't have a dream wedding planned out in her head, and he sincerely doubted it was the one they'd had at the courthouse. At the very least, he wanted to renew the vows they made to one another, even if it was only privately. This time it would be with love for her in his heart and the knowledge that the marriage was for life.

Ford sighed as he hit a bit of traffic, tapping his fingers on the wheel as time dragged. A buzz rang through the car and the display on his dash lit up with an incoming call from his sister. "Hey, Ginny. How are things in the tea business?"

"What the hell is wrong with you, Ford? I can't believe you would draw up divorce papers," Ginny shouted, her voice seething with rage. "Why would you do that to Millie?"

Ford's brow furrowed. "Whoa, Gin. Slow down. What are you talking about?"

Ginny huffed angrily through the speaker. "I'm talking about Millie finding divorce papers in your office. She was chatting with Jo and started freaking out. Now she won't answer her phone." His sister's voice started to sound more panicked. "Why would you file for divorce? I thought you loved her."

"I do love her." The reply was automatic. Professing his love for Millie would always be as easy as breathing, but he was so confused. "I didn't file any divorce—" *The papers from his father.* The papers he was going to shred but forgot about the second he stuck them in that drawer. Millie must have found them and thought the worst. He was such an idiot. Those papers should never have existed in the first place and now they had caused Millie to doubt his love for her. "Goddamn it!" Ford boomed, slamming his fist against the wheel. He was angry at his father all over again, but mostly he was angry at himself for being dumb enough to not burn those papers the second he saw them again.

"What is it?" Ginny squealed.

"I didn't file those papers, Dad did." Ford quickly filled her in on the rest of the story as his car crawled along the street. "I'm so stupid. You said Millie isn't answering her phone?"

"No," Ginny sighed. "Jo and I have both been trying to reach her for an hour. Mags finally showed up, so I can go drive by the house if you want."

"Thanks, Ginny, but I'm already on my way home. Thanks for calling and if you hear from Millie…"

"You will be the first person I call. Promise," she said before she hung up the phone.

While traffic was slow, Ford pulled out his phone and saw he had five missed calls from his wife. The stores he visited must have been in a cellular dead zone because he didn't hear one, and he never ignored a call from his Millie. He hit the "redial" button, but she didn't answer.

"Screw this," Ford said aloud as he pulled off the main street and took another route home. There was no way he was letting Millie think the worst for one more second if he could help it.

When he finally arrived home and rushed inside, he searched the house until he found Millie asleep on the couch, clutching the divorce papers in her hand. The sight of dried tears on her face broke his heart, and he wanted to go back in time and kick past Ford's ass again for keeping those papers around. Ford sat on the couch next to her and started to stroke her hair gently to wake her up. She finally stirred, blinking her eyes open.

Ford leaned down to look at her. "Hey, sweet girl."

Millie's eyes filled with happiness before that look shuttered slightly. "Hey," she whispered, her lower lip wobbling. She held the divorce papers out to him. "When I saw these papers, I thought you didn't want me anymore." Her moist eyes stared up at him, her expression questioning. "I knew it had to be something else though because you love me. Don't you?"

Ford sniffed, his own eyes getting wet. "Of course, I love you," he said, leaning down to kiss her lips. "I'm so sorry. I can tell you the whole story later, but the papers were not drawn up by me. I'm just the idiot who forgot to shred them." He rubbed his nose against hers and rested their foreheads together. "I've been a little distracted by my beautiful wife."

Millie let out a light laugh. "I've been pretty distracted too." She wrapped her arms around his neck and pulled him in for a tight hug. "I like being distracted by you."

"I like it too." He pulled back enough to reach up and feel her forehead. "How are you feeling? You don't seem to have a fever."

"I'm okay," she told him through a yawn, sitting up to stretch her arms. The sudden movement seemed to make her dizzy and she collapsed back on the sofa. "Whoa."

Ford hovered over her, his brow creasing with worry. "That's it. We're going to the doctor." He reached down and she took it, seemingly too tired to protest about the cost or anything, so she must feel horrible.

Ford slipped his arm behind her, helped her get her shoes on, and led her over to the garage and into his car. Once he was in the driver's seat, he started toward the only urgent care in town. He looked over to see Millie leaning against the headrest, a sad smile on her face. "Next time I'll get dizzy during office hours."

A small chuckle left Ford's mouth, but other than that he remained serious. "You've been sicker in the last few months than in the whole time I've known you. I don't care where we take you or how much it costs as long as we get someone to check you out."

"I thought you liked to check me out," she quipped, but the effect was slightly ruined when she yawned again immediately after. "Sorry. I have no idea why I'm so tired all the time. This stomach flu must be crazy." Ford hummed in reply, concentrating on the road until they were at the urgent care and he rounded the hood of his car to come get her. "I can walk you know." She gave him a wry smile, but she let him assist her into the building anyway.

"I know you can, but I'm here to help you, so I will." Ford paused at the door and looked down at her, his eyes shining with love. "I just want to make sure you're okay. I...I don't know what I would do without you, Millie." Now that he had her in his life, he couldn't imagine it being any other way.

Millie cupped one of his cheeks while kissing the other. "You won't ever have to find out," she vowed. "I'm sure it's just not having enough food in my stomach."

Ford nodded and led her inside. "We'll stop by the store on the way home and get you some saltine crackers."

After filling out the requisite paperwork and waiting almost an hour, they were finally called back by a nurse, walking through the white-tiled halls. The nurse stopped at a bathroom and handed Millie a small cup. "Oh, I'm not thirsty," she said, earning a strained smile from the older woman.

"It's for a urine sample," the nurse said blankly.

"Oh, I see." Ford saw Millie flush with embarrassment, but she seemed to brush it aside and did as the nurse asked. When she was finished, Ford followed her back to the small examination room, and the two of them waited patiently while the woman took her temperature and blood pressure.

"Vitals look normal. I'll send the doctor in and he'll be here as soon as he can." With that, the woman exited leaving Ford and Millie alone again.

"I'm glad at least everything appears normal," Ford told her, coming close to her and cupping her cheek. "Hey, when we get home, there's something I want to ask you."

"You can just ask me now. I doubt the doctor will

be here anytime—" Her words were halted by the opening of the door and a middle-aged man with salt and pepper hair coming through. Apparently, this speedy urgent care lived up to its name once you got back to an exam room.

"Millie," the doctor greeted her, flashing two rows of perfectly white teeth. "I see here you are coming in for nausea and dizziness. Is that right?"

Millie nodded. "Yes. There's a stomach bug going around, and I think that's probably what I have, but my husband wanted to bring me in and make sure." She beamed up at Ford and he felt a little better about things since she seemed to look better by the second.

The doctor chuckled. "Well, the kind of stomach bug you're suffering from is the kind that's going to stick around for a while longer if your urinalysis is correct." Both Ford and Millie shot the doctor a confused look and he smiled politely at the two of them. "The nausea is actually morning sickness. You're pregnant."

Ford's eyes widened and when his head turned to Millie, he saw hers were as well. "Pregnant?" Ford asked, the corners of his mouth twitching in the corners and his eyes never leaving hers.

"Yes. You'll have to make an appointment with your obstetrician to see exactly how far along you are, but you are definitely pregnant. Congratulations."

Ford huffed and smiled at Millie. He pulled her close, enveloping her in his arms and squeezing her tighter than he ever had. "Thank you," he whispered in her ear before leaning back to thank the doctor and shaking his hand. He thought about the new life growing in his wife's belly and smiled. They were having a baby, and he couldn't be happier about it.

The rest of the appointment went by with Ford only half paying attention. When they were finally home and sitting at the dining table eating a dinner that consisted mostly of white bread and crackers for her and a plate full of pasta for him, Millie gave him a questioning look. "How did I even get pregnant? I've been trying to figure it out since we heard the news. We used condoms the entire time."

Ford half laughed, half groaned, and put down his forkful of spaghetti Bolognese. "I was wondering that too, but I think I know how." He took a deep breath and exhaled slowly, hoping she wouldn't be too upset with him. "The condoms we used the first few times were ones I'd already had in my drawer. Until tonight when we found out about the baby, I didn't think about how old they might be. Turns out, pretty darn old."

Millie leaned back. "Huh." Apparently, she hadn't given any thought to the age of the condoms either. Ford certainly hadn't. He had been entirely too focused on being with her to check.

Millie's eyes peeked over at him and he winced. "Are you mad?"

"No," Millie replied immediately, easing his worry. "I've always wanted to be a mom, and there's no one else I would rather have a child with." Her hand found his on top of the dining table and she squeezed it. "Are you mad?"

"About the baby?" When she nodded, he shook his head. "Absolutely not. I'm so happy that you are making me a daddy. In fact, I'm so happy I can't think of a better time to ask you that question I mentioned earlier." Ford scooted out of his chair and dropped down to one knee before pulling a small box out of his pocket and presenting her with the antique engagement ring he purchased earlier that day. "Millie Legare, will you marry me?"

Millie giggled and smiled at him, her eyes wet

with happy tears. "Ford, sweetheart. We are already married."

"I know." Ford took the ring out of the box and replaced the simple silver band with the rose gold one. "But I wanted you to get a proper proposal and we're going to give you the wedding of your dreams." Millie had made all of his dreams come true, and he wanted to do the same for her.

"Thank you for wanting to give me those things, but I'm happy with the wedding we had. Besides, we have more exciting things on the horizon to prepare for," she said, placing a hand over their growing baby.

"We do." Ford's hand covered hers and he smiled, wondering how he got to be so lucky. "I can't wait to meet our little one."

"Me neither," Millie said, her smile turning coy. "Though, I think there are a few things we need to take advantage of before the baby arrives."

"Oh?" Ford asked, raising a brow and already raising up to his full height and helping her to her feet. He was fully on board with helping her out with anything she needed, especially the hormones that seemed to be causing her libido to go into overdrive.

"Absolutely. I want to take advantage of the time we have to ourselves while we can." She peeled off her sweatshirt and started backing up to the stairs, Ford following closely behind her.

Ford wrapped his arms around her and drew her close. "How about I give you a private showing of my Halloween costume." He kissed her lightly and walked her backward toward the stairs. "I'll give you a hint. It may or may not include a kilt," he whispered in her ear as he nipped at her neck.

"Yes. I definitely need to see that." Millie raced up the stairs, Ford on her heels, ready to give her a private romance novel cover modeling session, but the best part was that the two of them weren't a fantasy. They were real and they were together. Now and forever.

Epilogue

~Millie~

Another year's passing meant another birthday celebration with her friends. This year was Jo's pick, so of course they were at a rock climbing center. Jo had asked Millie if she should pick another place, but Millie told her no. At five months pregnant, there wasn't a lot of physical activity she was comfortable with doing that wasn't walking or yoga. Besides, Millie had never been very athletic anyway, so she mostly sat on the sidelines and cheered on her friends and their partners as they climbed up the wall.

The other person she was cheering on was her husband, who, for someone who had never climbed before, was infuriatingly good at it. Then again, Ford was good at everything. He painted the room that used to be hers and was now the nursery in two hours, he assembled the crib in one, and he already had car seats installed in both his and her vehicles as well as a baby seat on her bicycle. Ford was on top of everything when it came to her and the baby, and she loved everything about it.

What she didn't love was that her baby wouldn't have a set of grandparents in their life. Millie wrote to her aunt and uncle to tell them about the baby and got no reply. It wasn't surprising, but it was disappointing. However, she reasoned that it was better for the baby not to have to deal with flaky people coming in and out of their lives on a whim. She wanted better for her baby, and so did Ford. For his part, he had told his mother about the pregnancy and she wasn't happy. Ford's father still refused to speak to him unless it was related to a court case they both happened to be working on. It was sad, but

Ford said he was trying not to let it bother him, that there was no space in their lives for people who didn't love and support them, and Millie agreed with that. Besides, their baby would have plenty of support from her friends and their family members anyway.

Millie looked up and smiled as she watched Jo and Archer speed up the wall before turning to see Gigi and Cooper snuggling up against one another down below. They had all lived up to their challenges this year, and Millie was grateful that Gigi had the idea for them to try and stretch themselves a little. Both of her friends were thriving professionally and personally, and she was as well. The library outreach program had started on the first of the year with many seniors and some of the more disadvantaged members of the community utilizing the system to get books brought to them. Millie loved that she was able to help reach people who needed that lifeline. It was probably the thing she was most proud of in life besides the little baby in her belly.

A loud *oompf* drew her attention to her husband who had just landed on the ground, his hands and shorts covered in climbing chalk. Ford looked over at her with a wide smile before walking over to kiss her on the lips. When he pulled back, the affection and adoration on his face was almost blinding.

"How are my sweet girls?" he asked, resting a chalk-covered hand on her belly. They had found out about a month earlier that they were having a baby girl, and Ford couldn't have been more excited. "I can't wait to be a girl dad," he had said in the doctor's office, and he already bookmarked about thirty videos of how to braid hair on his laptop.

"We're pretty good, but we may need a milkshake on the way home to make us feel even better," Millie said, knowing he would give in to her request. Ford waited on her hand and foot during this whole pregnancy and she was trying not to get used to it, but it was hard. After a lifetime of taking care of herself, it was nice for someone else to take the reins for a bit.

"I think we can make that happen." Ford leaned down and kissed her again. "I was going to do one more climb, but do you want me to keep you company?" Millie lifted a book from her large purse and he barked a laugh. "Should have known," he said, kissing her forehead before heading back to the wall for his climb.

Millie settled in with her baby book. It was a pretty big switch from the romance novels she was used to, but she didn't read as much of them as she had before. She didn't need to. Millie had all the romance and happily ever after she would ever need right here.

Epilogue

~Ford~
Five Years Later

When he married Millie six years ago, Ford had thought it a temporary arrangement. As he watched his beautiful wife walk down the aisle that had been cleared in the field of wildflowers, each of her hands gripped by one of their children, he couldn't believe he had ever been so naive. Millie had turned out to be the best thing to ever happen to him and with each day that passed, Ford's love for her grew exponentially. Even now, he could feel his heart swelling as his gaze found hers, the love there shining back at him so bright that it rivaled the sun as it lay low on the horizon.

I love you, Ford mouthed to his wife as she passed their four-year-old daughter Julia and two-year-old son Marshall over to their Aunt Gigi. The two went happily to sit with their cousins and friends. After a kiss on the cheek from her two best friends, Millie joined him under the Willow Tree and took his hands. *Love you, too,* she mouthed back. As lovely in her gown today as she had been before, Millie looked like a fairy as they stood among the blooms, the floral design matching the wildflowers almost exactly.

Paying attention to the officiant was no small feat when the most amazing person Ford had ever had the privilege of knowing stood in front of him. Millie had insisted that she didn't need a do-over of their City Hall ceremony, but Ford had talked her into a vow renewal to recreate the wedding of her dreams. He'd spent the last six years trying to give her everything she wanted, and every time he asked what that was, she always answered the same way. *I already have everything I could ever want or need, Ford.*

That hadn't stopped him from trying to spoil her rotten every chance he got anyway, though Ford quickly learned that lavish vacations were no match for a night spent cooking with their small family. Millie enjoyed their time on the beach for their babymoon and the trip to the mountains when Julia was younger, but she lit up the most when they all simply spent time together at home doing something she loved. Ford also found that he enjoyed family life far more than he thought he had any right to. His favorite part of the day was when they would all sit on the floor of Marshall's room, reading a good book before bedtime.

Ford's gaze flicked to his children for a moment. Julia was the spitting image of her mother, even down to the thick-framed glasses. Ford winked at the little girl named after Millie's favorite author as he moved his eyes over to Marshall. The little boy looked a lot like Ford, but somehow he had ended up with his aunt's auburn hair. Named after the lawyer Ford had most looked up to, Marshall was the son Ford had always wanted but was just as afraid of having. It took many talks from Millie to convince him that he wouldn't mess with his own child as his father had him, but with each passing day, it became more and more obvious that Marshall wasn't him, and Ford wasn't his father.

Clifford and Theodora Davenport's absence was probably hardly noticed by anyone except for him and Gigi. The siblings had made attempts with their parents after their children were born, but they had been too stuck in their ways. It was sad, but Ford knew that it would be even worse to try and maintain a relationship that wasn't healthy. He wanted better for his children, his wife, and himself. As his eyes took in the small group of friends and found family they'd created, Ford smiled at each and every person who met his gaze.

Gigi and Cooper sat in the front row, his sister tearing up as she held onto Ford's children, her own two daughters looking like small princesses as they sat next to their father. Cooper was the owner and manager of the auto shop now, but more often than not he could be found playing tea party with his girls and his grandma Mags, who to everyone's delight was still kicking around and as spry as ever. Bob retired and now looks after his grandson. Currently, the toddler was bouncing on his grandpa's knee while his parents watched the ceremony, Archer's hand on Jo's pregnant belly.

Smiling, Ford turned back to his wife just in time to renew his love for her and the promises they'd made and kept before. After a kiss that was far less chaste than the one they'd shared in City Hall, Ford grabbed his wife's hand and raised it triumphantly as a chorus of congratulations and applause surrounded them. They walked down the aisle hand in hand and over to the tent that had been set up for a wedding breakfast, everyone they loved and who loved them ready to celebrate their union one more time.

Later that night as the two lay in bed, Ford turned to his wife, resting a hand on her small baby bump. "Was it everything you wanted?"

Millie placed her hand over his and beamed at him. "It was more beautiful than I imagined, and while I know I said I didn't need it, I'm glad we had the ceremony. There was something even more special about having everyone there." She leaned over and pressed her lips to his, each time feeling just as blissful as the first kiss they'd shared in his office. "Thank you, Ford."

Ford kissed her again, cupping the life they'd created together as he cherished the woman who'd made it all possible. "I'll always give you what you want, sweet girl, but you're welcome all the same."

"You know, I never thought I would find someone to love me, let alone be able to fill a whole field with people who love the both of us." Millie chuckled as she shifted, facing him more fully. "It's pretty crazy."

Ford shook his head, drawing her into his arms. "The only thing crazy about it is that it took me so long to see how much you meant to me. Now that I have, I'm never letting you go."

Millie leaned her head against his as she breathed softly. "I'm not going anywhere." For the rest of the night, they lay in bed holding one another, basking in the love that may have taken a while to realize but would last forever.

The End

EVERNIGHT PUBLISHING ®

www.evernightpublishing.com